Finding Katie

From the Finding Katie McDonald Series

By

Doc Richards

Dedicated to Linda Merrick—

Table of Contents

How It All Began
Dr. Michael Armstrong

It had been a great week. My class consisted of bright high school teachers, and my teaching style motivated them because I made the sessions fun. They reacted with enthusiasm to my hands-on method of teaching in which everyone takes part. It was summer in Montana, specifically Bozeman and Montana State University, one of the most beautiful places in the world. High mountains surrounded the city, and two ski areas remained open, although it was mid-August. A more romantic and soothing environment would be hard to find.

My name is Mike Armstrong, and I was twenty-seven and single at the time. I had just completed my Ph.D. in corporate finance from a large Tier I university in the South. Even though I was a faculty member at the University of Montana in Missoula, I taught this course in Bozeman every summer. I loved it there. The scenery, the activities, and the food all appealed to me, as did fishing in the rivers and streams avid fisherman that I was. Several lakes in the area were also virtually full of fish.

I always try to get to know my students, which was not much of a problem in this course even though it only lasted a week. One of the most exciting students at the session was an attractive woman who sat in the front row every day and listened to every word I said. She was beautiful inside and out with deep blue eyes and brown hair. Lindsay was shapely, and her smile lit up the night when the class went out to dinner at the end of every day. She accompanied me everywhere, and the attention was a little embarrassing because I could see the smirks and understanding grins from the other members of the class. They knew she had a massive crush on me.

When the class broke up after dinner each night, she would stay until everyone was gone and talk with me. I found out that she married a man who turned out to have contracted a severe illness and was not doing well. They had no children. She lived in Kalispell, just north of my home in Missoula. I made the trip north frequently for skiing, hunting, and fishing. Just north of Kalispell is Whitefish, the doorway to the Big Mountain, one of the best places to ski anywhere.

I was very professional with her as I was to all my students, although I would take her out, given a chance. We lived on the same floor of the dormitory housing the members of the class, and I would accompany her to her room in the evening. However, I never made any attempts at romance or anything beyond the professor/student relationship. At least not until our last night in Bozeman when after going to bed, I heard a quiet knock on my door. It was my friend, Lindsay, and she asked if she could come inside. I opened the door for her and offered her something to drink. She said she was okay and wanted to talk. I agreed.

She told me about where she taught, what she planned to do with her life, her dreams, her ambitions, and expressed her loneliness without a healthy mate. She began to cry softly and told me how much I had done for her that week, showing her and the class they could do anything they wanted. Goal setting and seeking were significant parts of my approach to life. She looked at me with those blue eyes and perfect lips and invited me to kiss her with just her eyes.

I had wanted to kiss her all week, but circumstances wouldn't allow it. Now that the class was over, we would both go home and only be a short (for Montana) trip up Highway 93, through the Mission range, from each other. I couldn't resist. Our first kiss was exciting and arousing, and we held each other and hugged and kissed until she dozed off in my arms. I pulled the sheet up over us and went to sleep beside her. Being there with her seemed to be the most natural thing in the world.

I can't explain it, I still don't understand it, but something happened as we slept together that night. We did not have sex until we awoke at the same time in the morning and shared loving smiles. The tension of the last evening and the nervousness we both experienced had vanished. We both felt that we should be together as we had been that night. It seemed right for us, and we hugged and kissed each other as if we had been lovers for years. She got a determined look on her face and, without saying a word, pulled my shirt over my head and removed my underwear. When she finished with me, she pulled the sheet off her, and I returned the favor.

"Make love to me, Mike. I have waited so long for this moment." She usually called me Dr. Armstrong, but she saw me in a different light this morning. I liked it. She was much smaller than I and very tight. I was gentle with her, and after a while, she took me all the way. I paused to let her relax and only began to move inside her when she could enjoy the feelings she had missed for quite some time. Her passion overtook her, and she moved with me in unison and closed her eyes. I kissed her. Her warmth and longing pleased me, and she came quickly. I slowed for a minute to let her recover some and resumed making love to her. I wanted to fill her with my passion, along with my semen. She came again, and I came with her, deep inside. I desired to make her realize that she was a special woman. A brief thought occurred to me that I might have given her a tangible, permanent memory of our time together, so I moved beside her and talked to her as a lover, which I then was.

"You are beautiful, Lindsay. Being with you last night and this morning was wonderful for me." I kissed her. We loved each other tenderly and lovingly and were good together. The time for us to go to breakfast and then the certificate ceremony was fast approaching, and I kissed her goodbye as she went to her room to prepare. I showered, put on my best suit, left my room for the last time, and put my bags in my car. Much to my surprise, she was ahead of me getting to the ceremony. I made my remarks congratulating the participants, and the Dean and I handed out the certificates and shook the hands of each student. Lindsay was positively glowing as she took hers from me with a big smile. She had gotten to me. We had lunch together as a class and went to our cars to make our trips to our respective homes.

Lindsay came over to me, and I asked her to sit with me for a while. She got in, and we talked. I thought we would see each other again, but she would not give me her phone number, which puzzled me. Oh, well, I knew I could find it. I kissed her goodbye, and we parted. Little did I know that we would never see each other again. A mutual friend told me later that her husband died shortly after her return home. She went into mourning, would not see me, and became somewhat of a recluse. Sometime later, I took a job in Texas, moved there, and our relationship ended. I think about her to this day and wonder what happened to her. Did she remarry? Was she still in Kalispell? I found out later that she was still there and had given birth to a child. I called her to see if she might want to tell me something, but she had nothing to say. I made sure she could find me if ever the urge came over her for any reason, but much to my chagrin, I never heard from her again.

Chapter One

Katie's Story

My name is Katie MacDonald, and I am twenty-one-years-old. My mom died recently after a courageous fight with breast cancer, and my father died before I was born. I never knew him. On her death bed, she told me her story and the truth about the man whom she had married and represented as my father. She finally said to me that when she got pregnant with me, he was so sick he was incapable of fathering a child. He was not my birth father, something I had always suspected.

My world fell apart at her death. Not only had I never known my ostensible father, now my mother, the woman who raised me, was also gone. We never had much money, just her teacher's salary, and she had made many sacrifices for me. The best thing she had done was to make sure I could pursue my passions for dancing and horses. She put me in dance classes at a very young age and was there for all my recitals throughout my life. Since she was a teacher, she had ins with a daycare facility that specialized in using dance to reach out to students. Later, when I entered the first grade, I joined my first real dance troupe. It all came naturally to me, and my passion grew. As I grew, I was also able to get various part-time jobs in the stables around the area and found a deep and abiding love for horses. They all seemed to react positively to me.

I had to cut way back on my dancing when mom got sick, and I took on the role of caregiver with the help of several of mom's close friends. I also had to cut back on my hours at the horse ranch where I was working. My schoolwork did not suffer, and I made excellent grades all through high school and was even able to attend and graduate from college. Between going to school, working, and taking care of her, my social life was non-existent. I loved people and had a boyfriend and a girlfriend but didn't get to see them very often.

In Kalispell Montana, the pickings were slim, and I settled for a cowboy named Cody from Wyoming for a couple of reasons. He was not there all the time, and I hated for anyone to try to smother me. He was a decent lover when we were able to get together, but something was lacking. My girlfriend had a husband, so that we couldn't get together often. But he cheated on her, and she knew it. When he was out, we could get together, mostly for going out dancing. We were not real lovers.

When mom died, I turned to them for whatever comfort and companionship they had to offer. My boyfriend must have seen that as his opportunity, and he pressed our relationship at precisely the wrong time. One night after an incredibly unsatisfying attempt at having a sexual encounter, he asked me to marry him and let him take care of me. That was the last thing I wanted or needed. He tried everything he could think of but made it all about him. He touched me, and I didn't respond at all. He pushed me down on the bed, held me there, and forced my legs apart to try to enter me. He couldn't because I had nothing to lube me at all. Besides, he always had trouble staying hard, no matter how much foreplay we went through. I threw him off me and left the bed, putting my clothes on as I went. That was it for him and me, and I went home and locked all the doors. I had to get him and his controlling ways out of my life. I was still hurting from my mom's death, and he had no idea, insensitive lout that he was.

After a few days, I went out with my girlfriend. She might understand. We went to a cozy little bar called "The Flame" and started drinking. The whiskey was smooth, and we both got drunk. She took me to her place. Thank God, we made it, and I passed out on the couch. When I awoke, my jeans and panties were down around my ankles, and she was licking me in her drunken stupor. I freaked out.

"What the hell do you think you're doing?"

"Just relax. I have wanted this for a long time," Diane said.

"No, no, I don't want this. I don't feel that way about you. Let me up!" She didn't. With all the strength I had left, I threw her off me, and she hit the floor hard, stunning her for a moment. I got up, rearranged my clothes, and left through the front door as fast as I could. She was hurling insults at me, calling me everything in the book. I walked home and again locked all my doors. I was all alone and feeling very sorry for myself. The horses I took care of always brightened my attitude, and when I felt better, even though the hour was late, I drove out to the ranch. They were glad to see me, and the gelding let me ride him around the corral bareback, which he seldom did. I felt better, but I knew I had to leave that place. Where to go? When I got home again, I removed my boots, lay down on the bed, and cried myself to sleep.

The next morning, I awoke with a tremendous hangover. The happenings of the previous several days came back to me. I saw the photo of my mother on my dresser and remembered her fondly. She was gone, Mr. Wyoming was gone, and now Diane was gone. Nothing remained for me there. I flashed back to the time I spent with mom in the hospital her final days when she told me the truth about my birth and the man who fathered me. He was a total mystery. I needed to get on with my life, so I earned my teaching certificate, moved down the road to Missoula, and took a job as a substitute teacher. I enjoyed working with the kids, but there was still something missing.

I realized that my ties to Kalispell and my old life were holding me back, so I gave all mom's things to the women's shelter and sold the house for what I thought was an acceptable price, knowing at least I would have no immediate money problems. When I was cleaning out the attic, I came across several boxes of scrapbooks that mom had kept all those years. My curiosity got the better of me, and I looked inside them. They contained clippings and articles from the last twenty plus years, including the year I was born. They fascinated me, so I took them downstairs and put them in my car. After I had collected everything I wanted to keep from the house, I sold all the contents, including the furniture, and went back to Missoula with my treasures. I had no idea what an effect they would have on my future.

I had lots of time to contemplate my situation and came to a firm conviction. My birth father had to be somewhere, and I determined to find him if I could. Mom had remembered some things about him, but not very much as her mind gradually slipped away. As she lay dying, she told me what she remembered. He was a tall man, athletic, and very attractive, and appealed to her immediately. She used to sit in his class and daydream about being with him. He was very personable and had just finished his Ph.D. She developed a major crush on him and flirted with him all week until the last night before the class was over, and they were to return to their homes.

Everyone in the class knew of her attraction to him; she did not try to hide it and even talked with some of her classmates about what they thought of him and if she should pursue her designs to the desired result. Everyone knew of her feelings except the man himself. She knew he liked her, but he was always very professional and never made a move toward her. After dinner the last night, she summoned all her courage and knocked on his door. He answered and invited her in. Mom told me very little about their encounter except that she stayed with him all night in his arms, cuddling and kissing. Early the next morning, they made love. It's incredible how sex in the early morning produces so many children, and she felt intuitively afterward that he had given her a baby.

Nine months later, she gave birth to me. The man I thought was my father was gone by then, and mom and I were on our own. She took terrific care of me as I grew, but there was always a nagging doubt whenever we talked about my dad. For one thing, I wanted to know if he had been so sick, how did he father a child. Until she died, my mom was always very vague about the specifics of their marriage, and I knew that taking care of him took a toll on her. From his photos, I could see no resemblance between him and me. He had straight sandy hair, and mine was black and curly. Mom's was brown.

Nonetheless, I didn't know until she lay on her death bed and decided to tell me the truth. Her revelation didn't surprise me, but I wanted to know everything she remembered. Finding my real dad did not become a compulsion to me until after her death, and I decided to get away from the toxic people in my life. I was alone and on my own.

I had no close relatives anywhere near me since I lived in northern Montana, and they were in Pennsylvania. We had never been close. My mom had left me some money, mostly in life insurance, because she used most of her assets to cover the cost of their respective illnesses. I had sold the house in Kalispell and had some money from that, but I was not wealthy. I wasn't broke either. I decided to try to find my birth father. From what my mom said, he sounded like a good man. Where to start?

I remembered my mom's scrapbooks that I had brought home with me after cleaning out the house. She was a dedicated saver of records and descriptions of importance in her life. I got them out and began to go through them. I found my baby pictures and others from the years in my life that followed. One covered the period in question and turned out to be very detailed.

I learned that she had taken continuing education classes every summer throughout her career. They usually lasted a week and moved around in many locations in the State, such as Helena, Billings, Bozeman, and smaller venues as well. I found the exact scrapbook covering the summer before I was born and discovered the class was in Bozeman that year at Montana State University. The flyer listed several instructors but had little detail. One seemed to stand out. He met her description of the man she thought was my real dad. In his promo photo, he wore a three-piece, gray pin-striped suit with a gold watch chain and had black curly hair just like mine. He was tall and very handsome, towering over the ladies in their class picture. There was my mom, very short but gorgeous, standing right beside him, gazing up at him adoringly. I knew I had found him.

The description said that he was an assistant professor at the University of Montana in Missoula. I looked carefully for his name and found it in the story under the photo. They listed him as Dr. Michael L. Armstrong, and I had a name to go with his picture. Now to track him down. I began my search at Montana State and tried to find someone who had been there at the time of the classes. No luck. No one even knew about the summer classes so long ago.

Next, I tried UM in Missoula. I had better luck there. Although many of his former colleagues had left for other jobs or died, I found the former dean of the college in which he taught, and he remembered him well. He told me he had moved to Texas and, as far as he knew, was still there. He even remembered the university where he taught and had visited there for a football game years ago. My search was progressing. I called his Texas school with my fingers crossed. Several of the professors there remembered him. I found out that, over the years, he had risen to the rank of full professor, earned tenure, and had gone into consulting and writing. He was not teaching there anymore. The academic vice president remembered him and even had an old phone number for him. I wrote it down eagerly, making sure not to make a mistake. The phone number was no longer in service.

I did an internet search for him and found that he had published profusely. Many of the articles included his photo, and much to my surprise, I looked just like him. His black hair showed flecks of gray later in his career, but he was just as handsome as he had been at a younger age. There was no doubt in my mind that the man in my mom's clippings was this man. How should I proceed? I didn't know whether he had other children if he had a wife, or how he would react to discovering an unknown daughter. I considered my options. I could go to Texas and try to find him, write to him, or find his current phone number and give him a call. I chose the latter. He might have forgotten my mom altogether or may not remember their night together. I decided to use her death as an excuse for the call since he had no idea that I was his daughter, at least not yet. I decided to sleep on my discovery and look for his number, and hopefully, make the call in the morning. I wanted to be sure my approach would not scare him away.

The next morning, I did an internet phone number search and found him in Dallas. I called his number, considering the time difference between Texas and Montana, and got his answering machine. I left the following message. "Dr. Armstrong, my name is Katie MacDonald from Kalispell, Montana, and I think you might have known my mom. Her name was Lindsay, and she attended one of your seminars in Bozeman over twenty years ago. She kept the clippings from that week and always wondered what happened to you. I am sorry to tell you that she succumbed to breast cancer recently, and I am letting people who might be interested know about her." I gave him my number and let him know I would be happy to tell him about mom if he wanted to know. It was all I could do at the time.

A week later, he still hadn't returned my call. I began to develop other strategies to meet him and decided a trip to Texas would be my next step when one evening, my phone rang. I didn't immediately recognize the number but answered it anyway. I thought it was more than likely a telemarketer and was surprised to hear his voice.

"Katie MacDonald, please."

"This is Katie."

"Hello, Katie. I am Mike Armstrong returning your call. How are you this evening?"

"Dr. Armstrong. I hoped you would call me back. I am fine. My mom talked about you from time to time. Do you remember her?"

"Yes, Katie, I remember her well. She was special to me, although I never saw her again after the course was over. Is her husband still living?"

"No. My mom survived him by many years, and he died before I was born. I never knew him."

"Please accept my condolences for the loss of your parents. Are you married?"

"No. I focused on my studies and finished them while I took care of my mother during her illness."

"Then, you are alone?"

"Yes."

"Did your mother ever say anything about me?"

"Yes, I know a great deal about you and her, Dr. Armstrong. She told me just before she died."

"After you were born, I called her hoping she would tell me about you, but she didn't. She was recovering from her marriage and the death of her husband. She was not free from her memories at the time. I respected that and left her alone, not wanting to cause problems for her. She was a powerful woman."

"Are you married, sir?"

"I am divorced."

"Do you have any children?"

"No, Katie, my marriage was very short, and I never was blessed with kids."

It occurred to me that that was about to change.

"Have you ever been to Texas? he asked."

"No, I haven't, Dr. Armstrong. I have heard a lot about it, though," I joked with him.

"How did you find me, Katie?"

"Before she died, mom told me all about her husband and how he was physically unable to father a child. She told me about a professor she met at a continuing education seminar and that she and he had become close. I always suspected that the man she had married was not my father, and she confirmed my suspicions. I found your name and picture in her scrapbooks and looked for you or anyone who might have known you in Montana. The former Dean at UM told me about your move to Texas. I searched for you on the internet and found you. I called the school where you taught, and one of your colleagues knew your current occupation and an old phone number. I called but found it disconnected. I searched further, and an internet phone search gave me this number.

Now you have called me back. I must say I am impressed that you are so well-known in academia."

"Thank you, Katie. What you seem to suspect is possible, although your mom never talked with me about you. I could be your father, but I would like to know for sure. Your mom and I had a brief affair, and nine months later, you were born. I could be wrong, but I have wondered all these years if I have a child in Montana."

"Is there a way we can find out for sure?"

"Yes, Katie. We can both take DNA tests and compare the results. That will tell us for sure."

"How do we do that?"

"Go to your local drugstore and ask for a saliva test kit. I will do the same, and we will send them to a lab for testing. We should have the results quickly. Are you willing to do that?"

"Yes, Dr. Armstrong. I would like to know for sure before I get my hopes up too high."

"Can you do it now, Katie?"

"Yes. Where do I send it?"

"Do you have a pen and paper?"

"Yes, right here."

"Then write this down." He gave me the address.

"Have it sent overnight, and I will do the same. When the test lab gets the two kits, they will analyze them and call with the results. We should know in just a few days."

"I will call you back when I have mailed it. Will you be there?"

"Yes, Katie, I will stay here until you call me back."

I rushed out to the pharmacy and got the test kit. I filled the tube with my saliva and sealed it, taking it straight to the post office and sending it overnight with all the pertinent information included. Then I went home and called Dr. Armstrong to tell him the kit was on its way.

"When they call, and they might call both of us, I'll let you know."

"Thank you, sir. I'll be waiting."

I had trouble sleeping that night, and my inability to concentrate evidenced my distraction all the next day. The horses sensed my change in attitude and let me love them all. I left work for home and waited patiently for a couple of days, hoping the phone would ring. My wait was not long, but it seemed like it took forever. Dr. Armstrong finally called me back.

"Katie?"

"Yes, Dr. Armstrong. Do you have the results?"

"Yes, daughter. I am your birth father."

I was speechless. The tests proved Dr. Michael L. Armstrong was my birth father. I cried.

"Don't cry, daughter. The test results are wonderful news."

"I know. I am thrilled to know the truth after all these years. Would it be possible to meet you?"

"We should meet. I want to meet you too."

"Are you sure, Katie?"

"Yes, Dr. Armstrong, I am sure."

"When can you come?"

"I have some things to do around here, but I can come soon. What would be good for you?"

"I just got back from a weeklong, overseas trip and will be here for some time to come. I'll arrange for your flight, and you can come in the next few days. Where will you fly from?"

"I live in Missoula now, so that I will leave from here. Will you check what is possible?"

"Yes. How does Saturday suit you?"

"That will be fine."

"I'll have the tickets ready for you at the airport. I hope you can stay awhile. I would like to get to know the woman who is my daughter."

"I would like to get to know the man who is my father too. Knowing about you opens an entirely new life for me. I can't wait to meet you."

"What is the best way to contact you with the arrangements. I have this number on my caller ID. Do you have email and social media as well?"

I gave him both. "Will you meet me at the airport in Dallas?"

"Yes, Katie. I wouldn't miss it for anything. I have an extra bedroom for you, and we can spend some time getting to know each other. Would that be okay with you?"

"Yes, sir." I hesitated. "What would you like me to call you?"

"Let's decide that when you get here. What would you like to call me?"

"How about Dad?"

"I never thought I would have a daughter or ever be called Dad. That would be wonderful. I am so glad you found me, Katie. My life is starting anew too. We can live our new lives together, I hope. See you on Saturday afternoon."

"How will I know you?"

"We will know each other when we meet. I just know it."

"Yes, we will. Goodbye, Dad. Until Saturday."

I started packing the necessaries and gave the rest to charity. My wreck of a car sold for a few hundred dollars, and I had nothing left to keep me in Montana. I could transfer my bank account to wherever I might end up and looked forward to my new life, which would begin on Saturday. I notified the ranch owners of what was happening and went to say goodbye to the horses. Everything, including me, was ready. Saturday morning, I called a cab to take me to the airport and took one last look at the mountains in the distance. I would miss them, but I had no regrets. My plane took off right on time and flew to Denver for my connecting flight to DFW International Airport. As we headed farther south, I felt my new life beginning. Many questions ran through my mind. What kind of man would my father be? Would I like the guys in Texas? What would I do when I got there? I knew I would find the answers to those questions. On the way, I was even able to take a nap. When I awoke, we were descending into the Dallas area.

Chapter Two

I Meet My Dad

Could this be happening? My mom wanted me to find my real dad. Otherwise, why would she have documented everything knowing I would find it? I think she must have loved him very much. She did it her way, and now I had found my dad after so many years. The whole thing was fantastic, surreal.

I was sitting beside a gentleman who was older than I, and he welcomed me to Dallas, giving me his card. He said if he could do anything to help me get acclimated to call him. If everyone in Texas was that friendly, it must be a welcoming place. I saw this massive airport below us as the pilots turned off the downwind and base legs and onto our final approach. After landing, we must have taxied for at least fifteen minutes before we arrived at our gate. Planes seemed to be everywhere in this great airport. Everything is genuinely bigger in Texas.

The terminal was massive and very modern. I followed the signs for baggage claim with nervous anticipation. My dad was meeting me there. As soon as I went through the gate, I saw him. He was unmistakable. He saw me too. I rushed over to him, and he took me in his arms and hugged me tightly. I hugged him back.

"Hello, Katie. Welcome to Texas."

"Hello, Dad, you are just as I imagined you would be." I kissed him on the cheek, and he kept holding me. I began to cry tears of joy.

"You are so tall, Katie, much taller than your mom."

"Another thing I got from my real father."

"But, you have blue eyes with that black hair."

"I got them from my mom. It all makes sense now, the way I look, taking after both you and her."

"You are beautiful, daughter."

The baggage conveyor started up, and I found my bags.

"These are mine." My dad picked them up, put them on a hand

cart, and we exited to the parking lot. I took one of them, and he took the others. He had parked his car close to the terminal, and it took us only a few minutes to walk to it. He opened a door and put my bags in the back, and then escorted me to the passenger door. I loved the softness and smell of the leather upholstery in his Lincoln SUV, and we were soon past the exit gates and headed north on a big interstate highway. The land was flat and spread out on all sides. Shopping centers and office complexes lined the road. I had never seen anything like it before.

"How do you like it?"

"It's amazing. Is all of Texas like this?"

"Oh, no. East Texas is heavily forested, and out west, there are mountains and deserts. Lakes and rivers are everywhere. We must go on a tour so that you can see it all."

"Where do you live, Dad?"

"I live on a ranch near a lake about an hour north of the airport. I think you'll like it."

"Dad, if I seem somewhat uncomfortable, please understand what I am going through now. My mom is gone, and I am on my own. I cut all ties before I left, and can handle starting my life over again, but to find you and meet you causes a very uncertain situation for me."

"Katie, I think I understand. I am nervous too, but your mom planned this from what you have told me, and she wanted us to be together."

"There must be people in your life that are close to you. Do you have a girlfriend?"

"Yes, Katie, I have several girlfriends. I spend most of my time with a lady named Jackie, and she is special to me. She is going to like you since you are so much like me. If it's okay with you, she will meet you soon."

"Wow! It's a whole new world for me."

"I want you to know that I realize you are a grown woman and can do as you please. Talk to me. Let me know what you are thinking and feeling. I hope this works out, you and me together, but it might not. If you have problems with anything, let me know. You are my daughter, and I am your Dad, but fate has thrown us together unexpectedly. Your mom saw to that."

"Whatever happens to us, you should know that I love you, Dad. I knew when I first saw you at the airport. You must promise to talk to me too. Maybe we can make this work."

A single tear trickled from his eyes. Mike was a good man, and I hoped he would be the father I never had. I finally understood my mom. She was a wonderful woman. Those two should have been together, and I am living proof that they were, at least once.

As we traveled through the Texas countryside, Dad pointed out some interesting things. He showed me vast expanses of land, several rivers, and things gradually thinned out as we proceeded north. I loved what I saw even though it was different from the mountains of western Montana. The country was wide open, and there seemed to be no limits. We left the highway and moved onto rural roads, went through several towns, many of which had squares in the middle of the towns, some with majestic courthouses, and into the boondocks of Texas. He finally turned into a narrow road on which I saw several houses. At the end of the road were a gate and a large house situated with a marvelous view of a vast lake. We were at home.

My Dad pressed the remote attached to the sun visor, and the gate opened. He drove to the house and parked in front of the garage. The house was large and very spread out. Close by, I saw a barn and several horses in the surrounding pasture. One of them was a beautiful palomino who seemed curious as to who this new person was. We would get to know each other quickly. The woods went all the way down to the lake. It was a beautiful place. We got out of the car, and he took me and my bags inside. I was nervous but not frightened. I knew I had nothing to fear. I was at my new home, and he was my real Dad. I shed a few tears when all that hit me. He put the bag down and held me. "It's okay, Katie. You are home now and with me, as you should be. I have been waiting for you for such a long time. I hope you will be happy here."

"Thanks, Dad. Everything is all so new to me. My real Dad, in a new place, and having no idea what is going to happen next. It's all so exciting but scary, just the same."

"Let's put your things in your room, and I'll give you a tour."

"I would like that very much."

He led me to a bedroom furnished very tastefully with a feminine touch. I thought of Jackie immediately. A dresser with a mirror was against one wall, and the closet was huge. I sat on the large bed and found it to be very comfortable. It had windows which let in light and bedside tables with lamps. It was all lovely.

"I must admit that I didn't put this room together. My friend Jackie did it when I told her that my real daughter, whom I had no idea even existed, was coming to Texas. I hope you like it. She has excellent taste and is all woman."

"I love it, Dad. It is beautiful and so comfortable. When do I get to meet Jackie?"

"She is coming for dinner this evening, and you will meet her then. Why don't we look at the rest of the house and the grounds before she arrives?"

"It is a huge house. I like it a lot."

"I hope you will be comfortable here."

"I know I will."

The far wing was mostly living and sleeping space and very well done. But the main area was my favorite. It was a true indoor paradise. The kitchen took up one entire end of the open room, large and fully equipped. Next to it was a casual living room with comfy furniture and many male accessories. The walls were rustic and covered with what I recognized as barn wood. The floors looked to be from the same material, although they were smoother and finished with what I guessed was semi-gloss polyurethane. It was gorgeous. The master suite was next, behind large oaken doors for privacy. The suite had a fireplace, and vents for central heat and air were strategically located around the rooms. It must be very comfortable in both the Texas summer heat and the depths of winter.

The most prominent part, however, was the panoramic view through the windows, which surrounded the whole floor, providing views of the lake, pastures, and woodlands. Rolling hills formed the horizons at a distance, not mountains, but they were enticing just the same. I stood in awe, unable to speak. The place was going to be my home. Happy tears started again.

"Do you like it, Katie?" Dad asked.

"I love it. It is quite different from Montana, but it is magnificent, just the same." I went over to him, and he embraced me in a fatherly hug. I couldn't believe what was happening to me.

"Would you like to meet Rex, my Irish Setter, and the horses?"

"Yes, especially the horses, but I need to rest for a minute. It is all so overwhelming."

"Come over here, Katie, and sit with me." He led me over to the leather couch and went to the sliding glass door that led out to the deck that surrounded the house. A gorgeous red dog came in, excited, and a little reluctant to come to me. Dad sat down beside me and beckoned him over. I let him smell my hand, and he approved. I petted him, which he loved, and he put his massive head in my lap. I kept petting him and talking to him. He loved the attention.

"Rex, this is Katie, she is my daughter whom I have never met before. Be her friend and take care of her."

The big dog knew what Dad was saying and curled up on the floor at our feet. "You have a new friend, big boy." Rex just lay there with his head raised, looking very majestic.

"He is so handsome, Dad. How old is he?"

"Rex is five and has been with us since he was a pup."

"Do you mean you and Jackie?"

"Yes, Katie. Jackie frequently stays with me here."

"Are you planning to marry her?"

"We have discussed it, but our lives are so wonderful the way they are, we don't want to spoil that. We love each other deeply and have become soul mates. I hope that isn't a problem for you."

"No, Dad, not a bit. I am sure she and I will be great friends."

"I hope so. Jackie has been the only woman in my life for some time now. With you being here, I now have two."

"Is that going to be a problem with her?"

"No, Katie. I just told her about you, and she is excited. She has no children either. I think having you in our lives will be something she has always wanted."

"Dad, I haven't had much to eat today. Do you have anything to munch on until we have dinner?"

"How about an old Texas favorite, chips, queso, and salsa?"

"Sounds wonderful. How about a Texas beer?"

"One Lone Star coming up. I think I'll join you."

"Sounds fantastic. Show me where things are in the kitchen so that I can help out around here."

"Come with me, Angel."

"No one has ever called me that, Dad. I like it." We went into the kitchen, and he showed me where things were. We opened two bottles of ice-cold beer, and I loved it with my first taste. He made fresh queso and opened a jar of salsa that he and Jackie had made themselves. The salsa was a little spicy for my taste, but the restaurant-style chips were fresh and crisp and helped with the spiciness. Soon I was in Tex-Mex heaven. Our beers didn't last very long, and we opened two more. I couldn't believe I was drinking beer with my real dad. The whole situation made me very happy, and it showed in my smile.

We took seats at the dining table and munched, drank beer, and loosened up with each other. My new dad was an excellent conversationalist, and we laughed together and toasted our unique situations and finding each other. The last toast was to my mother. Dad said, "And here is to Lindsay

MacDonald, Katie's mother and the mother of my only child. Wherever you are, and I think I know where we both want to thank you. What you did was very good for all of us."

"Here's to my mom, whom I loved so much," I finished the toast. We shed a tear together. Both of us knew we were getting close to each other. We had both loved my mom, not for the same reason, but that bond was strong between us.

We finished our snack and opened two more beers when we heard someone coming in the front door. Neither of us had heard the car drive up outside. The door opened and in walked a gorgeous blonde, tall and graceful, with a bright smile on her face. She saw us immediately standing in the kitchen and came over to us. Dad put down his beer and embraced her, giving her a big kiss. I knew she must be Jackie.

"Did you save one of those for me?" she said lightheartedly.

"Of course, my dear. I want you to meet Katie, my long-lost daughter."

"Hello, so pleased to meet you, Jackie," and I extended my hand to shake hers. She didn't take it. Instead, she took me in her arms and gave me a big hug. She stepped back when Dad handed her a beer, and she looked at me after taking a swallow.

"Katie, my dear, you are beautiful. I had no idea. You look just like your father."

I was somewhat embarrassed by that, ducked my head, and said, "And you are the most gorgeous woman I have ever seen, Jackie. I see why my Dad loves you so much."

"We are going to get along just fine, Katie," she said as she gave me another hug. This time I noticed her perfume—White Shoulders. Jackie was no ordinary woman.

"What are you guys doing besides drinking beer and eating chips and queso?"

"We are getting to know each other."

"How was your trip, Katie?"

"Exciting and full of anticipation, Jackie."

"Let's go sit and let Mike take care of us. Lord knows we both will be taking loving care of him now." I went with her to the sofa and sat beside her. Jackie was a person whom I hoped I would get to know very well.

"Tell me, Katie. Is there a special guy back in Montana who is sorry to see you go to Texas?"

I avoided the question. "I had a good friend there, but I spend most of my free time, of which there has been very little lately, with a circle of friends. We do a lot of things together. We ski together in the winter, hike, run, and go out. My school, working with the horses, and taking care of my mom, have taken most of my time." Jackie knew I wasn't telling her the entire truth. She was a very aware lady, and she did not pursue the subject.

"What are we doing for dinner, Mike? I'm getting hungry already."

"We have plenty here, but I was thinking about taking you two lovelies out to Al's for some fresh Gulf seafood. What's your preference?"

I responded immediately. "Let's go out. I want to see more of the place where you live."

"For a while, at least, you live here too, Angel." He used my new pet name again, pleasing me very much.

"You've got it. If Jackie agrees, Al's it is."

"I would love to dine there tonight, but I need to get ready. Would you like to come with me, Katie?"

"Thanks, Jackie. I would love to."

"Excuse us, lover, and make me a vodka martini. You know how I like them, medium dry and on the rocks. Katie and I will be back soon." She took my hand and led me into the master bath. It was luxurious and had everything anyone could want. When we got there, our conversation turned to girl talk.

"Katie, just between us girls, what's the story with this guy friend you have in Montana?"

"I knew you picked up on that. Cody is one of the reasons I wanted to come here."

"Let me guess. Cody wants something permanent from you, and you are not ready."

"How did you know? He wants to marry me, and I have no intention of doing that. Sometimes the situation gets to be more than I can handle. I have had enough emotional issues for a lifetime already. Sometimes I wish he would move back to Wyoming and be a cowboy again, leaving me alone."

"So, you left him."

"Not just him. He suspects but doesn't know. There are others."

"I do not doubt that, as gorgeous as you are."

"How did you handle that situation when you went through it?"

"How do you know I went through it?"

"As attractive as you are, there is no way you didn't."

"I regret to say that I had to break some hearts."

"Been there, done that. But now you and my Dad are together, and unless I miss my guess, you love each other very much."

"He is an amazing man, your Dad."

"For my mom to have fallen for him so hard, he would have to be."

"How did you find out about Mike and your mom?"

"For years, I suspected the man to whom she was married had not been my real father. So many things didn't add up. He died before I was born, and I didn't share any personality traits with him. Then I found out that his illness prevented him from fathering a child. Mom didn't tell me the truth until she lay on her death bed, having battled her cancer bravely but in vain. Even as she lay dying, she still loved Mike, and she left me clues so that I could find him. She didn't want him to see her in her last days, so she kept everything secret until then."

"She raised you by herself?"

"Yes, and she was a wonderful mother. I miss her so much." My tears flowed, and Jackie took me in her arms and comforted me. I liked her already.

Chapter Three

Dinner with My New Parents

"She did what she thought was best for you, Katie."

"When she knew she was going to die, Mom realized I would be alone, so she put me on the path to finding my real father, and here I am."

"This must be an emotional time for you, my dear."

"Yes, it is, but I feel so much better now that things are coming together as they should have all those years ago."

"This may sound selfish, but I am glad I found Mike and now you. If he had married your mom, I would never have met him."

"Are you in love with him, Jackie?"

"Yes, Katie. He is the smartest, most generous, and loving man I have ever known."

"Do you think you two will marry someday?"

"I hope so, Katie, but when the time is right for both of us, we'll know. Are you ready to go to dinner?"

"Give me a few minutes to wash the airplane off me and change into something more appropriate, and I'll be ready."

"Can I help?"

"I would like that very much, Jackie. My things are in my room. My room! That's hard to comprehend."

"I know it must be."

"Thank you so much for decorating it for me and getting everything ready."

"It has been a pleasure. Mike only told me what was going on a few days ago, and I wanted you to have a place that was all yours."

I hugged her and led her to my room. My traveling clothes went into the clothes hamper, and I washed my face before putting on a skirt and blouse, so I looked more like Jackie. We went back to Dad.

"There you two are. Did you have a good talk?"

"Yes, Mike. Katie and I are going to be great friends. This lady is something special."

I ducked my head and blushed at her words.

"She is going to be a great daughter. You couldn't have done better if you had chosen someone."

"She's her mother's child he said. Are you ready?"

"Yes, let's go have some fantastic Gulf seafood."

"I'm ready," Jackie responded.

"Me, too," I agreed. We took the Lincoln, and Mike headed out with his woman and his daughter together for the first time. I was so happy to be with them. My first outing in Texas was exciting, and being with Dad and Jackie was marvelous. I looked forward to the excellent food and getting to know my new family.

Al's looked like a dump outside, but even this early in the evening, the full parking lot indicated there was quite a crowd there. Dad let the valet service take care of the SUV, and we went right in. The staff only needed a few minutes to prepare our table, and we took our seats.

"May I recommend something tropical to drink? The Piña Coladas are fantastic as are the Mai Tais."

"A Piña Colada, but not too sweet for me," I responded, "maybe followed by a mojito?"

"Another excellent choice, Katie. How about you, Jackie?"

"I'll have what Katie is having, please."

"Make that three, waitress."

"Excellent, sir. I'll bring them out while you are deciding on your dinners."

"This is all new to me, Dad. What's good?"

"The Gulf is known for its oysters and shrimp. I like my oysters on the half shell and my shrimp either fried or sautéed."

"Okay, Dad, I must admit that I am used to seafood from Alaska and the northern Pacific, but these Gulf dishes sound wonderful. I'm looking forward to giving them a try."

"I love my oysters, too, Katie," Jackie told me. "Would you like to share a dozen on the half shell as an appetizer?"

"Sure. It will be my first time for raw oysters."

"What else, Katie?"

"Are the shrimp fresh?"

"They are probably alive as we speak."

"In that case, I will have a fried platter, please."

"Good choices for your first Texas seafood dinner."

The waitress returned with our drinks, and Dad offered a toast. "Here's to both the women in my life, especially the one we didn't expect."

"To Katie," Jackie echoed.

We tasted our drinks, and I must admit, the freshness of the coconut and pineapple was a new experience for me. I loved them.

The restaurant quickly filled up after our arrival. A line out the front door developed, and people were waiting for their seats. Dad had timed our visit perfectly. I looked as the waiters delivered dishes to the surrounding tables. It all looked delicious, whether fried, sautéed, or boiled. The Mahi dish looked terrific, and I had to ask what it was. Everyone seemed to be enjoying themselves in a relaxed environment while they ate their dinner. I liked Al's very much, and we ordered refills for our drinks. I asked Jackie how she and my dad had gotten together.

"Believe it or not, I was one of his students in graduate school. He looked so good in his three-piece suit, and all the girls had crushes on him. We waited until the class was over before we even thought about going out together. A mutual friend asked us both out for lunch but didn't tell us he had invited the other. Then he didn't show up, and there we were."

"That's a fantastic story. I bet you two were surprised."

"We have never seen him again after that episode. I still think he must have been an angel sent from heaven to get us together," Jackie told me.

"And now you have a daughter you didn't know about."

"Life is full of surprises," he said.

"What do you do, Jackie? If I may ask."

"Your dad turned me on to corporate finance so strongly that I decided to follow that path. He did me a favor, and I love working in the field. Besides, it gives us something in common."

"And now you have me. Is there any chance I might end up with a new mom to go with my new dad?"

"We'll explain that to you when we get home, okay?"

"Sure, Dad. It's going to take a while to get to know each other." Jackie had changed the subject much to my relief. I was afraid I had committed a faux pas.

Our waitress approached the table with a large tray of fresh oysters on ice, numbering more than a dozen. Dad wanted some too. They showed me how to eat them with the lemon, horseradish sauce, and saltine crackers. I watched Jackie eat one and did as she had done. To my great surprise, it was delicious. "That is so good!" I said.

"They are excellent roasted and even fried too. An oyster po' boy is a famous sandwich around here, especially when they are fresh and newly shucked."

"I can see why, Dad." We finished the oysters, and I was already feeling satisfied.

A busboy took away the empty platter, and our waitress brought our entrees. The shrimp smelled terrific, and I watched my dad dip one in the tartar sauce served with it. I did as he had and was rapidly picking up the proper ways to eat Texas seafood. The shrimp was the best I ever had. It was so fresh, and the breading flavors were subtle but delicious and new to my palate. I was going to love Texas food, and I must admit I ate heartily at Al's.

Dad and Jackie offered dessert at home if I wanted some, and we took our leave from the restaurant. The line was still out the door. We returned to the house and Rex, who greeted us energetically. He liked me, and I felt gratified about that.

The three of us took seats in the living room and relaxed after dinner. I was curious to know what other culinary opportunities awaited me. Next, I wanted to sample Texas barbeque, having heard so much about it. "That was excellent, Dad, Jackie. I loved the oysters and shrimp. Next time, I think I will try something else on their menu."

"There are many dishes from which to choose. Al's is very popular around here."

"I could see that just being there. But can we try Texas barbeque next?"

"I imagine we could work that into the menu. What do you think, Jackie?"

"Angelo's?"

"Perfect. Fantastic place to do a sampler."

Dad put his drink down on the coffee table and looked at Jackie. She nodded her head. He began to talk with me. "This evening you asked us a question to which we delayed our response. Would you like us to explain it now?"

"If it's something you want to keep between yourselves, just say so. I will understand."

"It's not that, Katie," Jackie said. "We have come to grips with it, and our love has gotten us through it."

"You see, Katie, Jackie, and I tried for years to have a child, but it never happened. We wanted to know why, because we both wanted a child."

Jackie took up the story. "We both got tested, and the results showed that I am unable to get pregnant due to some unknown issue with my female parts. It was a blow to both of us."

Dad continued, "We tried everything from fertility drugs to in vitro, but nothing worked. We have a wonderful relationship and want to be together even if we can't have children. Our happiness is dependent on loving each other and nothing else."

"We like living this way and see no reason to formalize our relationship with marriage. It may happen someday, but so far we have seen no need for it."

"If you are happy, I see no need for it, either."

"Thanks for understanding, Katie."

"I agree with you."

"Now, I have a question for you."

"Okay, Dad, what is it?"

"Ever since I found out about you when you tracked me down, I have wondered about this. Have you ever seen your birth certificate, Katie?"

"No, Dad. I asked mom about it, but she never told me or showed it to me. Why?"

"I knew it listed your mother, but I was wondering who it included as your father."

"I don't know, but I have always thought her husband was my father. He should be the one listed."

"I took the liberty to find it in Kalispell before you left to come here. Katie, he is not listed as your father." He handed me an envelope, and I opened it. A copy of my birth certificate was inside. I unfolded it and looked carefully at what it said. It had my date and time of birth, the doctor who delivered me, but where my father's name should be, the space was blank. I looked up at him with a significant question on my mind.

"What did you mean when you said I might get another mother out of this?"

"It might be a perfect time for Jackie and me to marry, especially if we have a daughter."

"When you said things would change, you weren't kidding."

Rex raised his head and put it back in my lap. I petted him affectionately. He looked like he was asking me an essential question.

"We know the truth now. Do we go to see a judge, and have you added as my father?"

"Yes. We will be official."

"Jackie, are you ready to be a part of all this?"

"Katie, I am not getting my hopes up, but yes, I'm on board."

"Now that we know, does that mean you two will marry?"

"Yes, Katie, I believe every person should have two parents. We should have done it long ago."

"I don't want to be the reason for that. The decision must be yours. Be sure that even if I had never come along, you would have done it anyway."

"But you did come along, dear Katie, and I, for one, am so glad you came into our lives."

"Thank you, Jackie. I am glad I found you too."

We stayed up late that night and talked more. I told them about Montana since Jackie had never been there, and Dad had moved away over twenty years ago. They explained to me about Texas and how they were there to stay because they both loved it so. I learned about the horses and told them I knew how to ride and wanted to help take care of them. Finally, we went to bed together, so that I would not awaken alone, with me on one side of Jackie and dad on the other. Because it had been a long day for me, I went to sleep quickly and slept very well until morning in Jackie's arms. The smell of coffee and breakfast awoke me. I dragged into the kitchen, and Jackie handed me a cup of coffee. She was off on Sunday and could spend the entire day with us. I looked forward to it.

We rode horses all over the property, including a gallop along the beach at the edge of the lake. I loved my new home, and I was beginning a love affair with Texas. I asked my dad where he planned to put the pool.

"How did you know I was planning a pool?"

"It makes sense. We are in Texas, you have a lot of room here, and you know Jackie and I would love one. Where is it going to go?"

"Jackie, how did my daughter get to be so smart?"

"She is your daughter, Mike. She has some of your best traits."

"We don't know that yet. We will know soon, dear Jackie."

We rode back to the barn, brushed the horses, and turned them back out in the pasture after feeding them their treats. I loved the one I rode, whose name was Mandy, and planned to take care of her myself. Dad rode Romeo, the palomino whom they had left intact due to his championship bloodlines. To say he had spirit did not tell half the story. I resolved to get to know him and looked forward to our first ride together.

Seeing my Dad and Jackie so happy stimulated my sexuality, and I wished I had already found a nice man to love. My thoughts aroused me, and I excused myself for a few minutes to make sure everything was okay. I returned to them much more stable in my emotions.

Chapter Four

My New Mom, Jackie

After lunch, Dad and Jackie took me out to their chosen pool site and showed it to me. Secluded and very private, I immediately knew they had chosen well. "Let's call the pool company tomorrow and get them out here. I will be here even if you two are working and will make sure they do it right. Deal?"

"How can we refuse an offer like that?"

"I'm all for it," Jackie agreed.

"Then call them, Dad, and let's get started."

They came a few days later and laid out the site with a large pool and a spa. It would take them several weeks to get it all done.

We returned to the subject of our relationship. "I will contact my lawyers tomorrow and get them working on this. The first thing to do, I think, is to have your birth certificate amended to name me as your father. With the DNA evidence, that should not be a problem. Would you like to change your last name to Armstrong, Katie?"

"This is all happening so fast. It's making my head spin. Can the three of us discuss it? I know I am beginning a new life, and I don't know what I want in many aspects of it. Finding you, my actual father needs to sink in before I start making decisions such as that."

"I understand. Yes, Katie, we can and will discuss it, the three of us."

"Yes, Dad. The three of us."

"Jackie, will you marry me?"

"Whoa, Dr. Armstrong. Aren't you going a bit fast on all this? I agree with Katie. We all three must understand what is going on with all the changes happening to us."

"What is this, a revolution by both women in my life, together?"

I looked at Jackie, and she looked at me. My smile told her a lot.

"Mike, now that Katie is here, I finally have another woman to whom I can talk. I've missed that. You are wonderful, and I love you dearly, but she and I need to talk."

"Can I be a part of your conversation?"

"Later, maybe, but for now, I need to talk with the woman who likely will become my daughter and best friend. Can you understand that?"

"Yes, Jackie. All this is new to me too."

"I know, my love. We need to get to know each other since we are together this way so unexpectantly."

"I think I will make a trip to the store or go take care of the horses. You two stay here and relax. I'll be back."

"Thanks, Dad."

"This may take some getting used to."

"We know, Mike. We'll talk together as three very soon."

"Okay. I'll see you both later."

Jackie gave him a hug and a kiss, and I hugged him. He left us alone to talk.

"Jackie, you know him far better than I. How do you think he took that?"

"He is trying, Katie, but he hasn't entirely come to grips with our new situation yet."

"I can understand that. Now instead of a girlfriend and no immediate need to marry, he has both of us. He must be thinking about taking care of me too."

"No doubt. If I may ask, why did changing your name not appeal to you?"

"You are in the same boat, Jackie. How do you feel about changing your name?"

"When or if we marry, I am not sure I am going to change it at all. I certainly don't have to. It might be somewhat different for a daughter."

"Why so? I don't want to forget my former life and my mother, who raised me alone, and whom I loved so much. It is too early now, and I don't know my Dad or how I feel about him. Is something causing you doubts about marrying him? You have been together for a long time and never married. Does my being here change that?"

"I don't know yet. You see, there is something about me Mike doesn't know."

"There is someone else in your life, isn't there?"

"How did you know?"

"It's not another man, either, is it?"

"Katie, is it that obvious?"

"To me, it is. You see, Jackie, the nights in Montana, can be very long and lonely. My Wyoming cowboy just did not fill the bill. He was frequently gone, and I sought another for company. To be honest, she found me."

"Is that part of the reason you were willing to leave and come here?"

"Yes. I wanted to leave that all behind and begin anew."

"Did your mom know?"

"She suspected. You see, the only way she could cope with her husband's illness and death was because she became close to a nurse at the center where he had his treatment. She had the same talent I have, being able to recognize women of similar interests."

"Do I get to meet the people in your life?"

"No, I'm afraid not. Mr. One-Way Wyoming Asshole is someone I never want to see again. My gal friend has a husband, and we were not intimate with each other. Even if we go up there, I don't want to replay those old tapes."

"Wow, Katie. You have had a lot to happen to you in a short time."

"Yes, Jackie, I have." I started crying softly. She came to me and held me firmly. I felt I had found a friend in my possible Mom-to-be.

"It's going to be all right, Katie. You are a courageous young woman, and I feel you can handle just about anything that might come along."

I raised my head to look in her eyes, and they reassured me. Then she lifted my chin, smiled at me, and kissed me full on the lips. The softness surprised me, and I felt the wonders of her embrace. I pulled back from her with more questions than answers then returned her kiss. She felt love in my arms, and I let myself go to enjoy our newfound closeness. My future Mom? At that time, she was just an attractive, sexy woman who was getting into me while I got into her. I forgot Mike and all my past for those few moments and just enjoyed having this beautiful woman love me. I didn't care what the repercussions might be. I needed her.

"Jackie, you are hot as hell. How are we going to be a mother and daughter and share our love? My sex drive is powerful, and I want that part of my life back."

"You are not my biological daughter, Katie. The fact that I might be married to Mike has no bearing on us."

"And when we sleep together as we did last night, you will know it as well as I do?"

"We will figure that out when it comes up."

"I have never lived with a lover before, man or woman. Can you tell me what that might be like?"

"I wish I could, dear Katie, but I don't know much about it either. We will just have to find out together."

"Then what are we going to do?"

"We are going to decide together what to do. I love Mike, but he has no clue what to do with two women in his life, so it's up to us."

"We have no clue what to do with him, either."

"That's true. Our plan will have as its major goal to make us all happy. Only the two of us can determine what that is going to be."

"I know that in time I will come to love my Dad. For now, I need you, Jackie. I have no one else. I am in a strange place with people I don't know. My entire world has changed, and I need a friend. Please don't leave me, Jackie." I hugged her lovingly.

"Don't worry, my child, my lover. We will be together, no matter what."

"What are we going to tell Mike?"

"Mike? That's the first time I have heard you not call him Dad."

"I know he is my Dad, but I don't feel that father/daughter relationship yet. We have had so little time together. Might I meet your girlfriend, Jackie?"

"That might be a problem, Katie. If I don't leave Mike, she is more than likely gone."

"You have me now. Do you and Mike have a good sex life?"

"Not really. At least not what I want."

"I'm sorry."

"Don't be. I take care of myself. I am not sure about Mike."

"Do you think he has other women in his life?"

"I know he does. A woman in every port as the old saying goes."

"Then why do you live together?"

"Living together with our other interests seems to be the best situation for us right now."

"And now I have come along. Am I upsetting your apple cart?"

"You have already upset mine, Katie. I am not sure I can be your mom and your lover at the same time."

"So, we have an issue, then."

"It would seem so."

"What are we going to do?"

"My first instinct is not to marry Mike and leave things just the way they are."

"I don't want to lose my identity, Jackie."

"Do you feel that if you change your name, you will do that?"

"That is a distinct possibility."

"I see. Then we get Mike to do all the right things that he should do, but neither of us becomes an Armstrong?"

"Yes. I want everyone to know who my birth father is, but I don't want to lose Katie MacDonald. Can we do that?"

"Yes. We will tell Mike what we want, and he will go along."

"What about your marriage to Mike?"

"If by some miracle I can bear him a child, then I will marry him and become Mrs. Armstrong. Otherwise, things remain the way they are."

"I love you, Jackie. Thanks for everything."

"I love you too, Katie, although I never thought it would happen. Maybe the two of us should go away by ourselves for a while."

"Mothers and daughters go on trips together all the time. Do you think you could marry Mike and adopt me?"

"How did you know what I was thinking?"

"It seems like the perfect solution, Mrs. Armstrong."

"And you would take our name, Katie Armstrong?"

"It would be an honor, Jackie."

"Are you ready to bring him back to our discussion?"

"If you answer one question for me."

"What would that be?"

"Can I sleep with you?"

"Do you mean both of us?"

"No, just you."

"Yes, my dear. And I will take you as my daughter whether I marry Mike or not."

"Then, it is settled. You and I have a man together who is going to love us and take excellent care of us. You and I will love each other and take care of our man. We are a pair, no matter what happens. Agreed?"

"Agreed. Let's not invite Mike back to us yet, though. I want to get to know you better first. I want to feel your touch, and I want to explore your mind, soul, and body. Will you let me do that?"

"My thoughts exactly, Jackie. We are going to be very close, I think. We might as well begin now." She kissed me a lover's kiss and touched me all over, raising my sexual energies in a way I had never known before. I melted into her arms and responded to her deep within me. I knew my move to Texas was the right thing to do. It was right.

Jackie took me back to their bedroom and put me on the bed, looking up at her. She was so beautiful! I pulled her to me and kissed her romantically. I needed her, and she would not get away until I found out what I wanted to know. I needn't have worried. She took the lead with me, removing my clothes piece by piece. As she did, she touched me all over, beginning with a kiss, then her hands moved down to my breasts, and she rolled my erect nipples between her fingers. I closed my eyes and let her do as she pleased. She was an excellent lover.

When she removed my panties and touched my extreme wetness, I rose to a higher plane. She knew how to please me, and I was responding to her with my real sexuality. No one had ever aroused me the way she did. I opened my eyes in total rapture, and she smiled a huge smile my way. I placed my hand behind her head and pulled her down. She got the message, and the next feeling I had was her tongue licking my clitoris, going around it repeatedly, and trailing her kisses across my labia and down as far as she could go. I was flying, and she knew it. She raised her head to focus on my love button as she slipped a finger in my vagina, making me explode in my first orgasm in many weeks, one I needed badly.

She didn't stop with my first one, just took a short break and went back to what she was doing. "You taste so good, Katie, and I love the way you respond to me."

"You knew what I needed exactly, Jackie. Love me until I pass out under you." She started moving her finger in and out of me instead of just leaving it there. She flipped my clitoris with her thumb as she used her tongue to take me back to ecstasy. I raised my leg between her legs and moved her hips with my hands, so she was rubbing against me. She went into her world and moved with me stimulating her clitoris as she worked on mine. I came again, and she came just after I did. Her orgasm shook her entire body, and I was glad she came so quickly. I fell limp under her but didn't pass out. She collapsed on top of me and held me tight. What a lover! We stayed in our embrace for a long while and took up where we had left off. I rolled on top of her and kissed her the way she had kissed me. She responded at once and moaned at her pleasure. I made her come powerfully even after what we had done already. She showed me what a real loving relationship could be. Texas was going to be a lot of fun.

Chapter Five

Our First Night Together

"I am getting sleepy, Jackie. It has been an exciting day. Is Mike coming home anytime soon?"

"I'll call him. He's probably with his drinking buddies."

She called. "Mike, this is Jackie. Are you having fun?"

"Yeah, sweetheart. It's a good time for us guys."

"I think Katie and I are going to bed. It has been quite a day."

"You guys go ahead. I won't be too long."

"We'll hold you to that. We had a wonderful talk, and we have some things to tell you, but probably not until morning."

"Are you working tomorrow?"

"I think not. If I do, it will be from here. I want to spend some time with you and Katie."

"Sounds good to me. Sleep well, my love."

"We will. Join me when you get home."

"You know, I will. See you soon."

Jackie ended the conversation and leaned over to kiss me. "I hope he gets home in one piece. He sounded somewhat out of it."

"I would imagine he has done this before?"

"Yes, but he always makes it back, even if he has to get someone to drive him or take a cab."

"What do you think his reaction will be when he finds us in bed together?"

"You want to sleep with me tonight?"

"Yes, Jackie, more than anything."

"I want that too. Let's take a shower together first and take things as slowly as we can."

"May I bathe you?"

"That's what I had in mind, Katie. And then I can bathe you. Does that sound good?"

"I can think of nothing I would like more."

"No reservations; fully involved with each other?"

"Yes, Mom." I chuckled.

"Don't laugh. I still think marrying you would be wonderful for both of us."

"We can have everything we want and keep the love of the man who cares for us.

"Yes, we can. Let me introduce you to our shower. I think you will like it."

"If you are there with me, I have no doubt."

Jackie took me by the hand and led me to the back of the house and the master bath. When we got there, she removed my clothes so erotically that I was dripping wet again, and my nipples were hard and pointing out. I helped take hers off and marveled at her as well. She caressed me, and I was flying. This woman knew how to please another woman. That was clear to me. She took me into the shower after having adjusted the water temperature. I loved her caresses when she bathed me and tried to remember what she was doing to me so that I could do the same to her. No need to say, I was highly excited.

"Katie, you are beautiful. I love your body, so firm and young. You must excite everyone who sees it."

"Thanks, Jackie. Sometimes that is a problem."

"Katie, will you give yourself to me again tonight?"

"Yes, Jackie. I am yours to do with you as you wish."

"Let's dry off and go to bed."

"In yours and Mike's bed?"

"Yes. Won't Mike be surprised when he comes home and sees both of us in bed together?"

"He might take the hint."

"He won't realize what's going on until in the morning."

"LOL! I think it will be great."

"He is going to want sex when he wakes up."

"Then I will leave and go make coffee."

"Good plan. I will take care of our man, and then we can spend most of the day together, like Mom and daughter."

"Ha-ha. That is funny. Somehow, I don't think he will see it that way."

"I guess we'll just have to see."

"Love me anyway?"

"Yes, Katie. We are going to be inseparable."

"I would like that. Can we get some sleep now?"

"Yes, let's put on our nighties and snuggle up. I would love to sleep with you all night."

"I want that, too. Jackie. Tomorrow morning is a brand-new day. I think it is going to be a good one."

"I do too, Katie."

We got into our nighties and slipped under the covers together. Jackie was so warm and soft, and yet she was a dominant lover. I made love to her, arousing us both again. When we went to sleep, we were very close to each other in our embrace and our emotions. We slept well together.

My dad came in after we were asleep, and seeing us both in their bed must have surprised him. He didn't wake us when he slipped in behind Jackie and embraced her, but I knew he was there. Sleepily, I snuggled closer to her and went back to sleep. Being there seemed to be right for me. I must have turned over at some point because when we woke the next morning, I was facing away from her and backed up into the curve of her body. She was soft, warm, and comforting. Sleeping in her arms was very natural, and I was so glad to have a new bed partner.

She and I awoke together to the smell of coffee and bacon coming from the kitchen. Dad was already up and had slipped out of bed very quietly so that he didn't wake either of us when he left. We put on robes and followed him.

He gave both of us a cup of coffee, which we accepted quickly, taking sips to begin the day. It was good. "How are the two most important people in my life this morning?"

"Good morning, Mike," Jackie said as she kissed him.

"Good morning, Dad." I kissed him on the cheek.

"Sorry we missed your coming home last night," Jackie opened the subject, knowing full well that he would take it from there.

"Imagine my surprise when I found the two of you sound asleep in each other's arms, looking for all the world like lovers who had just discovered something between them."

"It was nice, Dad. I love Jackie, and being with her makes me feel right at home."

"I love Katie, too. We just kind of fit together in many ways."

"I am so glad to hear that. You must have had a productive talk."

"We did, and we made some decisions about things."

"Am I privy to what you have decided?"

"Yes, of course. We will tell you after we have some breakfast. Will that be okay?"

"Yes, of course. You must tell me everything."

Jackie and I looked at each other, questioning that, but we would tell him enough to satisfy his curiosity.

"How do you like your eggs, Katie?"

"Sunnyside up with runny centers."

"Just the way we like them too. I'll put them over toast?"

"Sounds delicious." I looked over at Jackie, and she smiled back at me. Dad saw the whole thing.

"Okay, you two. What's going on?"

I took Jackie's hand in mine and kissed her on the cheek. "We think we might be soulmates, Dad."

"No, we know we are soulmates, last night proved it without a doubt," Jackie responded.

"Here. Have some breakfast. Orange juice?"

"Yes, Dad, thanks."

"Jackie?"

"Sure, Mike."

"Let me warm up your coffee."

We ate, joked, and had a wonderful time. Being with these two was natural, and I rejoiced deep within me that things were working out this way. As he promised, Dad waited until we finished eating and had cleaned things up before bringing up our conversation of last night.

"What questions did you answer in your chat last night?"

"We are going to take things slowly, Dad. That was number one."

"We also decided, at least Katie did, that she wanted to have her birth certificate amended to list you as her biological father."

"The DNA tests prove that beyond a doubt."

"Undoubtedly, as you say, but it will probably have to go before a judge up there. I'll get my lawyer on it right away. Anything else?"

"Yes, once you are officially father and daughter, we will address the name thing."

"I don't want to lose Katie MacDonald completely just yet."

"Jackie, have you made your decision about us?"

"Once we get the relationship thing worked out, and we see how our family is shaping up, I will give you my answer. If we do marry, I do not want to try to take Katie's mother's place. Any relationship between Katie and me has to be new so that her memories will remain of the kind, caring woman who gave her birth."

I squeezed her hand as a thank you gesture.

"That is very wise, Jackie. Besides, it might be a little awkward for a mom to have a love affair with her adopted daughter."

Both Jackie and I almost fell out of our chairs when he said that. He grinned that knowing grin of his at seeing our reaction. He knew for sure at that point.

"Don't look so surprised. From the time I came to bed last night and saw you holding on to each other so tight, until this moment with you sitting close and holding hands like that, I realized that there was something special going on between you. Jackie, I know that Katie is not your first lover, either. Now that the cat is out of the bag kiss her, and we'll go on from here."

Jackie did precisely that with a tender, loving kiss. It was a little strange to be kissing her in front of my dad, her lover.

She bade me good morning and moved toward Mike and kissed him too. "Thank you, Mike."

"I love you both, and I want you to be happy. If that means you will be together, so be it. One thing, though. Don't let me make a mistake about who my daughter is and who my lover is when we are in bed. That just wouldn't do."

"No, it wouldn't. We'll be careful."

"Okay, Jackie. Now for this other thing."

"You mean, Katie and me."

"Yes. What happened between you last night?"

"Full disclosure?"

"Yes, Jackie.

"Okay. Here it is."

"Let me explain, Jackie."

"Go right ahead, Katie."

"When I first laid eyes on Jackie, I was immediately attracted to her. She is a combination of my mom and my special girlfriend in Montana and even more beautiful. Dad, she kissed me, and I melted in her arms. We talked, kidded with each other, and carried on like we were lifelong friends. Neither of us had any idea what our familial relationship was going to be, but we knew there was a spark between us. She captured my heart and wouldn't let me go. I knew she felt something for me too."

"I love you, Katie. You are not a little girl, you are an adult woman, and I would rather you be my lover than my daughter. You already had a wonderful mom, and I am not her. From what you say, you have fond memories and will always remember her."

"Have you done anything together yet?"

"You mean, have we made love to each other? Yes, we have, and it was wonderful. I needed her more than I ever needed anyone. That might never happen again, but Jackie is the best kisser I have ever known, and she sends chills all up and down my body."

"Where does that leave me?"

"Don't worry. We aren't going to run off with each other and leave you. It leaves you with two wonderful women who love you very much."

"Do you still want to be my lover too, Jackie?"

"Of course, Mike. You might be surprised to know that until Katie came to us, I had not been with anyone else but you for some time."

"Now I have something to tell you both," Dad began, "we all slept together last night although you were asleep when I came to bed, and that is okay. I liked it very much. But when we make love, Jackie, I am not sure how I will feel if Katie is in bed with us."

"I have my bedroom, Dad. That'll not be a problem for me. I will just go to my room if that is what I need to do. We must discuss this further, though. I'm an adult now and know about sex. You two can have sex all night, and I hope I can watch it. Might that be possible?"

"It's okay with me."

"Thanks, Jackie. By the time that happens, who knows what might have happened between you and me?"

"We'll try to find some way. If I can accept the fact that you two are in love with each other and keep an open mind about that, I might be able to accept having my adult daughter as a part of the family lovemaking. It might be possible, Katie."

"We are not the typical family, that's for sure."

"I hate to skip out on you two, but I must do some work in town today. I'll get ready, and you guys feed Rex and take care of the horses. They could no doubt use some company this morning."

"Leave it to us, Dad. We'll take care of them."

"I know you will. Take care of each other too. Jackie, I haven't seen you this happy in a long time, and having you here, Katie, is wonderful. Just save some for me for when I get home. I shouldn't be gone all day."

Dad went in the back to shower, shave, and put on a suit. He left us, and when he was out of earshot, I asked Jackie,

"Did he just give us permission to pursue our mutual interests?"

"I think so. Let's go feed Rex and bring him in. It might be an excellent time for the two of us to take a ride together, too."

"I'm a little nervous, Jackie."

"You mean about being with me?"

"Yes. You and I must plan carefully where we all go from here."

"I have some ideas about that. We can continue our talk when we are alone."

"That would be very good. Now kiss me, and let's get things rolling around here."

"The first thing to do when we get Mike listed as your father is to set you up financially. He should put you in his will, make you a beneficiary in his insurance policies, open a bank account for you, and get everything else done. He also should add you to his health insurance policy, and we need to find you a good doctor. His lawyers can take care of most of that. We also must take you shopping. Are there things in Montana you want or need?"

"No, I let them all go. I took care of my mom's effects shortly after she died by donating them to the local women's shelter. I am sure she would have wanted it that way. I do have a bank account there containing the proceeds from the house and my car. I want to move it down here."

"Good for you. Once we get all this squared away, we can begin to decide on names and marriage plans. I didn't want to saddle Mike with a wife who cannot give him children. Now that you are here, that might change. I want you to have two parents and might marry him and become Mrs. Armstrong. You can decide later what you want to do. How about Katherine MacDonald Armstrong? Could that work for you?"

"It might at that. I want to do something special for Dad."

"What would that be?"

"I want to make sure the pool gets built. You and I can do it as long as Mike pays for it, of course."

"Of course. That is a wonderful idea, Katie. I can see both of us lying in the sun, soaking up the rays. We'll do it for him."

"Can he afford it, Jackie?"

"Mike has done well for himself. He can afford it."

"Is there anything else we need to decide?"

"Yes, whether we are going to continue our love for each other here, the couch, or in the bed?"

I kissed her passionately, and she responded. It felt so good after all the things that had happened to me. I let Jackie lead the way. She was the new love in my life, and she was an excellent lover. My sexual anxiety dissipated as she made love to me, and I was happy again.

Chapter Six

In Love for the First Time

In Montana, I dated because I thought I should. Frankly, very few of the guys up there appealed to me. That might be the reason I gave a couple of girls a try. They were friendly, and we had some things in common. With my schoolwork, my job, and Mama getting sick, that all ended abruptly. I had to stay with her because her health insurance would only pay a portion of the expense of cancer, and paying for a caretaker was not possible. I was glad to do it for her because she raised me by herself and loved me dearly. It was not an easy time. Then she died, and her struggle was over.

For a while after her death, I tried to get back to myself, but that person had evolved. I was a new me, and then my search for my dad began. The essential point is that I had never been in love before, although I wanted someone in my life in the worst way. Now I had Jackie, and she could be that loving person for me. I found my father, and I also found her. I hit the jackpot. We both would take care of Mike but in very different ways.

"Where do you think he is today, Jackie?"

"Unless I miss my bet, he is taking care of arranging things for you. He knows what he needs to do."

"I hope he arranges some things for you too, Jackie."

"Thanks, hun. What I need most is you."

"I need you too, Jackie."

She embraced me, and we kissed. I did so love kissing her.

"Would you like to take a horseback ride together?"

"Yes, I want to get to know the horses. Tell me about Romeo."

"He is a stallion and is very spirited. Very few people can ride him. At least he won't let just anyone get on his back."

"He reminds me of my favorite in Montana, although he was a gelding. He had spirit too. Do you think we could go to a rodeo sometime?"

"Yes. There is always a fair around here somewhere, and the animals and their riders can be fascinating."

"Their riders?"

"Yes, this is Texas, you know. The cowboys around here are the real thing, although there are some wannabes too."

"I love to ride. My next horse is going to be Romeo."

"Are you sure you are up to it?"

"Let's change and go meet him."

"Okay, Katie. You are on."

I had brought my riding boots, several pairs of jeans, and a few shirts with me from Montana. It felt good to put them on again. Jackie looked great in her riding outfit. We went down to the barn and into the corral. The horses were across the pasture, munching on the grass.

"I guess we'll have to go get them," Jackie said. "Sometimes, they don't want any human company."

"Watch this," I answered. I used my usual call, and the horses all raised their heads. When I gave them a "Cumba ho," they trotted over to us and came into the corral through the gate I had opened. I took Romeo by the neck and hugged him tightly. He nuzzled me in greeting. Jackie was amazed.

"That was amazing. How did you do it?"

"Horse talk, Jackie. I learned it just before puberty, and it works every time. Soon, with enough training for them, they will come without a call."

"I had no idea you knew about horses."

"I love horses. Which of these harnesses is Romeo's?"

"This is his," she went under the shed and brought one out. "But getting him to take the bit can be a problem. He is very headstrong."

I patted him and talked to him as I put the reins over his back. I massaged his mouth and lips and the underside of his head. He loved the attention and opened his mouth when I inserted my fingers and massaged his gums. Quickly, I put the harness on him and buckled the straps. Then I put the reins over the top railing of the corral and let him know I wanted him to stay.

"His blanket and saddle are over there," Jackie pointed.

He was doing well, not at all trying to leave. I took the reins off the corral rail and put them over his head and back behind his neck, all the time petting him and talking to him. He whinnied and shook his head. That was my cue. I led him away from the side of the corral and, in one move, mounted him bareback. He pawed twice but didn't try to throw me off.

"Good boy," I said to him, "would you like me to take you for a ride?"

He raised and lowered his head, signifying his consent, and I took him out of the corral and guided him into the pasture. He loved it but wanted me to let him loose. I slacked the reins, leaned forward until I was right behind his head, and urged him to go. He did, putting his head down and breaking into a fast trot and then a smooth gallop. When he discovered I was not going to fall off and was with him all the way, he sprang into his fastest gait and let me feel his muscles and his strength. I rode him entirely around the pasture twice. He began to pant, and I reined him in and let him walk. He was quite an animal. I fell in love with him immediately. Jackie had bridled and saddled Mandy and joined us while I let Romeo cool down. I took him back into the corral and dismounted. He turned his head to me and gave me another whinny.

Jackie rode a little longer and joined us as I was getting a bucket filled with soap and water. Romeo loved his bath, and when I brushed him down, he looked like he was heaven. I filled another pail with oats and let him eat and drink while I finished grooming him. I had made a fast friend. Jackie just brushed Mandy since she had not sweated during their ride. We left them eating their oats in the corral. I left the gate open, so they could get back to the pasture when they finished, and we returned to the house. Romeo moved his head up and down again and said thanks to me with a snort. I couldn't help but smile.

"I saw it, but I still don't believe it," Jackie said when we got back in the living room.

"You don't believe what?"

"That you handled Romeo as you did and even rode him bareback at full gallop. How did you learn all that?"

"I have been riding since I was a child and got a part-time job when I was twelve. Horses have been a major part of my life since then."

"Mike is not going to believe it either. Even he has trouble with Romeo."

I just smiled and hoped she would be interested in my equine experiences.

"Can you share your secrets with me?"

"Sure, but later. Right now, there is something I want more," I answered.

"What is it? You know I want to please you."

"Jackie, I want you to make love to me again, but I have doubts about myself." I ducked my head and turned away.

"What's wrong, Katie. I thought you liked being together."

"I do, Jackie, more than you know, but aside from last night, I have almost no experience with beautiful women."

"Have you ever been with another woman before me?"

"Yes, but it was a disaster."

"Would you tell me about it?"

"After it ended with my cowboy, a good friend and I went out together one night and had too much McNaughton's. It's a Canadian whiskey and is very smooth. Well, we went to her place, and I must have passed out because when I awoke to what was going on, my jeans and panties were down around my feet, and she had her head between my legs, doing things to me that I didn't like. I left with her shouting at me some nasty words. Things like a tease, bitch, and some others I don't need to mention. That ended it with us."

"No one else?"

"No. Most men turned me off, and I surely did not love or care for her in that way. It might seem old fashioned, but I always thought I should feel something for someone whose bed I shared." The memory caused me to start crying. "I don't want that to happen to us. You see, I love you, Jackie, and now that you are in my life, I can't imagine not having you there."

"Oh, my dear Katie. I had no idea. Your love life has not been a good one, has it?"

"No, Jackie. It has been horrible. Does that change things between us?"

"No, it doesn't. I was in your shoes at one time, and it was not that long ago. We'll get through this together."

About that time, when she was holding me close, we heard Mike coming back. "I need to get myself put back together for my Dad."

"No, you don't. You are Mike's daughter, and he will be here for you no matter what. I'll tell him we have had girl talk and some sad things in your past came up. He's mature and knows women well enough to understand and even try to help. If he wants to hold you to comfort you, let him. Nestle on his chest with your head beneath his chin and let him be your father. He needs that."

"You know him very well, don't you, Jackie?"

She just smiled at me and nodded her head. "Stay here with me until he comes in."

"Thanks, Jackie, I will."

She was holding me in a loving embrace when he walked in. He immediately saw that everything was not okay, and he came over and sat on my other side and put his arms around me too.

"What is wrong, honey? Jackie?"

"We have had some girl talk, Mike, getting to know each other. Katie has had some sad events in her life, and we are working through them."

"Is there anything I can do?"

"You are doing it, Dad. I have never had a dad to hold me."

"You do now, Katie, and Jackie as well."

"I know. Thanks to both of you for taking me in. You didn't have to do that, you know."

"We wanted to do it. We both were excited when you called me until you got here. Now, we are so glad you came into our lives."

"Katie has had a rough time since her mom got sick. She had to put her own life on hold to take care of her. Now that she is with us, she wants to begin anew and live her life fully and without reservation."

Dad hugged me and kissed my cheek. "And you will, Angel. We will make sure of it."

"Thanks, Dad. I feel better now."

"Then what I have to tell you should make you feel even better."

"Have you been busy today, Mike?"

"Yes, Jackie. The wheels are rolling."

"That's great, Mike."

"How are you doing, Katie?"

"I have something to share with you two. It is the letter my mom wrote to me just before she died. I think it will give you some idea of what I am trying to get past."

"My dear daughter, Katherine. If you are reading this, then I am gone. My lawyer sent it to you at my instruction. First, let me thank you for taking care of me during my illness. I am sorry you had to suspend your life for a while and take a break from your dancing and your horses, but I hope you will forgive me. I have left you several clues so that you can find your birth father, and I hope you will follow them and find him. He is a wonderful man, intelligent, handsome, and caring. I regret not having had him in my life. You see, I was very much in love with Dr. Armstrong, although our lives lay along different paths.

"I hope you will find him and that you can give him a chance in your life as I was not able to give him in mine. He called me after you were born, and he knew what had happened. I would not let him in. I wish I had. Now, things are different. My most sincere desire is that you might have the opportunity to meet your father and become a part

of his life. He will be good for you and needs you. Take loving care of him, Katie, and be to him what I was unable to be. I love you more than anything else in the world. Have a wonderful life. Your mom, Lindsay."

I was crying my eyes out when I finished reading it to them. They both had tears in their eyes too.

"A message from her after her death. I love this letter, but she wanted me to get past it. That is why she sent me to you, Dad. She did not know about you, Jackie, but she wanted more than anything for me to be happy. I must let her go, but I need you two to help me get past that. I know I am where I should be here with you. She set it up, and she continues to take care of me even after her death. Now, you are all I have. She knew you would be what I needed to go on."

My dad and Jackie both embraced me and let me know everything would be all right. It would take some time, I thought, but I believed them. My dad and his companion, whom I was growing to love, would see to that. I was in excellent hands, put there by my loving mother. They both held me until my tears subsided to make sure I was all right. The three major parts of my life came together that day, my Mom, my father, and a loving, caring woman named Jackie. It was a time of transition for me. I was leaving the past and its trials behind and going on to my new life. I was ready.

"That's enough sadness for a long while. Mike, my dear, Katie rode Romeo bareback this afternoon. It was quite amazing. She knows horses."

"You rode him bareback? How did you catch him?"

"I called him, Dad, using horse talk. He came easily."

"Did he fight the bit?"

"Not at all. Romeo is a magnificent animal."

"Bareback?"

"Yes, I love to ride a spirited horse that way. It gets us closer than sitting on a saddle."

"Did he try to throw you?"

"No, he behaved perfectly, and he is fast. I rode him at full gallop until he got winded."

"Amazing. You learned a lot in Montana."

"Yes, I did. What did you do today, Dad?"

"I paid a visit to my attorneys and got them started on amending the birth certificate, modifying my will, changing my beneficiary designation, and getting you included on my health insurance. I had them also make sure that if something happens to me, both of you will have this place as your home. Then I went to my bank and had them include you on all my accounts. Our DNA evidence opened doors readily.

"Can you have my Montana bank account transferred down here? I sold the house and my car and put the proceeds there. I thought it might be best for me to turn loose of my old life completely except for certain mementos and the good memories. I will keep this letter from my Mom and her scrapbooks, for example, but my life is here now with you two. Finding my new way will take some time, but it will happen."

"Sure, Katie. Give me a bank statement, and I will take care of it. Is anyone hungry?"

"I am Dad."

"Me too, Mike. What do you suggest?"

"I don't want to cook. How about Angelo's takeout?"

"Ribs for me," Jackie responded.

"I have no idea about Texas barbeque. Your suggestion about a sampler might be perfect."

"Good idea, Katie. I'll see to it. Does anyone want a beer?"

"Yes."

"How about Shiner Bock this time?"

"Yes, an excellent idea, Mike. We should introduce Katie to all the Texas beers, from commercial to the craft brews."

"Three ice-cold bottles are coming up."

"Feeling better, Katie?"

"Yes, Jackie. Sorry about the crying jag."

She took me in her arms and cuddled me as Dad brought the beers. "You deserve to be emotional after the life you've lived. I am just glad we were here to give support."

"I have no idea how I would ever handle all this otherwise. My mom knew I would need people who loved me, and she set it up. I am so glad it worked."

"We are too, Katie. Our lives are enriched by your being here."

"Okay, dinner is ordered. It will be here in less than an hour."

"Sounds good, Dad. After we eat, I might want to go to bed early. I am tired and think it is about time I spent the night in my room. You two need some time together."

"I think it has been wonderful having you sleep with us," Dad commented. "I am getting used to having my two favorite women sleeping together in our shared bed."

"She doesn't sleep with us, Mike. She sleeps with me. I sleep with you. I love being in the middle with you both, and I don't want to change anything."

"Are you sure?"

"Yes, Katie. Besides, when Mike leaves for work, we are together. I can hold you and sleep in your arms without having to change beds. Our places are already warm."

"Are there any eligible young cowboys around here?"

"Katie, dear. Do you miss having a man in your life, one just for you? One who is not your father?"

"Both those things. I think finding out about Texas men might be a lot of fun."

"I found mine, and I would bet there is one out there for you too. Maybe a selection, knowing how gorgeous you are."

I ducked my head and blushed a little.

"How do I go about meeting them?"

"Do you want another cowboy or a young professional in a suit?

"No more cowboys unless I find an exceptional one. The well-dressed professionals were not in the majority in Kalispell and Missoula."

"We have some time before dinner arrives. Would you like to take a walk?"

My dad thought that was an excellent idea, and he got up to go with us.

"Sorry, Mike. We need some girl talk. Why don't you get things ready for us to eat, and we will be back in a few minutes?"

He smiled and sat back down. "Okay, girls. Have a good walk and an even better talk."

Jackie and I smiled at him, and she gave him a little wave as we went outside.

"I know there must be some things you don't want to say in front of your father, but you and I have a different relationship. Thanks for being willing to talk to me."

"I must talk to someone. Despite you two, I am lonely for my own man. I have needs and have ignored them for so long. It is time for me to go on with my life, including my love life."

"Were you close to anyone in Montana?"

"Several guys interested me, but I knew none of them was right. After my first lover, I woke up to the fact that many men only wanted to be with me for a night so that they could brag to their friends. I got very tired of that. They were boys, not men."

"I can understand why you were popular. You are a knockout. Do you have boots and a hat?"

"Nothing dressy, just my riding duds. I left all of that in Montana with my other excess baggage."

"Do you enjoy sex, Katie?"

"With the right man, it's wonderful. I had that once, but he moved out of state. I never saw him again."

"That must have hurt."

"It did. Mama got sick just after that, and I haven't been with a man since. It has been a long time, Jackie. I miss being cuddled, caressed, and loved."

She took me in her arms and hugged me tightly. "You have been very strong through all this. Mike and I will start working on some ideas as soon as I can talk with him."

"Do you think he knows I am a woman with desires and needs?"

"He has never had a daughter before, and he thinks all women are virgins when they meet him, but he realizes they are human too. He probably thinks the same way about you."

"Well, I am not a virgin. I am very passionate, and I need the close interaction only a lover can provide. I could always get back into riding again. I was pretty good at barrel racing and even learned how to rope and subdue a steer. I like rodeo and met some interesting men there."

"Have you ever been interested in other girls?"

"Yes, but don't even a hint about that to Dad."

"He might be more understanding than you think."

"I know that he loves you and you love him, but I find you exciting, Jackie."

"Is that why you embrace me so tightly when we sleep and love me so deeply when we are together alone?"

"Yes, I love being held by you and kissing you. Something is developing between us, at least until you marry my Dad?"

Jackie checked to see if anyone could see us and satisfied that we were truly alone, she answered me by laying a passionate kiss on me, making me melt in her arms again. She pulled me close and continued kissing me so wonderfully. Jackie answered many of my questions with that kiss. I embraced her, and when she drew back from me, I kissed her. It was my answer to her. We both were breathing hard. I kept holding her in my embrace, and she kept embracing me. Some way, I was going to get her alone again, in bed or somewhere else, and make mad, torrid love to her. Our first time together was her show, but the next time would be mine. We parted and looked deeply into each other's eyes. She smiled at me, and I smiled back. We had strengthened our girl to girl bond. I felt much better. I had found my first Texas lover, and I was falling for her.

We heard the delivery truck arrive and headed back to the house, holding hands. Mike would just have to deal with us. He smiled when he saw us happy together and welcomed us back for dinner. Jackie kissed me before we went in. He saw that and came to embrace both of us. He could see that we had gotten much closer during our walk.

"Anyone ready to eat?"

We went in and took our seats at the table. Dad brought us two more beers, and we drank a good portion of them in our first swallows. We were both thirsty, and the cold beers were excellent. I loved the Shiner Bock. Next, he brought the food to us. Jackie's ribs looked good, and he put my sampler in front of me. He had ordered brisket for himself and passed the sauce around. I had eaten something called barbeque before, but this was an entirely new experience for me. It smelled heavenly and tasted great. Jackie was right, the ribs were excellent, and the sauce added many flavors to them. I liked the brisket too, and the sausage had character but was a little too hot for my taste. The pulled pork needed something more. I learned that most people served it on a hamburger bun with sauce, onion slices, and pickles. I was not very impressed with it. Nonetheless, the meal was excellent overall with the potato salad and beans. I loved it.

We three slept together again that night, and I hugged Jackie, very close to me. Dad held her from the other side. The happy days passed quickly, and I grew closer to Jackie and close to Romeo. We spent the next weekend together, enjoying each other's company, and Dad went to work on Monday morning. When he came home, he had fantastic news.

"My lawyers called me today. The judge approved the amending of your birth certificate. I am now officially and legally your father, Katie. I am so happy. We will get a copy of the revised version in a few days."

"That makes me happy too, Dad. Now there is one other thing."

"What would that be, daughter of mine?"

"Now that we are official and legal, I want to change my name."

"Do you want to become an Armstrong?"

"Yes, Dad. I liked Jackie's suggestion that I should become Katherine MacDonald Armstrong. It includes a link to my past and a hope for the future. That is how I want to be known. Can you get that done?"

"Katie Armstrong? It has a ring to it." My Dad hugged me and told me he could. I was pleased about becoming his daughter officially. A feeling of serenity came over me. Jackie smiled radiantly at my decision. We were officially a family.

Chapter Seven

Some Nightlife for Us

"I want to celebrate."

"Here or somewhere else?" Dad asked.

"I want to go out someplace that has champagne and a fun crowd along with a chance to dance, let my hair down, and just enjoy my new family."

"I know just the place," Jackie volunteered, "and we don't have to get too dressed up. There might be some single men there too."

"Sounds like just the place. When do we leave?"

"As soon as we change clothes. Boots we can dance in, and wide belts with fancy buckles. We can fix you up with whatever you don't have. Want to come with us, Mike?"

"Why don't you two go, and I'll join you later?"

"Okay. I would love that. An evening with my new almost daughter, Katie Armstrong."

I smiled at her and Dad. "Make sure you come to have some bubbly with us, Dad."

"I wouldn't miss it for the world, my lovelies."

"Then let's get ready, Katie."

"All right. Let's go."

It didn't take us long, and we were on our way. Jackie drove, and I was delighted at what happened. Celebration with Jackie would be a lot of fun, and I would get my first look at Texas guys. I hoped one of them would want to dance. I knew the two-step, the cotton-eyed joe, and most other Texas dances from the honky-tonk in Kalispell. It could be a fun evening.

We got there, a place called DJ's in Dallas. It had two floors with a large opening between the upper level and the lower deck so that everyone could see everyone else. A large bar was in the center of the lower floor, and a good crowd had already gathered. We paid our cover and went to the bar.

"Champagne, Jim. We are celebrating tonight." Jackie knew one of the bartenders.

"Right away, Jackie. Who is this with you?"

"Let me introduce Katie, our new family member. We just found out that Mike is her birth father, a secret for over twenty years."

"Welcome, Katie. I hope you like DJ's."

"Does the J stand for Jim by any means?" I asked.

"How do you think I got this gig as a bartender?" He joked as he reached for the PA microphone. "Everyone, welcome Katie to our fold."

A spirited, "Welcome Katie," issued from the patrons.

I bowed to them and thanked them for their greeting while Jim opened a bottle of excellent Brut and served us. I toasted DJ's and took a swallow as others toasted me, making me feel extraordinary. Jackie gave me a hug and a big smile.

"I think they like you, honey. See anything you like?"

The music began. A lot of it was classic country. The first song was "Cherokee Fiddle" by Johnny Lee, and I just started moving to it. A blonde guy named Brian came up to me, took my hand, and gently pulled me to the dance floor. He was an excellent dancer, and soon we were getting a lot of attention. I was so glad I had learned the Texas dances. His smile was beguiling, and he made me happy I was there. Another great looking guy took Jackie away as well, so Jim put the champagne bottle back on ice. We danced on and on. The music and the company were unmatched in my experience. I was enjoying the evening.

My Dad came in, and Jackie and I decided to take a break. I gave Brian one of my cards with my cell phone on it, and we returned to the bar and our unfinished bottle of bubbly. Jim poured one for Dad and emptied the bottle to Jackie and me. Our family was complete, and we toasted each other and continued our celebration. One of the girls grabbed Dad and pulled him to the dance floor. My Dad could dance! The girls lined up to get a chance with him even though they were much younger than he. He loved the attention.

Jackie and I shared knowing smiles and finished our drinks. We waited to go back to the dance floor, watching him charm all the ladies in the place. He was something else. The DJ put on Cotton-Eyed Joe, and Dad joined in the dance line. The next selection was the Sweetheart Schottische, followed by a tune to which the line did the Freeze. Dad stayed with them all the way. When the DJ put on Achy Breaky Heart, two gorgeous girls moved to either side of him in the line, and he danced along with them with a massive smile on his face. They turned out to be two Dallas Cowboys Cheerleaders. Jackie and I joked that we had lost him.

Then two handsome Texans came up to us and asked us for a dance. Of course, we hit the dance floor again. The cheerleaders captured Dad, and he bought them drinks at the bar. He must have said something about why we were celebrating that night because when my dance ended, and I walked back to him, the two girls greeted me warmly. They nicknamed me "Montana" and wanted to know everything about me. Jackie came back to Dad, and I found myself between the two girls, laughing and joking with each other. I enjoyed them. They were not anything like I thought they would be. We talked about boyfriends, girlfriends, and Montana. They told me about how they became cheerleaders and what it was like to dance at AT&T stadium. I found out about the goodwill work they did and the problems of having a love life as a cheerleader. They told me they were close friends and roommates. I could see there was more than the obvious between them. They were vague about their boyfriends and loved going out dancing together. I began to get the picture, and I liked them.

"Mike is your birth father, and you didn't know about him until recently?" Helen asked. She was a natural redhead and didn't try to hide her freckles except for a little powder to smooth them out some. Her friend was Estelle, a gorgeous brunette with black hair like mine, long and straight. They both had plenty of it to flip in their routines. In a way, I envied them. They invited me to a party they were having for their fellow cheerleaders and some football team personnel next Saturday night. It was at the stadium and sounded like a lot of fun. "Please bring your Dad and Jackie. They are well known to us, and we all like them."

"Yes, he is one of our favorites and is an excellent dancer," Estelle added.

"That seems to run in the family," Helen said. "Katie, we watched when you were dancing, and some of your moves were very familiar to us. We dance some at our parties, mostly as a group. It's somewhat of a rehearsal for game day. Would you like to dance with us?"

"I would love to. We did a lot of your routines in my dance classes. You say it is next Saturday night?"

"Yes," Helen replied. "Just come to gate number one, and we will have security bring you to us. Say about eight?"

"Do I get to spend some time with you two?"

"That's why we invited you, Luv, we want to get to know you better," Estelle answered.

The hour was getting late, and the crowd was thinning out. "I'll be there. Can I come alone and leave my Dad and Jackie to their own devices that night?"

"You bet you can, hun. Why don't you plan to stay with us afterward?"

"Are you sure you want another person in your plans?"

"That is no problem. We can't mingle after ten o'clock with men. We will all be staying together, sequestered until the game on Sunday. Want to come?"

"I am just a simple girl from Montana. All this is so new to me. Are you sure it will be okay with the other girls?"

"We are sure, Katie. We'll send a car for you if you give us your address."

"That would be fantastic, but I live with Mike and Jackie up near the lake. Is that too far away?"

"Leave it to us. Then it's a date?" Helen wanted to confirm.

"Yes, I wouldn't miss it for the world. Dallas, here I come."

They both hugged me, and Estelle went over to Mike to get the address and phone number, setting everything up.

Helen and Estelle hugged me goodnight and took their leave. I thanked them, and they left together. The party and meeting the girls was going to be so cool. The car would come for me on Saturday afternoon at six and take me on the adventure of my life. I told Dad and Jackie what had happened, and they expressed their surprise and amazement. It had been a great night out in Dallas.

"The first thing we must do is take you shopping. We will make sure you dress to kill for this party."

"Okay, Jackie. What should I wear?"

"Leave that to me. When I was a Dallas Cowboys Cheerleader, I learned a lot."

"You were a cheerleader?"

"Yes, for quite some time. It was a lot of work but worth it."

"I had no idea. Does Mike know?"

"Yes, he knew me before that period of my life. He was very supportive."

"I can't believe they invited me to their party."

Jackie chuckled. "Do you have any idea what is going on, Katie?"

"No, to be frank, I am in a state of disbelief. To have two new friends who are Dallas Cowboys Cheerleaders is beyond my wildest dream."

"That's one reason I took you to DJ's. It is a little-known hangout for the girls."

"My Dad is very popular with them."

"They know him from when I was on the squad, and they are all in love with him."

"Now it makes some sense. What else do I not know about my Dad?"

"You will find out as time goes by. Mike is an incredible man, Katie."

"That's becoming very evident."

"What else is going on?"

"They are auditioning you, Katie."

"What? No way."

"They know who you are since you are Mike's daughter, and they saw you dance and charm all the guys in the place. You have style, training, and a magnetic personality, just the type of girl they constantly look for."

"I did take dance for many years and only stopped when Mom got sick. But a Cowboy Cheerleader? I don't know about that."

"Go to the party and meet the girls, without your father and me. Have fun, and enjoy the scene. Be a part of the group, and I can guarantee they will talk to you."

"You did it for several years?"

"Yes. I could have stayed with the group longer, but I wanted a life of my own and someone who loves me. Mike is that guy. The girls all envy me for being able to capture his heart and follow my dreams."

"Is tomorrow too early to go shopping?"

"No, dear. Tomorrow is the day you begin your journey as a Texas girl and leave your Montana ways behind. I know you will love it."

Jackie took me several places to look for my Texas wardrobe. We shopped for boots, jeans, belts, belt buckles, shirts and blouses, neckwear, and hats. I even found a bandana I liked, which I could use in several ways. Jackie approved of what we chose and took me home to show Dad.

"My next Cowboy Cheerleader, my daughter. I am not sure I want you to go to that party alone."

"Don't worry, Mike," Jackie reassured him, "she will be well chaperoned. The guys at these parties, if there are any, must behave, or they will never get another invitation. It will be just fine."

He came over to hug me. "Do you want to do this, Katie?"

"Yes, Dad. I do."

"If you need us, all you have to do is give us a call."

"I know. Thanks."

"Want to see my new wardrobe?"

"I would like that very much. How about a fashion show?"

"Let's go, Jackie. I need your help."

"I'm right behind you."

We showed him my first outfit, jeans, boots, a belt with a beautiful buckle, a shiny linen shirt, and a George Strait hat. He loved it and the several variations on the same theme that followed. He liked them all. Our last outfit was very different. It included boots, tights, and a classic tan brushed leather skirt with a beautiful blouse. The skirt had a fringe, and the outfit was impressive. He loved that outfit best of all. I was ready to do some boot scooting, looked the part, and felt very comfortable in that outfit. Dad decided that was the one to wear to the party. He thought I would be irresistible.

I was not so sure. I needed to have a long talk with Jackie. "Okay, Jackie. How should I conduct myself at this party?"

"Katie, you just go and enjoy yourself. If there is dancing, you dance. If people want to talk with you, talk with them. Relax. Have fun. Don't drink. Let Helen and Estelle introduce you around and take care of you. Everything will be fine."

"You say they are auditioning me?"

"Yes, it's the way we work."

"What if I don't want to be a Dallas Cowboys Cheerleader?"

"Don't decide that until you know the people and the organization. It will take some time, but you will be able to dance again, and I know you love dancing. Give them a chance, and if you decide it is right for you, go for it. Look at what a wonderful experience it can be."

"Jackie, I am just a girl from Montana. I don't know anything about all this. Why would they want me?"

"You are a gorgeous, personable woman. And you can dance. Being a cheerleader is a lifelong commitment, and you will be a part of the organization for a long time. At least give it a chance if they want you to join them. I think you will be a fantastic member of the organization."

"I have no expectations beyond the party. I am going to enjoy it, and I look forward to meeting the other girls. It should be fun."

"That's a great perspective on the situation. You are going to do well, Katie."

"Thanks, Jackie. I am excited, nervous, and have to sort through some things."

"Do it later, my dear, after the party. You will know much more then."

"I have no idea what I am getting myself into."

"You are in control, Katie. Do what you want to do."

"If I could just decide what that is."

"You will know. Believe me."

"Okay, what's going on with my girls?" Dad interrupted us.

"We are just getting ready for the party."

"You will be fine, sweetie. Has Jackie explained things to you?"

I went over to him and gave him a big hug. "Yes, Dad. I am not going to worry about all that. Just enjoy partying with the girls and getting to know them. Jackie, you say there *will* be dancing?"

"No doubt about it. These girls love to dance. They may even show you some of their moves."

"Good. I can see whether we had it right in my dance classes. We used to emulate your routines in practice."

"You know our routines?"

"Yes, most of them. Of course, we were never as good as the real thing, but it was fun."

"That's great. Let me show you some basics we follow."

"Okay. I'd love to see the moves."

"This a DVD that all the girls get. We'll watch it through and then practice some."

"You're serious about this, aren't you, Jackie?"

"Yes, Katie. I am."

"Well, put it on, and let's look at it."

The first lesson was a basic outfit. It was all there, from the boots to the shorts, the blouse, and the vest. It also covered the evolution of the uniform from Cowbells and Beaux in the early days to today's attire. Minimal changes have occurred along the way.

The next section covered how to stand in line with everyone together and the necessary DCC walk and basic dance moves. The Cheerleader walk was very similar to the Temptation walk, which was second nature to me. The rest of the DVD explained the current routines in use, many of them devised long ago. The dance routines for several country/western songs completed the video. How much I already knew amazed me. I had learned about their dance routines and steps and realized we had been very close in our Montana efforts. When I began to dance with Jackie, I was right with her the whole way. She gave me some pointers on hand position and their smiling technique, which could last a long time and become tiring. To say I loved it all would have been an understatement.

"You are a natural, Katie, as if you had been doing this for years."

"I have, Jackie, ever since I was sixteen."

"You are going to have a fun Saturday night and Sunday. I am envious."

"Thanks, Jackie. I am very excited about it. Saturday night. And Sunday?"

"Yes, and Sunday. If you stay with them Saturday night, they will make sure you have a role at the game. Enjoy it!"

"My first chance to dance with the Dallas Cowboys Cheerleaders, not just practice anymore. These are the real girls. Can we go over it all again?"

"Yes, of course, Katie. The sharper you get, the more impressed everyone will be."

We danced together and had fun with each other every day until Saturday. Dad would watch us sometimes and usually left us with a smile on his face and a shake of his head, showing his total surprise at how good we looked together.

I also got to know the horses much better, which relaxed me, and I rode at least one of them every day. Finally, Saturday morning came, and I began to get ready. I packed a bag and put on my new outfit after letting Jackie do my hair and makeup the way they should look, given where I was going. Because of her help and support, I was not nervous—excited, but not tense. Right on time, a long, white limo with the Cowboy star on the front doors pulled up in front of the house. I was going to open the door, but Jackie stopped me.

"The chauffeur will come to get you. Just be cool and calm. Don't carry your bag at any time. Let them take care of you. I'll get the door."

She opened it. "Miss Katherine Armstrong, please."

"Just a second. I'll get Katie. Here is her bag." He stowed it in the trunk and returned.

"Have fun, Katie." She kissed me and wished me luck. The chauffeur showed me to the open door, and I got in. Helen and Estelle greeted me and beckoned me to sit between them. The driver closed the door and took his place behind the wheel. When we started, Estelle poured me a glass of the champagne they were drinking and handed it to me. It was delicious. Helen offered a toast.

"Here's to Mike and Jackie, whom we all love and their wonderful daughter, Katie. Welcome, dear."

Estelle seconded the toast.

"Thank you, girls. You make me feel wonderful. I am happy to be with you again."

"Bottoms up!" Helen directed as she drained her glass. "Enjoy it. This bottle is all the drinking we will be doing tonight. Must maintain dignity, right?"

"Yes," Estelle answered.

"I'm good with that," I added. One more each, and the bottle was empty. I was too excited to drink, anyway.

"Katie, may I steal a kiss, please?" Helen asked. I kissed her. She was an excellent kisser, just as Jackie was.

"Don't leave me out," Estelle wanted the same.

She kissed me, and I soared. Would they all be this affectionate? I had my doubts, but time would tell. We talked during the ride to Arlington, and I relaxed in their company. They had a way of putting a girl at ease. When we arrived, our driver went straight into a door on the side of the stadium. Other limos were there before us, and girls were walking out to the field. Helen and Estelle walked with me into the vast arena, where about fifty girls were chatting with each other. In just a few minutes, we were all asked to take a seat, and I went with my companions. The plush chairs all had names on them, and right between Helen and Estelle was one with my name on it, Katie Armstrong, just like all the others.

The girls wore a variety of outfits, from boots and jeans to skirts and blouses. There was not a single cowboy hat anywhere. They knew how to do their hair, just as Jackie had done for me. Thanks to her, I looked like I belonged there. I was very comfortable. Carolyn Sanders, the new president of the Dallas Cowboys Cheerleaders, greeted us from the podium and welcomed us to the event. She introduced the guests, including me, and I rose to my feet and gave them the DCC curtsey, just as Jackie had taught me. They shared glances and approved.

"We are going to have fun tonight and have a little rehearsal for our game tomorrow. Guests are welcome to join us if you wish. Let's start with our traditional warm-up. Take your places."

When Helen, Estelle, and the other girls got up from their seats, I got up with them. Helen looked at me approvingly and placed me between Estelle and herself. Everything Jackie had taught me, from spacing in the line to the DCC stance, came back to me. I felt as if I belonged there. The first song the DJ played was one I had memorized, none other than Billy Ray Cyrus's Achy Breaky Heart. I started on cue and didn't even have to watch any of the other girls. Anyone would have thought I had been a cheerleader for years.

The number ended, and I took my stance along with all the others. Song followed song for the next half an hour. There were recordings by George Jones, Hank Williams, and Hank, Jr. Many of the girls were breathing hard, including Estelle. Not me. Elation filled me, and I had no room in me for fatigue.

"Would you like to take a break?" Helen asked.

"No, no way. I am having a blast. Let's go on to the next thing."

"How's your high kick?"

"Bring it on."

We kicked for several minutes, just a kick, shuffle, kick again. Not everyone on the squad could do it for long.

Half the squad went to their chairs, knowing what was coming. The rest of us closed ranks, forming one line with our arms across each other's shoulders. A darling blonde named Cheryl took Estelle's place beside me. The music began, and I knew exactly when to start. The kicks came quickly to me, and I concentrated on staying together with the others and raising my legs exactly as high as they did. I could have gone higher. These girls were professionals, and I tried my best not to stand out.

I was beginning to get winded as Helen said, "Get ready for the split." I sensed when it was coming and went down in unison with all the rest. We flipped our hair forward and then back to give us all the tousled look. It was very sexy. When the leaders released us, I popped right back up and resumed the stance. I had done everything they had asked us to do. Helen walked with me back to our seats. A few minutes later, Mrs. Sanders came to join us. Or I thought that was what she was doing. She walked directly over to me.

"Miss Armstrong, would you come with me, please? Some people would like to meet you."

I looked over at Helen, and she smiled and nodded her head.

Mrs. Sanders took me through a door under the stands and into the locker room. In an office just off the main hall, she introduced me to a woman named Kelli, one of the directors of the squad. She motioned me to have a seat and sat at a table with me in the corner of the office.

"Katie, it's great to meet you. Do you know who I am?"

"Yes, I do. You are a director of the Cheerleaders."

"Please call me Kelli. You know, Katie, you looked terrific out there. If I may ask, how did you learn our routines so well? You looked just like one of the girls."

"Thank you, Kelli. I have been dancing since I was six, and when I turned sixteen, I joined a troupe that used your routines to warm up and sharpen their skills. Over the last few days, I have worked with Jackie, and she prepared me for the party and rehearsal."

"And Mike Armstrong is your father. Did he adopt you?"

"No, after my mother died, we discovered that he is my birth father. We went through all the legal steps and had my birth certificate amended to include him in that role in my life."

"So, he is your natural father?"

"Yes. I live with Dr. Armstrong and Jackie now."

"I see. You three finding each other is a blessing. We in the organization think a lot of him. He has been a great friend to us."

I just ducked my head and smiled. "We know."

"Now down to business. Katie, we need someone like you to fill a current vacancy we have and want you to join us and become a Dallas Cowboys Cheerleader. Is that possible?"

I just sat there with a look of surprise and disbelief. "You want me to be a Cheerleader? You flatter me, Kelli. Being a part of this organization has been a dream of mine since I was little."

"Then you are interested?"

"When do I start?"

"You have already started, Katie, your audition ended a few minutes ago. We know a lot about you, and we know your parents. Plus, you can dance. In a few minutes, Helen and Estelle will escort you to our locker room, where you will find your locker and a set of uniforms. Jackie gave us your sizes.

Dress and return to the field. We will find you a place, and you can rehearse everything we have planned for tomorrow. Is that all right with you?"

"Oh yes, Kelli, and thanks for the chance to live my dream."

She hugged me and sent me back to the field, and Helen, who hugged me and congratulated me. The other girls welcomed me, as well. Just like that, I was a Dallas Cowboys Cheerleader. It would be quite a significant part of my life.

Chapter Eight

The Newest Cheerleader

We found my locker quickly. Rather than being on one end or the other as I expected, it was right beside Helen, with Estelle was just a few spots down. Helen showed me the proper undergarments and how to wear them. First came the Peavey tights, and I opted for tiny panties under them. Then came the demi pushup bra, and I could put on my shorts, boots, blouse, and vest. Helen approved of my look. She touched up my hair, and I was ready. She had dressed when I did as she showed me what to do. We were ready. I couldn't believe how I looked in the mirror that everyone used on their way out.

Since I was tall, they put me close to the middle of the line. Helen was two girls down from me, and Estelle a little farther down from her. We picked up our pompoms and headed for the field of my dreams. Our routine began even before we got to the football field. We danced out in a double line and took our places. I just followed the other girls and smiled as Jackie had taught me. No outsider could tell that I was brand new. Everything balanced, and I wondered whose place I was taking. I found out later that she took a leave of absence several weeks ago when she discovered she was pregnant. The line now had its balance back, one of the reasons my audition was not as extensive as usual. We did our pregame routine. It was not difficult, and I nailed it on the first try. Our directors did not want a repeat. We broke into our four groups in our game time configuration and did much the same things we had done earlier only this time, no kicks and no splits. Most fans would be watching the game instead of us, but we did our thing as best we could. I loved every minute of the session.

Afterward, Kelli sought me out and congratulated me on my performance and for being truly a member of the team. "Are you ready for your first game, Katie?"

"Yes, Kelli. I'll get a good night's sleep and be here a little early so that I can take all of this place in."

"That'll take weeks, I'm afraid. Quite a few of the girls still don't know their way around. Helen and Estelle will bring you and make sure you are all right."

"Thanks, Kelli. I can't wait."

"I should be thanking you, for knowing so much about what we did when you came to us, and for filling a vacancy that has been somewhat of a problem. You have made us whole again, and all the girls on the squad delight in having you and your talents. Now have some fun tonight and get to know the girls."

"I still can't believe this is happening, Kelli. It's beyond my wildest dreams." She hugged me and welcomed me again, this time with a kiss.

"You are going to be great, Katie. Helen will show you about our makeup artists and hairstylists. You won't have to do any of that. They will take care of everything."

"I'll see you in the morning, Kelli." With another hug, she turned and left. Helen found me and took me in hand. We took off our uniforms and put them in the hamper for cleaning. A new, fresh one was in my locker for tomorrow. I took a deep breath as we dressed, Helen took me to our limo, and we headed to our hotel. As soon as we were in our room, a large one that would accommodate up to ten of us, I called home. Jackie answered.

"How did it go, Katie?"

"I am officially a Dallas Cowboys Cheerleader. They hired me on the spot after our rehearsal. I have my locker, wore my new uniform, and practiced with all the other girls. Kelli has been great to me, and so have the others. I am so excited and will be on the field in my place for the game tomorrow."

"That's wonderful. Where are you, Katie?"

"Helen and Estelle were as good as their words. I am staying with them tonight. I am also staying with the entire squad. They have us sequestered in a hotel near the stadium on a floor dedicated just to us. Will you and Dad be watching tomorrow?"

Dad answered me. "Yes, Katie. We wouldn't miss it for the world." They were on the speakerphone.

"They all hold you both in high esteem, you know? Jackie, they see you as my mom."

I could hear her weeping softly.

"We are so proud of you, Katie. Where are you in the line?"

"Due to my height, I am in the middle. Helen is two girls to my left, and Estelle is just down from her."

"Are you sure this is what you want to do? You had your doubts."

"I am sure, Mom, I mean, Jackie."

I knew Dad heard my slip of the tongue.

"The directors are summoning us to a meeting, and this will be the last chance for us to talk until tomorrow. I love you both, and I will try to do my best for you."

"Do it for yourself, Katie. Just having you as our daughter makes us very happy."

"Thanks, Mom and Dad. It is going to be a great ride for us. I must go now. Watch for me at the game."

"We will, Katie, I promise."

"Goodnight to both of you. I will miss you tonight."

"We'll miss you too, honey. Have a great debut, and enjoy this improbable chance given you. We love you very much."

"I love you both too. Until tomorrow." I had to go to the meeting and hung up the phone, excited but a little sad at not being at home with them for the night. My exuberance quickly overcame my anxious feelings, however, and I went with the others to our meeting. We had dinner there, and I felt much better, my energy restored. After dinner and a pep talk from one of our directors, we returned to our rooms. Helen asked if she could sleep with me, and I accepted. We changed into our nighties and crawled into bed together. After a goodnight kiss,

I went to sleep in her embrace, warm and comfortable until morning.

They awakened us at six o'clock. The game was at noon, and our leaders wanted us to have plenty of time to get ready. We visited the group bathroom, and everyone went through their morning routine. I was still sleepy until I realized what was going to happen. Helen smiled at me and shared the excitement of my first time on the field with the girls. We went to breakfast, which was light and contained energy foods and coffee or tea. They took excellent care of us on this game day. After breakfast, we boarded the buses and headed for the stadium. I was barely able to contain my excitement. As the limo driver had done, the bus driver drove us inside the stadium and stopped very close to our dressing room. After a brief meeting to make sure everyone was there and feeling good, we went into the hairdressers and makeup. Doing all of us required a couple of hours, even though many people were working. They did my hair first with a shampoo and blow-dry. Then the finishers took over. They curled, brushed, and made me look fabulous.

Next came the makeup room. The walls had stations all around them, lighted mirrors, a place to work, and two chairs, one for us and one for our artist. It was impressive. I took a seat where indicated and tried to relax. My artist took one look at me and smiled.

"What do we have here? A fresh face? Welcome honey. I look forward to working with you. Just put yourself in my hands, and I will build on your natural beauty and make you look fantastic."

"I'm all yours. Work your magic."

"Okay, you can look in the mirror as I do my thing. First, we are going to clean your skin so that I will have a blank canvas with which to work."

After the cleaning, she did my brows and moved on to my eyes. I watched her every move. She used a little shadow on my lids and liner to define them, and a little mascara was all she needed to thicken and lengthen my lashes. I knew I had to find out what products she was using. She put a light foundation on my face and blush on my cheekbones. I saw where she was going. The lip color she used came from a tube, and she applied it with a brush. It set up quickly and would not smudge. She worked on me for over an hour and sent me to my locker to dress. We were right on time. I looked terrific, better than I had ever looked before.

Helen was at her locker when I got to mine and told me I looked fantastic. I blushed a little and thanked her. Now for the uniform. When dressed, I knew I would look good as a member of the squad. I finished dressing right on time, and they called us for warm-ups. I followed Helen, excited and so nervous I forgot my pompoms. I hurried back for them and took my place in line. The girls were as excited as I was. They gave us the signal to begin, and we left for the field after the second verse of an old standard, "Looking for Love" by Johnny Lee. The crowd roared when they saw us even though not everyone had arrived yet. I was beaming for my first time on the field with the Dallas Cowboys Cheerleaders. I was in my element and danced my heart out all through the game. When it was over, I didn't even know who won. I dressed but left my makeup on, grabbed my bag, and exited the locker room.

"Katie," it was Kelli. "You have some people here to take you home. She pointed to a couple standing outside. It was my Dad and Mom. I ran over to them and embraced them both. Jackie started crying.

"You are so beautiful, Katie. Kelli got us tickets so that we could see your debut, and we watched you the whole way. You were wonderful."

Dad embraced me again. "You are amazing, dear daughter of mine, and did very well."

Helen walked up and greeted them, giving each one of them a hug. "You two have quite a daughter. I have never seen anyone take to being one of us as readily as she did. She is great."

"Thanks, Helen. Can we drop you off somewhere?"

"Thanks, Mike, but I am meeting someone in a few minutes who will take me home. I'll see you next week, Katie. It's an away game, so that we won't be involved, but I wouldn't be surprised if they need you, anyway."

"Thanks, Helen." I gave her an intimate hug and kissed her goodbye. "Thanks for everything."

"Will you take me home now, Dad? I'm exhausted."

"Certainly, honey. Let's go. Kelli got us a parking place close by, and we can get out of here easily."

"I would like that, and I have to tell you everything that happened in the last two days."

"Then, let's go home, my two lovely ladies. I look forward to spending some time with you both."

We reached the car, my Dad got behind the wheel, and I moved to the middle of the front seat between him and Jackie. She put her arms around me as I said, "What a week! Meeting Helen and Estelle, practicing with you, Jackie, and then my visit to the stadium, which turned out much better than I had even imagined. It all wore me out."

"Let me hold you on the way home, Katie. That's what moms do."

I relaxed in her arms, and the next thing I knew, Dad was putting the car in the garage. I had slept all the way home even though it was early evening. I realized I was exhausted, mentally, and physically and just wanted Jackie to hold me.

"Could I have a drink?"

"Sure, Katie. What do you want?"

"Vodka and orange juice, please." Dad got up to make it, but before he returned with it, I was fast asleep.

"I think our little girl is tired, Mike."

"She is not a little girl anymore, Jackie. She is a full-grown woman and is hot as hell."

"Let her sleep. If she wakes up, we can get her something to eat and put her to bed."

"I am going with her."

"I want to play the game back since we recorded it. My daughter might have had a good TV shot. If she did, I want to keep it."

"Okay. I'll hold Katie for a while, and you can take over. She has had one wonderful week, and deserves to be held and loved on tonight."

"I agree. Our daughter has made us proud and has found something in her life after all those hours in the dance studio and all the other things she has done to keep herself in shape, despite the troubles she had for so long. She already sees you as her new mom. Will you marry me, Jackie? I would love to make it official."

"Yes, Mike, I will marry you. Until now, I was not sure, but now I am. We will raise our daughter together in the right way."

"I think her mom took care of that. Our job is to help her as she finds herself as an adult."

"Yes, you're right. I could use something to eat myself. What do we have back there?"

"I bet we can find something."

They did. I slept until morning.

When I awoke, I was in Jackie's embrace, warm and comfortable. Dad was already gone. My mind was not sure what had just happened. I went to the restroom to take care of things and saw my face in the mirror. I still had my game makeup on, and my hair looked good even though I had slept on it. The glitter was still in it, and I knew that yesterday was not a dream. I wanted a shower and to take off my makeup. Jackie followed me into the bathroom. I turned to her and said, "It was not a dream, Jackie, it was real, but it all seems like a blur."

"Yes, my dear Katie. It was real." She hugged me and told me how proud she and my Dad were of me. "You did very well, sweetie."

"The party, the sequester were wonderful. I danced my heart out, and they put me on the squad, showed me my locker, put a uniform on me, and I was a Dallas Cowboys

Cheerleader. I got some sleep with Helen, and the next day, I was on the field with my dancing buddies and over one hundred thousand people watching us. I just wish I could have seen it for myself. When you guys showed up, and everyone welcomed you, my heart was soaring."

"You *can* see it for yourself. Your Dad recorded the entire game, and we made a collage of our daughter's debut with the squad. We can see it whenever you wish. But first, use some of this to remove your makeup and then take a shower. I know you must want one in the worst way."

"What was that you said?"

"You mean about the video?"

"No, about me being your daughter."

"After you went to sleep last night, your Dad asked me to marry him. We have talked about it for a long time but never seriously considered doing it. I said, yes."

My joy at what she had said showed all over me, and I hugged her tightly. "That is wonderful news. We are truly going to be a family now."

"Yes, we are my daughter."

"We are going to raise some eyebrows. You are much too young to have a daughter my age."

"That's not all we are going to do, either. I think I will get my old uniform out, and we can take pictures together as Dallas Cowboys Cheerleaders. Don't you think that will be fun?"

"Undoubtedly. You can dress for the reunions too. We are going to have a blast with this."

"Yes, we are. Now go take off your makeup and shower, and we will look at the video. I want you to see it."

"You know, mom, I don't even know who won the game."

"You must have brought the team luck. Our team won going away."

I smiled at her and began removing my makeup. It was not an easy task and took me a while. Then I took my shower and felt like a different girl. It was good to be back to myself, but I couldn't wait until the next home game when it would all happen again. I think Jackie knew the feeling. After my shower, I dressed and went to find her. She was cueing the video and ready to play it for me. I was excited.

We had some yogurt, granola, fruit, and coffee as we got ready to watch.

"Ready?"

"Yes, play it, please."

The first images were of us marching out doing the Cheerleader's walk. The squad looked great. "Watch closely now. Here you come."

The cameraman must have had his camera resting on the turf because the shots were from ground level. We all smiled for the camera as they had taught us and looked great. I came into view, and in just a few steps, there I was. It was my first appearance on live TV, and the cameraman raised his camera and zoomed in on me. I gave him my best smile and a little wink. I couldn't believe how good I looked in the uniform and with perfect makeup and hair. It didn't look like me. We marched on and split the line in two, going to our positions for our pregame routine. Another camera found me, and I took the stance with my pompoms at my side, and my chest pushed out just a little. The other girls did the same thing. They took another headshot of me and moved to the other girls. I had gotten lots of exposure for some reason, possibly because I was new, but how would they have known?

We split into two groups, did our routine, and they gave me a few more seconds on camera. We danced into our double line, forming a tunnel for the players. There I was again, near the head of the line. The players gathered on their sideline, and we girls went to our initial positions in four groups to entertain the crowd. We were well-received as usual and went into our dance set as the teams took the field. Everyone in the stands watched the kickoff, and we went into our first routines. I was having a blast. They picked us up when we rotated to the next position, and I was on TV again. They also went down the line at the end of the half, and I got more exposure. Just before the game was over, we marched back to our locker room, and it all ended.

"Do you want me to play it again, Katie?"

"Not just yet, mom. I want to let it sink in some first."

"Your Dad took a copy of this DVD to work with him and is undoubtedly showing it to anyone and everyone who wants to see his new daughter. He is a very proud papa."

Tears came to my eyes, and I hugged Jackie very tightly. "Did I do okay, Jackie?"

"Better than okay. You were amazing, Katie."

"Thanks for all you did for me in this. It happened because of you."

"Don't forget your Dad. They asked him for permission to approach you even before the party. He assented. He knew you were perfect for the cheerleading squad."

"Have you and Dad talked about a date yet?"

"No, but there will be plenty of time.

"This is too much for me even to contemplate. I get to go to my parent's wedding. How often does that happen to a girl?"

"In your case, only once, and not only are you going to be there, but I want you to be my maid of honor."

"It will be my greatest honor, Mom. Are you going to invite my fellow cheerleaders?"

"Of course. I will need several of the girls to serve as bridesmaids. We'll have to do it on an off weekend, so they can have as much fun as they want at the reception."

"Oh, Mom, it sounds delightful."

"Thanks. Now we need to talk about you."

"What do we need to talk about?"

"The first thing we are going to do is take you to the training headquarters in Frisco. It's called the Star. Everyone trains there, the team, the cheerleaders, everyone. It is the hub around which the Cowboys organization revolves. The next step awaits you there."

"It sounds great. What will I learn?"

"The dieticians will put together a healthful plan for you that will keep you in shape and give you the energy you will need as you go on as a Cheerleader. Then, they will custom tailor a fitness program to keep you fit and strong. The directors haven't introduced you to the more demanding moves yet. We refer to them as graduate cheerleader school."

"You mean the sky kicks combined with the power splits?"

"Yes. Can you already do those?"

"My favorite, mainly because they come naturally to me and most girls can't even do them, no matter how much they practice their stretching and balance. Yes, I can do them."

"Is there anything you can't do in the squad's repertoire?"

"Jackie, I have been practicing all this since I was sixteen. If they have something that I haven't seen yet, let them bring it on. I know I will be able to do it."

"Have you learned gymnastics?"

"Yes. Flips on the balance beam are still somewhat of a puzzlement, but I can do everything else, including the rings and the raised bars. I spent years learning that, and I enjoyed every minute of it."

"Try to hold back some when you first begin there. Gradually you will be able to let it all loose. The program will make you better at what you can already do."

"I can't wait!"

"All thoughts of men had vanished from my thoughts. I was delighted with the way things were."

Chapter Nine

Training for Real

Dad had a long day at work, but he got a lot done and could relax the rest of the week. His colleagues loved the video from the game, and he received many congratulations on his newfound daughter. He came home smiling from ear to ear. It was good to see him so happy. I could tell, however, that his joy had new roots that evening. We had some dinner, and he invited us to come with him to the couch. Neither Jackie nor I had any clue what was going on until he took a little red box out of his pocket and kneeled before us.

"Jackie, we have been together for a long time, but never saw the need to formalize our relationship. That time has come. We have a daughter who needs us and whom we need. I want us to be a family in every sense of the word." He opened the box revealing a gorgeous diamond engagement ring. "Jackie, will you marry me?" She gave him her left hand, and he slipped the ring on her. It fit. Jackie took one long look at it, and the tears welled up inside her.

"Yes, Mike. I will marry you, I will adopt our daughter, and I will be your wife and Katie's new mom from this day forth."

Dad kissed her deeply, and they shared a loving embrace. It occurred to me that not only was I going to be at their wedding, but I was also there now as they became engaged. I looked up as if to ask my mother in heaven if it was all right with her. I felt a warm, loving feeling envelop me, and I knew she was giving her approval. Dad took Jackie to bed, and I stayed in the living room so that they could have some privacy for a change. I felt a tear come to my eyes and just sat there for a while, knowing that tomorrow, I would be back in the gym and eating even more healthily than ever. I thought of the video and wanted to watch it again, all by myself. It was still in the player, so I started it up and sat back to watch. I saw things that I had not noticed the first time Jackie played it for me. I hoped we would have a session just to evaluate the video as a team.

I was at the end of the video when the phone rang. I hurried to answer it so as not to disturb my Dad and Mom-to-be. A cheery voice said hello. It was from Helen. "Hey, Montana, could you use some company this evening? I had something bring me out this way and hoped I could stop in and see how you have recovered from all the excitement."

"Yes, Helen. I can't think of anything I'd like more. I have so much to tell you. When can you get here?"

"Give me about fifteen minutes, and I'll give you a hug and a big kiss. I have missed you."

"Come on, girl. I'll be waiting."

"Don't you need to let your parents know?"

"No, that is one of the things I want to tell you. They just became formally engaged and are back in the bedroom, not likely to emerge for some time. Now get over here."

"On my way, girlfriend."

I knew I would have some company that evening and hoped even longer, and I watched for her car. She had guessed right and drove up about fifteen minutes later. I rushed out to her and got my hug and kiss. We went in, and I offered her a drink.

"I had better not since I am driving," she said.

"Then you will just have to spend the night with us."

"I would love that."

"Good, then it's settled. How about a rusty nail?"

"I would love one." I made two, and we toasted each other, our friendship, and the cheerleaders. Being back with her was excellent.

"So, what is this big news?"

"Jackie and my Dad are going to get married, and I'll have a real mother again. He gave her a ring after dinner."

"That's fantastic, Katie. Congratulations. Things seem to be working out for you."

"I have been living a dream for the last week, thanks to you and Estelle."

"Dad made a video of me from the network broadcast. Would you like to see it?"

"Yes, very much."

"I was just watching it. Let me restart it." I did, and we watched intently.

"Wow, Montana, you got a lot of coverage in that video. They must have liked you."

"I'll get Dad to make another one for the entire squad."

"Excellent idea. I would love to see it. Have you recovered completely yet?"

"I'm not sure I will ever recover, Helen. It was all so overwhelming."

"Would a kiss help?"

I saw no reason to say anything, just moved toward her, and answered her with an embrace. Our kisses got hotter and hotter. Soon, we were making out in earnest.

"Will you let me sleep with you tonight?"

"Yes, Helen. I usually sleep with my Mom, and she sleeps with my Dad in their big bed, but tonight is special for them, and they don't need me with them. I thought I was going to sleep alone tonight, but having you with me would be wonderful."

"There is one more thing, Katie. Would you let me make love to you?"

"You mean, go all the way? Not just kissing and hugging?"

"Yes, I think I fell for you that night at DJ's. You were so beautiful, and you are probably the best dancer I have ever known, a natural?"

"It has been a long time since anyone wanted to sleep with me, and since I had sex with anyone except Jackie."

"I thought I saw a spark between you two."

"You are very observant, and I love her very much, but she is in love with my Dad, and I respect that. We have been together, and she is a wonderful lover. She healed me inside. I love to sleep together with her. Aren't you in a relationship already?"

"It ended some time ago. I am a single now."

I reached for her and hugged her. "I feel an attraction to you, too, Helen. Could we go slowly and see what might develop? I am so unsure about myself in a relationship. They have never gone very well for me."

"Yes, Katie. We can go slowly. We slept together the night before the game with several other girls in the room with us. I wished they would make other arrangements and go somewhere else, but that is not the way it works with a DCC sequester."

"If we sleep together, just the two of us, things will be different. I need to get to know you better. Are you working out tomorrow?"

"No. My regular training sessions give me a day off after games, then it is back to the gym, and I will not miss that."

"Jackie is planning to take me there for exercise and consultation on my diet. We could go there, just the two of us, and Mom and Dad can spend time together now that they have become engaged officially. They might appreciate that. Have you eaten?"

"No, I was going out to dinner with this guy, but my being a cheerleader intimidates him. He broke our date and is no doubt gone now. Good riddance if you ask me.

"You date guys, then?"

"Yes, my encounters with my own sex most of the time are diversions. I feel differently about you."

"Why don't we fix you something to eat and we can talk before we go to bed."

"Then we are sleeping together?"

"Yes, my dear Helen. We are going to sleep together tonight."

"What are you going to tell your mom and dad?"

"I'm not going to tell them anything until they see us together in the morning."

"Can you get away with that?"

"I think so. If I know those two, they will be busy with each other all night. Come to the kitchen with me. I know we can find something delicious. I must make sure my new girlfriend is well-fed and has plenty of energy."

"For things to come later?"

"That's the idea, lover."

We found all sorts of good eats in our search. Helen ate well, although sparingly. I understood. When she was okay, we returned to the couch. Dad and Jackie were still together in the master suite. I freshened our drinks, and we relaxed with each other.

"Tell me about your living situation, Helen."

"There is not much to say. A couple took me in when I was tiny, and I never knew my birth parents. The guy my 'mom' was with left us when I was young, and she had two more youthful children to raise. She never was legally my mother. She just gave me a place to live. I left to lessen her burden and am on my own. I wouldn't have it any other way. If I don't have a place to stay for the night, I go to the cheerleader rooms close to the Star. I do okay for myself."

"We have plenty of room here, Helen. I bet Mom and Dad would welcome you. I am hoping mom and dad will find their love and want to spend most of their time together. I think my days of sleeping with them are over. When they go on their honeymoon, you will have to stay here with me. We will have a blast, we two Cheerleaders. Every single guy in Dallas will come running."

"When we are not practicing, exercising, or on a trip ourselves."

"I will feel much more secure under the wings of the organization."

"Yes, that is a real bonus."

We talked for several hours more, and when we both began to yawn, I invited Helen to come to bed. I took out nighties for both of us. We changed into our bedclothes, washed our faces, brushed our teeth, and crawled into my bed. The funny thing was that it was the first time I had slept in it myself. Helen was warm like Jackie, and we kissed goodnight and held each other firmly. We were tired already, and the rusty nails helped us toward sleep. We awoke together the next morning with the sun shining into our room and the smell of coffee brewing. I kissed Helen and didn't want to leave her and her warmth. It was time to meet my parents as an engaged couple and to let them see that Helen had spent the night with me. I was excited, but Helen was cautious. We put on robes and house shoes and headed into the kitchen. Helen wanted to stay behind me, but I took her hand, and we walked together.

Jackie saw us first and gave me a good morning kiss and then turned to Helen. "I am so glad to see you again, Helen. Mike and I were concerned that Katie might get lonesome without us, but I see you kept her company."

"Yes, Mom, and she kept me as warm as you do."

She kissed Helen too and turned to my dad. "Look who is with us, Mike. It's Helen. We shouldn't have worried about Katie at all."

"That's two nights we have slept together, and I love it," Helen joked.

"Do I see something going on here?"

"No, mom. We are good friends, although we have discussed going further. Helen is into guys as I am. We are excellent together, though. She is going with us to the Star today for a workout and to get me started with the day-to-day activities of the squad."

"In that case, you two go together. Mike and I have some things to take care of."

"Really? What things?"

Dad answered. "We have a ring, and now we need a license. On your next day off, tomorrow I believe, we are going to a judge and get married."

"Now? So soon? That is wonderful news. What else?"

"We are going to begin the process to have Jackie adopt you, make you legally her daughter rather than a stepdaughter. Is that okay with you?"

I turned loose of Helen's hand and rushed over to Jackie. "Yes, oh yes, it is another dream come true." My tears started flowing, and Helen came over to me with misty eyes as well. She hugged Jackie and me.

"I am so happy for you all. Congratulations."

"If you agreed to be a witness, Helen, we would appreciate it," Dad invited her.

"You want me to be at your wedding?"

"Yes, Helen," Jackie answered, "and we are so glad you are here with us. Can you stay for a while?"

"You want me to stay with you?"

"Yes, we will need some time for a honeymoon, and Katie needs you. Having you here gives Mike and me the freedom to enjoy our marriage and still be assured that Katie gets the guidance she needs as the newest Dallas Cowboys Cheerleader."

"Leave that to me. We will get Katie through as a team. Once she knows what's in store for her, things will go smoothly."

Mom and Dad were holding each other. She looked up at him. "See, Mike. Our Katie is going to be here with Helen, and I would think other cheerleaders as well and will be fine while we are gone. Would you two like some coffee?"

"Yes, Mom, that would be excellent."

"Then, have a seat, and I'll feed you."

"May I help, Jackie?" Helen asked.

"I would like that very much, Helen. Come on over here."

Dad sat by me at the table. I had to hug him. "I am so happy for you. Don't worry about us. We will be fine."

"Oh, my dear Katie. Life changed when you called me that day and came to Texas. You have made me very happy, Angel."

"My new life makes me happy too, Dad. When mom died, I didn't know what was going to happen to me. You have taken me in and done such wonderful things, the two of you. I never dreamed it would be like this."

"You have made fifty new friends and are well on your way."

"I might invite some of them to come here for a party when the chance presents itself. Would that be all right with you?"

"As long as you are escorted and have security. The DCC are a great attraction, and I want to make sure you are all well cared for when you do."

"Helen and I will arrange security with the organization. If Carolyn or Kelli would like to join us, they will certainly come with security."

"If we have a DCC party, security is a given," Helen offered.

"Yes, they take excellent care of us," Jackie agreed.

"Don't worry, Mike. Everything will be just fine. All we must do is marry and enjoy our honeymoon together. We'll talk about giving Katie a brother or sister too."

Helen found that overwhelming and excused herself for a bathroom break. I went with her. She hugged me very tightly, and I kissed her. "Welcome to the family, Helen. I think you are going to be adopted."

"I might just want to spend time with you while they are gone."

"We'll have plenty of time for that. Let's finish breakfast, dress, and go take care of business, okay?"

"Can we spend the entire day together?"

"Yes, and the night too. We are going to get your things and move you in over here, at least for the near future."

"Here?"

"Yes, Helen. You must stay here, at least while they are gone. Would you like that?"

"I would, Katie. We'll do good things together."

"Yes, we will. I am so excited about today. I feel it is a rite of passage for me."

"Let's go get it done and come back home so we can celebrate with your parents and spend some time together."

"Sounds good to me. Workout clothes?"

"Yes, they will give you a locker in which to store your things. You can even get them washed and cleaned for you there. I'll show you all about that."

"Sounds good to me. Let's get ready and go. Your car?"

"Yes, I think it will get us there."

"Good. I don't have one yet. Soon, I hope."

Mom and Dad were dressing when we left. There was a new bond between them, and they looked so happy and right together. I was glad we didn't have to go all the way to the stadium in Arlington. Frisco and North Dallas were much closer. It only took us thirty minutes to get there. Helen drove into the gated parking lot and found a space. My excitement was evident. We went to the private entrance and did not have to go through the main entrance and lobby. It took us directly to the dressing rooms. Then she took me to the cheerleaders' offices where she introduced me and told them I was there for initial familiarization. I went with the lady named Mrs. Rogers, who greeted us, and Helen went to start her workout. They gave me a folder with rules, guidelines, and schedules. By the time I finished, I could see I had a lot to learn.

Mrs. Rogers gave me a keycard for the parking lot and an access code for everything else. I could get into the facility, park my car, and record my visits. She detailed a first workout program and discussed diet with me. It was just before noon when she let me go. Helen was waiting for me and took me to the gym used by the cheerleaders. The players had their own on the other side of the complex. She explained the machines and how to use them and took me through one set of each of my exercises to make sure I knew how to do them. I left feeling invigorated rather than tired as I had expected. The main goal was stamina and flexibility, and I could see how the routine accomplished those goals.

Our next stop was the cafeteria. I looked at my prescribed diet, which contained a great deal of protein, mostly plant-based, such as legumes and salads. I watched Helen get her food and closely followed what she did. To my surprise, the food was quite good. It contained almost no fat and minimal carbohydrate. The meal satisfied me completely. I suspected we were going to eat well there.

By early afternoon, we finished, and my first visit to the Star ended. I felt tremendous and hugged Helen as we left. "Where are the other girls today?" There had been no one there but us.

"They are taking the day off to rest. Tomorrow things will begin all over again, and we will start getting ready for the next game. Kelli and the other directors will no doubt have some new things for us to try. Are you game?"

"Yes. I want to learn everything I can. I love dancing and being a member of the team. Whatever they throw at us, I will be ready."

I left with Helen and put my hand on her leg as she drove. The way we smiled at each other, I knew I would have a lover even though Jackie was marrying my father and going away for several weeks. My fantasies were very active all the way home. But now they were about Helen.

Chapter Ten

A Wedding in the Family

We went back home and found Dad and Jackie already there. Dad showed us the marriage license proudly, and Jackie kept her arms around him. They were inseparable. Helen and I congratulated them and hugged them affectionately. They both were beaming and so happy that Helen and I had to smile at them.

"When is the ceremony, you two?"

"Tomorrow at ten in the morning if you are both available then."

Helen said, "We wouldn't miss it. Count on us. We can arrange our schedules around that."

"When are you leaving on your trip?"

"We have airline reservations for early tomorrow afternoon. You guys are going to be on your own for a couple of weeks."

"Can you tell us where you're going?"

"I haven't even told Jackie yet. We'll let you know when we get there."

"Okay. Can I use your car while you're gone?"

"Sure. Are you getting used to Dallas traffic?"

"I think I can handle getting to and from the Star. I have no intention of going anywhere else."

"Sure. I'll leave you a key fob."

"Thanks, Dad."

"How did your first visit go, Katie," Jackie asked.

"It was impressive. I have some work to do."

"Don't worry, I'll take care of her while you're gone," Helen volunteered.

"I know you two will get along just fine."

We looked at each other. "You bet we will, Dad. We are becoming sisters. I think we should have a celebration dinner tonight."

"Go out or stay here?"

"Let's take Helen out with us. She has been a little lonely lately."

"Great idea, Katie, I know just the place," Mom said. "We will dress up a little and have a great evening."

Helen had brought clothes with her when we stopped to get her things. She would be fine. While mom and dad were gone, I planned to take her shopping and get identical outfits for us too. We would have an excellent time.

We excused ourselves to get ready and let Jackie and Dad go to their room and do the same. We fixed our hair and put on our makeup. We were going to look fantastic! We wore skirts and blouses with short boots. I gave Helen my string of pearls that were perfect with her long red hair and outfit. I put on a gold necklace, and we were ready.

The little place Dad and Jackie took us, named Guido's, specialized in New Orleans cuisine, from seafood to gumbo and everything in between. I toasted my mom and dad and announced they were finally getting married tomorrow. That got a lot of attention. Helen and I were as close as the sisters we wanted to be the entire time. Just as we were finishing, some jerk approached us and announced that he had seen us at the Cowboy game. "You are both Cowboy Cheerleaders, aren't you?"

"I'm afraid you have us confused with someone else," Helen rebuffed him. "We're just sisters out with our parents on the eve of their wedding."

"Your parents. They are just getting married?"

Dad took over. "Don't look so surprised. We have been living in sin for over twenty years and just decided to make it legal."

"Oh, I see," he said through an alcoholic haze. He didn't, but at least he turned around and walked off. Two bouncers who knew mom and dad were standing close. Dad waved to them and showed them we were all right and motioned for them to come over to us so that he could introduce Helen and me. They would remember us, we were sure.

Aside from that one occurrence, the rest of the dinner was excellent. Dad picked up the tab, and we headed back home. We talked for a long time and found out a lot about their relationship. They asked us questions too. I was glad they avoided the subject of Helen and me, but we got to know each other better. She was a hit with them, delighting me. It got late. Mom and Dad headed for bed, and Helen and I were not far behind them. Tomorrow was their wedding day, and we planned to do our exercises after they left for the airport. We needed to get some sleep, but I wanted to talk with Helen, just the two of us. We got under the covers, and I embraced her. Can we talk, Helen?

"Yes, Katie, I need to talk to you too, and there is no better time than right now."

"What's on your mind, Helen?"

"I love sleeping with you, and I have feelings for you that are surprising to me."

"I felt it the moment we met."

"You did? Why didn't you tell me?"

"I wanted to dance with you that night, slow dancing."

"OMG, Katie. Are we going to have an affair?"

"No one, man or woman, has ever turned me on the way you do. I have tried to resist you because I wanted to find out how you felt. We have become close friends, and I don't want to jeopardize that. Understand?"

"Yes, I think I do."

"Would you let me explore your body closely?"

"You want to explore my body. Yours fascinates me. You are so fit, and you move so well in the dances, I am curious how I can be more like you, dear Katie."

"You are an ivory doll, Helen. Your hair, your breasts, your hips, all make me crazy."

"No one has ever said that to me."

"Well, it's true. I get excited when I am with you. What do you think it is, Helen?"

"I don't know. I am so inexperienced in things like this. Most of the girls are straight and moon about guys all the time. I do too, but I feel there is more."

"Do any of the players turn you on?"

"No. I am not into football players, no matter how much money they make."

"Why not?"

"Their mentality is not conducive, at least for most of them, for closeness with anyone but themselves. The players' egos have been inflated by those who want something from them."

"Have you ever been in a close relationship with another woman?"

"No, have you?"

"Once in Montana, but only Jackie here."

"Jackie? Your soon-to-be mom?"

"Yes, I mentioned that to you. We are hot together. Jackie is great."

"How is that going to work out when she is your mom?"

"I think I am going to need someone else."

"Maybe me?"

"Yes, Helen. We can live together, work together, play together, and love together. I want to explore that."

"What if someone finds out?"

"I think Jackie already suspects. She is very wise."

"But what about our Cheerleader colleagues?"

"What about them? I am sure some of them like other girls too, more than likely in addition to men. I don't think it will be a problem for us."

"Hold me, Katie. I need to know you care."

I embraced her tightly and comforted her fears. This woman was getting to me. It could be that I felt needed and horny at the same time, a deadly combination. I made up my mind to love on her that night. Hopefully, we would find something special. We had plenty of time.

I took the lead with her after that. Our kisses were hotter and deeper, and I felt something I had never felt before. I kissed her on the lips and brushed her hair with my hand going down to her breasts. I kissed them through her nightie and then removed her top. She lay there with me, looking lovely and receptive to what I was doing. My chance to feel her warm wetness had come. I kneaded her breasts and sucked on her nipples, which became long and firm. To my delight, she was responding to me. I kissed down her tummy until I came to the beautiful clump of red hair just above her girl parts. With all the courage I could muster, I pulled her panties down, and when she didn't object, I buried my face in her womanhood. She parted her legs for me and started to moan softly. She was already very wet, and I tasted her nectar. I licked her from the opening of her vagina up to her clitoris. She grasped the bed covers and moved beneath me. I had her. She was going to go over the top with me, my new girl lover. It all made me happy.

When she came, she flooded me with her juices, and I kept up what I was doing. After several more climaxes, she curled up in a fetal position and reached for me. I joined her and kissed her passionately. She began to cry.

"What's wrong, Helen?"

"Nothing is wrong, dear Katie. I am thrilled right now. I have never felt this way. Promise me you won't leave."

"My dear, Helen. Let me hold you all night tonight, and you will know that I have no plan to leave. I think I am falling in love with you, and we are going to use whatever time we have together to find out."

"I love you, Katie."

"And I love you, Helen. We are going to be great together. Do you need anything before we go to sleep?"

"No, Katie. You are all I need."

"Sleep well, my love. Tomorrow is going to be a historic day."

"I know. Hold me and never let me go."

I embraced her and stroked her hair until she dropped off in a deep sleep. I followed quickly behind her. We kept each other warm all night.

Jackie woke us in the morning. We were still sleeping in each other's arms. She sat down on the side of the bed and watched us for a while. I felt her presence and woke to her broad smile. She leaned down and kissed me, encouraging me to turn over to her. I pulled her head down to me and returned her kiss. Helen awoke when I turned over and snuggled up to my back. Jackie broke our kiss and moved over me to Helen, kissing her tenderly.

"My two beautiful girls together. How I wish I were in bed with you both."

"Come on in, Mom." We moved apart to make room for her, and she got under the covers. We two embraced her back and front. It was a tender moment for all of us on the day she and my Dad were going to marry. Mom relaxed with us sharing her kisses.

"Let's get up, girls. It is going to be quite a day."

"Yes, it is. Come on, Helen, let's join the party for breakfast."

"All right, Katie. I would love a cup of coffee."

"Me too."

We wore our robes into the kitchen, and Dad poured coffee for us. A fruit plate was in the middle of the table, and we ate. It was good. The Greek yogurt and granola topped everything off, and we were wide awake and full of morning energy.

After we ate, we dressed nicely and headed for the judge's office, arriving a little early. Judge Nation welcomed us and asked us to sit. He wanted to get to know something about us. Dad took the lead and explained how he and Jackie had been together for quite a while and how I found him and that our DNA showed him to be my birth father. I explained how my mother had died and left me clues to my father's identity. He asked about Helen, and she explained that she and I were best friends and were both Cowboy Cheerleaders. He also said he didn't see any problem with the adoption process. Approval should come through in the next few weeks. He congratulated us and, after receiving the marriage license, had us stand before him as Mom and Dad took their vows.

He ended, "By the power vested in me by the State of Texas, I now pronounce you husband and wife. You may kiss the bride." Dad kissed her first. Then I kissed her, followed by Helen. It was a happy time for us all. Dad shook the judge's hand, slipped him a couple of hundred dollars, which he would not accept, and thanked him. We all headed for the car. They had done it, and our happiness showed through everything else.

We returned home, and Mom and Dad changed into their traveling clothes, gathered their bags, and awaited the limousine. When it arrived, I made sure they had their boarding passes, and we shared goodbye kisses all around. We waved at them happily and wished them a good trip before we went back into the house.

"It's just us for a while, Helen."

"I know. Let's go have lunch and workout so we can come home and spend the evening together."

"Sounds like a plan to me." Helen drove dad's Lincoln to the Star, and we had a great lunch in the cafeteria with the other girls who were there. There were quite a few that day. We exercised together, and no doubt, were the topic of conversation for many of the others. It was evident that Helen and I had something going the way we worked with and looked at each other.

Estelle came over and said, "Hi," and worked out close to us. It was good to see her again. She asked what was going on, and we told her about Dad and Jackie marrying and being on their honeymoon. I told her we had the house to ourselves and invited her to join us. She readily accepted then proceeded to explain to all the other girls about my Dad and Mom. I had two parents for the first time in my life, delighting the girls.

One of them told Carolyn, and just as we were completing our routines, she came over to us and hugged Helen and me and congratulated us both. Helen looked puzzled that she got the same as I. Carolyn must have known something neither of us knew. We would find out what later.

"Dad and Mom permitted us to have a party for all the girls if we wanted. What do you think, Carolyn?"

"Let me see when we have a place in our schedule, how we can arrange security, and I'll get back to you."

"Thanks. Mike and Jackie are both very interested in participating in the organization again, now that Helen and I both are members of the squad."

"That's wonderful news, Katie. We will be glad to have them back. See you again tomorrow?"

"Of course. We will be here every day." She smiled at us and walked toward her office. Now everyone would know about Dad and Mom.

Helen and I walked out to our car and got in. I kissed her and told her I loved her, putting her at ease. She knew then that I still included her in my life and those of my parents. I drove home for the first time and had no problems. My confidence was growing about dealing with Dallas traffic, at least from the house to the practice complex. Helen sat close to me the entire way.

When we got home, I thought a celebratory drink would be appropriate and made two vodka tonics for us, light. We sat with each other on the couch and began to talk. The house was eerily quiet, so I let Rex in to give us some company. He loved Helen and settled on the throw rug in front of us. We petted him generously and loved on him.

"Katie, I have something on my mind. Can we talk?"

"Of course, Helen. Come closer to me and tell me what's bothering you."

"I am very happy for you and your parents and that Jackie is going to go through the adoption process to make you legally her daughter. You all will be delighted together." She put her head under my chin and snuggled me close. "I only wish something like that would happen for me."

"You said you were on your own and loved it that way."

"After seeing all the love among you three, I wish someone loved me that much."

"I know it must be a lonely life for you, Helen."

"Yes, it is. If it weren't for the Cheerleaders, I don't know what I'd do." She wept quietly in my arms.

"I love you, Helen, and I think mom and dad are very fond of you as well."

"Maybe they will adopt me too."

"We would be sisters officially."

"I could stay here with my new family. We could sleep together and never be apart."

"What a great idea! My dad would have three Cowboys Cheerleaders in his life. He would love that."

"Carolyn and the others would love it too. It would be great public relations for sure."

We both chuckled at that. "When things settle down again, and they get back, we will have a talk with them about it. If I know my parents, they might just go for it."

"Do you think there might be a chance?"

"I can be very persuasive, Helen. We will hit them with it while the bloom is still on the rose following their marriage."

"Oh, Katie. I love you so much."

"I love you too, Helen, and don't want to wait to have a sister. When they call, I will put a bug in dad's ear, suggesting that he notify his attorney to get things started. If they both agree, we can get the preliminaries going while they are away. You can be my wedding gift to them, another daughter."

It was around ten o'clock our time when the phone rang. I saw it was dad's cell phone, and I answered quickly. Helen and I were still in the living room with Rex, talking about things, among them the rehearsal scheduled for tomorrow evening. It would be my first.

"Where are you two?"

"We are on the island of Kauai in Hawaii for a few days before leaving for the South Pacific," Dad answered. "How are you two?"

"We are just fine, dad. Is mom there?"

"Yes, let me turn on the speaker." He did. "Can you still hear me?"

"Yes, dad. Helen is here with me, and you can talk with her too. Are you having fun yet?"

"Yes, we still had plenty of daylight when we arrived, and the flight was enjoyable. We are going to the beach in a few minutes and then dinner. What are you two doing?"

"We have been discussing something that I want to talk with you and mom about."

"Really? What is that?"

"Helen and I want to be sisters."

Silence from their end.

"Katie, dear, you are prescient."

"What do you mean, mom?"

"Your dad and I have been thinking about having two daughters but didn't know how to approach Helen about it. Are you there, Helen?"

"Yes, Jackie and Mike. I am here."

"What do you think about becoming our daughter? I am adopting Katie so that I will be her legal mother. Would you consider having Mike and me adopt you too?"

Helen broke down in tears. "Yes, Jackie. Being your daughter would make me very happy."

"I'll contact my attorney and get things started. I am sure Judge Nation will help since he has interviewed us. You will have some questions to answer about your birth parents and the people who raised you. Once that is all done, we will follow through with the final steps. Welcome to the family, Helen."

"Thank you, Mike. You have made me very happy. Have fun, and come back to us relaxed and tanned. Your daughters will be waiting for you."

"We'll send you a postcard everywhere we go. Enjoy yourselves, you two, and work hard with your Cheerleader friends."

"Thanks, dad. We will, and we told Carolyn and the girls about your marriage and asked if we could have a DCC party out here soon. She congratulated us and is arranging everything, including security. We just might have to have another to celebrate when you get home. You are going to have three of us in your family. Don't things change quickly sometimes?"

"Yes, they do, and all this is for the best. We will come home to both our daughters."

Chapter Eleven

My New Sister

"Tonight, I am going to return the favor you paid me last night, dearest sister. I feel happy and free for the first time in my life away from the squad. We are going to be together for the rest of our lives. Thank you so much for standing up for me and supporting your parents, our parents, plans for our family. How did you know?"

"They have been dropping hints, both verbal and non-verbal since the night we all met at DJ's. I thought they were planning for another addition, and they specifically spoke of giving me a sister or brother. I wonder if mom found out something about her health that made up their minds. They tried very hard to have a child early in their relationship, but mom recently found out she has an anomaly in her DNA. It causes problems with a fertilized egg implanting in the lining of her uterus. They want another daughter, and you are it."

"What is it about this place and this family? Do you make dreams come true?"

"Finding my father was my dream, and it happened, and I got Jackie as a bonus to be my mom. Yes, magic happens around here."

"I believe it. Let's see what magic we can create between us tonight. Are you ready?"

"Yes, sister Helen. We will sleep in the big bed tonight. Would you like that?"

"I just want to be with you, Katie. It has been a big day."

"Yes, it has, and tomorrow will be another chance for us."

"Can we try to find Estelle and get her to come over here with us?"

"Yes, Helen. We should see her at our exercise session. We will get her to come over here, and we can get ready for our rehearsal together. We are going to create our makeup and hair salon in a bedroom, and we can work on each other. You game?"

"Yes, but I don't have any money for that."

"Don't worry. Mike will take care of that, and when they adopt you, everything will work out. You are a beloved member of this family now, as am I. It is going to be fantastic."

"It already is, dear Katie, and tonight, I am going to make it even more wonderful. I hear the big bed calling us."

"Come with me, sister. I love you so." The night was spectacular for us. We loved together and went to sleep satisfied sexually. Helen was different from Jackie, but she knew how to love. We held each other again all night and relaxed the next day until we had to go.

We went to our rehearsal the next evening, and I thoroughly enjoyed it, but it was exhausting. Again, Helen and I both went through the entire thing. The leg lifts to the splits went well. That I could already do them amazed Kelli, and she smiled her satisfaction toward me. I got a few pointers to refine my technique, and she was delighted with her recruit. I was way ahead of many of the old-timers.

Helen and I talked with Estelle and invited her again to join us at the lake. "Are you sure? You two seem to have something going yourselves."

"My dad and mom are planning to adopt Helen, too. We are sisters and love each other very much. We are a family but want you to be a part of that. Please come and give it a try."

"That's wonderful, Helen. Katie, your dad, is going to have three of us in his family. Want to try for four?"

"As I recall, you already have a mother and father, Estelle," Helen answered with a smile.

"Very true, Helen. Okay, I accept your invitation. What should I bring?"

"Plan to stay awhile, Estelle. We have plenty of room."

"Then it will be the three musketeers?"

"That's the idea."

"Count me in. Can I ride with you over there?"

"Yes, of course, if you want. We have my dad's SUV, and we came over here together."

"Tonight?"

"Yes, right now. If you would prefer, you can follow us so that you will have your car. We have plenty of clothes for all of us, and you can go get your things tomorrow."

I hugged her, and so did Helen. "You know where it is, so if you lose us, just come on anyway. We are looking forward to having you with us."

"We have plenty of food and will feed you," Helen offered.

"Okay. I'll be there."

"Shall we?" I asked.

"Lead on."

In a few minutes, we were on our way, delighting Helen. She had missed Estelle. We were all tired after rehearsal but regained some energy from dinner. Estelle loved the house, and Rex accepted her readily. When we showed her the master suite, she wanted to know if we were sleeping there. We explained that we were since mom and dad were away. She hugged Helen and smiled.

We went back into the living room, and I made our nightcaps.

"You know, if you two are nice to me, I might never leave here."

"Give us tonight, and you can decide in the morning. We will do our routines early, and then we are planning to create a makeup station here for us to use. Interested?"

"You bet, Katie. I would love to help."

"Then, it is a plan."

"Yes," both Helen and Estelle agreed.

"Is it bedtime yet?"

"Yes, Estelle, it is. Come with me, and I'll get you something to wear."

"Make it light. I like to sleep with as little on as I can get away with."

"No problem. If you want to sleep without anything on, it will make things much easier."

"What do you mean?"

"We are all going to sleep in the big bed with each other tonight. I cannot be held responsible for what I do to you in my sleep," Helen chuckled.

"The three of us? In the same bed? I don't know if I can handle that."

"We have practiced with each other, dear Estelle. Now that you are here, we plan to enjoy you," I explained.

"You guys are too hot for me. Will I survive being with both of you?"

"It will be close, but I think we will keep you alive to love again," Helen said sexily.

"I'm ready. Take me to bed."

We did just that, and she survived the night. It was good to have another bed buddy. We put her between us and loved on her most of the night. We all got some sleep, though, and rose the next morning refreshed and very happy. Estelle seemed to fit in perfectly. The three of us had breakfast and headed out to the Star. The other girls had something new about which they could talk. Our smiles let them all know we were three.

When we arrived home, we went to check on the progress the pool people were making, and it looked like they were doing well. I hoped it would all be ready when mom and dad came home. We looked online for places that had the furniture we needed for our makeup center and found one that seemed particularly promising. We all got into the Lincoln with Helen driving and headed that way. Their showroom was full of different options from which we could choose. One stood out to us as being just what we wanted. It was very much like the stations at the stadium and had two seats with a perfect mirror and excellent lighting. The table had drawers for storage, and we all agreed it was the one. I gave the saleswoman Mike's credit card and the address where they were to deliver it. It would arrive tomorrow afternoon, and they would set it up for us. We were gleeful at our choice and began planning for using it to its fullest. Helen drove us home. I felt I could have handled the traffic, but Helen was an excellent driver. We talked on the ride back to the house.

I checked the mail. Aside from other items, I found a large envelope from dad's lawyers. I knew what it was immediately. We went upstairs, and I gave it to Helen. "I think this is for you, sis."

Dad was true to his word. The adoption questionnaire was in it. Helen began working on it at once. In about an hour, she had finished. "Do you guys want to see my whole life in a five-page document?"

"I would rather hear it from you, Helen. Have you checked to make sure it is complete?"

"Yes."

"Then put it in the return envelope and let's go mail it. I want this finalized as soon as possible. As I said, I am giving my parents another daughter for their wedding present."

"They are going to adopt you, Helen?"

"Yes, the plan is for Jackie to adopt Katie and for them both to take me. What do you think?

"I didn't believe it at first, but now I have seen the papers. Congratulations to both of you. I wish you all the happiness in the world." She hugged us both.

"Thanks, Estelle. We are pleased about it all."

The three of us drove to the nearest post office, just a few minutes away, and mailed the forms overnight back to the lawyers, starting the process. If all went well, it would happen quickly.

"Anyone up for riding the horses? They need to exercise every day."

"I would love to ride," Helen responded immediately.

"I thought you might. How about you, Estelle?"

"I rode some years ago, but not recently."

"No problem, you can ride Mandy. She is an excellent mount. Helen, you get Blackie, and I will ride Romeo. Let's put on our boots and jeans and go out to them. It'll be fun."

We took Rex with us, much to his delight. I called the horses from the corral, and they came running. The corral had come to mean human attention and a bucket of oats for them. I gave Helen and Estelle their bridles and showed them how to put them on. We put the reins over the top railing to let the horses know to stay there. I got their blankets, and we put them in the appropriate locations on their backs. Romeo was anxious to start and pawed the ground a couple of times, letting me know he didn't think I was going fast enough. I threw his saddle on him and cinched it tight, showing the other girls the cinch knot and how to tie it. I then fastened the bucking strap loosely, explaining that it should not be too tight. After checking to make sure everything was okay, I showed them how to mount from the left side after taking the reins in their left hands, and we were all up. I led them out into the pasture and slowly rode until they got their balance and felt comfortable. Romeo wanted to go faster, and I let him have his head. He leaped into a gallop, but the other horses stayed calm.

Romeo lived up to his constant need for attention as a three-year-old and was full of himself. I pulled him up and patted his neck, praising him and telling him how handsome he was. The big stallion loved that and started to prance like a show horse. He was a real lover, and he loved to have me riding him. I exercised him through all his paces and rejoined the others. They were enjoying their rides too, although their mounts were not as energetic as Romeo. I let him out once again and took him around the entire pasture until he was breathing hard and wanted to walk some. I made a note to myself to exercise him more frequently. He was getting a little lazy. Mike would be glad to have someone take care of all three of them.

I led the girls back into the corral and closed the gate. We removed their saddles and blankets and again dropped their reins over the fence rails. I got us three buckets with their soap and water, and we washed them and brushed them dry. They loved that and knew what was coming next. I showed Helen and Estelle where their oats were, and we gave them each a bucket, which they ate hungrily. We took their halters off while they ate, and I opened the gate, so they could return to the pasture when they finished. As we walked back to the house, Romeo whinnied his thanks before he and the others left the corral. We girls walked arm-in-arm happy and smiling at our ride.

We smelled like horses, so our clothes went into the hamper, and we headed into the shower. It was the first time Estelle bathed with us. Helen and I took turns with her. She enjoyed it and helped clean both of us when we finished with her. We dressed scantily and went in to make some dinner after making our selections from the liquor cabinet. All three of us were very happy. Estelle was fitting in well and was a delightful friend.

We ate a light supper and returned to the couch with fresh drinks. I started the conversation. "I am sure you both remember the outing to DJ's. The guys went kind of crazy over you."

"As I recall, you got a lot of attention too, Katie," Helen observed.

"Some guys were charming, and they could dance. Would you tell me what Dallas guys are like?"

"A lot of the guys that go there are looking for one thing and one thing only–a conquest for the night, but they are usually obvious."

"I guess my Dad got so much attention from the girls because they knew he was not like that and was a lot of fun."

"You got it, girl," Estelle chimed in.

"How would someone like me find the right type of guy?"

"What do you have in mind, sister?"

"Although I left my Wyoming cowboy because he was so controlling and wanted to tell me how to live my life to please him, I can't help but think that somewhere out there is a good man who appreciates women like us."

"The first rule is to stay away from the football players, especially the Dallas Cowboys."

"I picked up on that already, Estelle."

"Secondly, most guys who wear a suit during the day but dress up in their very attractive but useless fake cowboy duds to go out may fantasize about being a real one. They are usually escaping their very boring lives and many, their girlfriends or wives. You have to be careful with them."

"Are there any types that might have promise, Helen?"

"Yes, and they come along from time to time."

"So, one day, I will turn the corner, and there he will be?"

"Something like that. You must be happy with who you are and moving forward with your life if you want to find him. Be true to yourself and your life. Love those who love you and don't worry about finding a man. When you aren't looking, that's when he will come along."

"Unannounced and unexpected?"

"That's the way it works. Don't put up any evidence that you are desperate to find a man. Just let it go. When it the time comes, it will happen."

I thought for a few moments. Helen and Estelle exchanged glances. "That's what happened when you two showed up and became parts of my life. When you grabbed my Dad, Jackie, and I joked that we had just lost him." They both snickered at that scenario. "Then two guys dragged us off to the dance floor, and Dad gave you champagne until we returned. It was an auspicious evening for me."

Helen kissed me tenderly and said, "For us too, dear sister of mine. You just showed up, unexpected and unannounced, but there you were. I didn't even know Mike had a daughter and that he and Jackie had resumed their close relationship. As I said, unexpected and unannounced."

"For me too," Estelle joined us. "It was a great evening."

"What were you guys doing there, anyway?"

"As if we don't get enough dancing with the Cheerleaders, we both had an evening off and wanted to find some new guys with whom to dance. DJ's has patrons who are some of the best dancers around."

"When we saw Mike, we knew it was going to be a fine evening. He can dance!"

"I saw that when he hit the floor with you two," I agreed.

"Jackie knows that we all love him, and she is a good sport about sharing him. Besides, he loves it so much when he is with one of us."

"I noticed that too and will take him out myself some night. Dancing with my father will be a new thing for me, and I look forward to it."

"The party we are planning for him and Jackie will give us all a chance to dance with him."

"Estelle. That is supposed to be a secret."

"Oh, no. I'm sorry. Katie, I guess I let the cat out of the bag."

"A party? For our dad and mom, Helen?"

"Yes, sis. We'll do it as soon as they get back and rest up some from the trip. Carolyn and Kelli are planning it. They want it to be a surprise party at the stadium in their honor. Please don't let on."

"Your secret is safe with me. I won't say a word."

"Thanks," they both told me.

"Who is invited to this party?"

"All the cheerleaders, of course, and their significant others. Security will be tight. Kelli is going to put Jackie in a new uniform and try to get her to join the line for some happy dancing and reminiscing. It should be a real blast. Expect to wear your uniforms too, and they will take a shot of mom and daughters together."

"I want them to take care of our entire family, with you too, Estelle."

"The occasion is going to be well-documented, I assure you. No hard liquor allowed, of course, only champagne, and the Cowboys organization will foot the bill. It will be splendid."

Tears came to my eyes. "All this is happening, isn't it?"

"Yes, Katie, it is about as real as it can get."

I hugged them both and got up to gather myself with the excuse that we needed fresh drinks. They let me be alone for a few minutes, and I came back to them with the new cocktails and a smile. "I love you both so much, and I love the Cheerleaders and my new life with all of you. I am thrilled and happier than I have ever been before."

"Welcome to our world, Katie. We love you too."

"When are your folks getting back, Katie?" Estelle asked.

"They left less than a week ago, and they said they would travel for at least two. I would say we should look for dad and mom just before our next home game. They haven't said anything about coming home in their postcards, so that's just a guess. They both will be delighted to see you here with us, Estelle."

"Thanks, Katie, but I can't stay here all the time. I have other responsibilities to take care of, including my family. I am sure Robert wonders where the hell I am too."

"Robert?"

"An excellent friend now who may become more than that. He is self-confident, and my being a Cowboy Cheerleader doesn't threaten him at all. He is a little older than I am and has a good head on his shoulders."

"What does he do?" Helen asked.

"He is a stockbroker and does very well from what I have seen."

"I wish you the best, Estelle."

"Me too," I seconded Helen's comment.

"How did you meet him?" I wanted to know.

"Remember what I told you earlier? I met him just like that. It is our story."

"Can you stay here tonight?"

"Yes, I wouldn't miss it for the world."

"Then, we will make it a special one."

"I hoped you would say that. Shall we?"

Chapter Twelve

This Game is Going to be Special

We didn't have any more scheduled events until we would begin to prepare for our upcoming game. Helen and I went to the training table and the exercise room every day. I could feel my muscles getting more robust and more flexible, and it surprised me that both things could happen at the same time. My exercise program was having all the effects the trainers were expecting. They knew what they were doing. The routines got more natural by the day, and I devoted myself to my health and fitness. A very positive effect was that my periods were still regular, and I knew I should see my doctor again. I had a feeling I should do something about birth control even though I did not have a boyfriend and didn't expect that to change anytime soon. Helen and I were still inseparable.

The weekend came, and we took Sunday off for a break. Rumor had it that Kelli and the other directors were going to have us add to our routine, and if it worked, we would include it at the next game. One particular thing happened on Tuesday before the game. After we returned home from our daily routine, we found two packets from Dad's lawyers in the mail, one addressed to Helen, and the other addressed to me. In them were the final adoption decrees for both of us. I was now legally Jackie's daughter, and my name became as we had planned, Katherine MacDonald Armstrong. Helen officially became the legal daughter of both Dad and my new Mom, and her name was now Helen De Franco Armstrong, which included her former name. I didn't even know what it was until I saw the papers.

We hugged and kissed and shared our delight at being officially and legally now sisters. We were both joyous. I decided to try to contact our parents. I pulled up Dad's cell number and pressed CALL. Much to my delight, his phone rang on the other end. After a few rings, I thought he wasn't going to answer, but he did. "Hello, Katie! How are you doing?"

"Helen and I have some wonderful news for you both. The final adoption decrees came today, and you and Mom now have two daughters." I heard him tell mom.

"Katie says we have two daughters. The adoption papers came through." He handed Mom the phone. I guessed the speaker feature was not working well wherever they were. I put ours on speaker, anyway. In unison, Helen and I shouted out, "Hello Mom and Dad."

Mom began to cry. We both could hear her. "Oh, Katie, Helen, that is wonderful news. We are now a family."

"Yes, we are," I replied, "where are you?"

"We are in Auckland, New Zealand, after a wonderful visit to Sydney and Queensland, Australia. We took a fantastic cruise from there to here. It is spring in this part of the world, and this is a beautiful country."

"We miss you. Are you coming home soon? Can you make it back for the game this weekend?"

Dad came back on the line. "I'm afraid not, my two Angels. We have a couple of days here, and then we are going back to Hawaii for a while, Honolulu, this time. You know, luaus, roast pork, and even poi, not to mention Waikiki Beach and Diamond Head. We'll watch from there. Can you record it for us?"

"Yes, Dad, we'll do that. I can set the VCR on the timer and hope it works. They will sequester us again on Saturday night, of course, but we'll arrange for backup in case ours doesn't work. Helen De Franco Armstrong, your new daughter, would like to speak to you."

"Hello, Mom and Dad. I never thought I would be able to call anyone that, but I just want you to know how happy you have made Katie and me with your selfless acceptance of us as your daughters. We miss you and look forward to your return to us. Rex wonders where you are too. The horses are fine, well-fed, and we exercise them every day, all three of them with Estelle's help, and the pool is close to completion. It will be ready for you when you get back."

"We are so glad to have our daughters in our lives. You have brought us much joy. We must go now for a tour we scheduled. Have you been getting our postcards?"

"Yes, Dad. We kept them all. The places are beautiful."

"We will bring you here as soon as the football season is over. It will be summer here then."

"We would love that, right, Helen?"

"Yes, Katie. We are going back to celebrating our new sisterhood now, Mom and Dad. Come home to us soon."

"We are looking forward to being with you again, this time as a real family. Take care." They were gone.

"We tried," Helen shrugged.

"Yes, we did. It will be okay. We have a lot to do before the weekend, and they will be back shortly after that."

"I can't wait to hug my new parents. It's a dream come true for me." I hugged her tight as she shed a few tears.

"Let's get a couple of t-shirts that say, 'We are now sisters,' to wear to work out in."

"Great idea, Katie. I bet we can get them quickly and show the other girls that it happened."

"I would like that very much." We got online, ordered them, and specified overnight delivery. We would have them tomorrow. We couldn't stop hugging each other. Our happiness in being sisters and having new parents was overwhelming. We stayed together on the sofa for a long time, just hugging, kissing, and shedding tears of joy. For the first time, we both felt the closeness that only sisters can experience. We shared a light dinner later and went to the big bed together as sisters for the first time. Our relationship was no longer just a friendship or a love affair. We now had a permanent bond between us that would last a lifetime.

Wednesday would be our last big rehearsal, and wearing our new t-shirts, we went early to have dinner and do our exercises at the Star. The field there was identical to the one at

AT&T Stadium, and Helen and I did everything they wanted us to do. Several of the new additions to our routines came naturally to most of the squad, but some of them could not do the head turn, high kick, into the splits, as well as Kelli wanted us to do. Her solution was to group those of us who could do them well together in a shorter line and have us make the new moves to each side of the stadium as we swapped sidelines. The show would happen at halftime, and many times the networks ignored us to show excerpts from other games and commercials.

Carolyn notified the TV people that we were doing something special, something they had never seen before. Thursday and Friday, we went with our usual daily routines, including my practicing show moves with Romeo. When we went to the stadium on Saturday to practice for game day, they were there planning their angles and camera positions for best coverage. We then went into sequester as usual.

When Sunday came, Helen and I took full advantage to show our new moves for the cameras and audience, bringing praise from both Kelli and Carolyn, who could see we nailed them. It was the proudest moment of my brief time with the organization. More would come. Helen and I, along with others, gave them more options for their routines.

The new moves in the routine included extended high kicks, much higher than the standard ones we did as a squad. In these kicks, our legs went vertical, almost touching our faces as we kept steady on the other leg. I wondered if we were all keeping things covered during them. I discovered that several of the girls gave them quite a show. We did two sets of eight, then did a peel off from both ends to the middle of our shorter line, returning to our stance after each one of us did our kicks. We ended the routine when we were all standing again, jerked our heads away from the audience flipping our hair, and quickly back to the front. When our eyes straightened up, on the signal, we did radical splits in unison and stayed down with our heads bowed to the audience. They loved it and rose to their feet, giving us a standing ovation as they clapped and whistled their approval. We then rose and marched off the field, exhausted but satisfied. I had played to the crowd as had Helen and ignored the cameras. Later, I would see that the video contained images of my entire routine, both close-ups, and long shots. Our new line was a real hit in person and on the screen. Helen and I hugged each other and rested before we retook the field for the second half.

We emerged to thunderous applause. The rest of the half went according to plan, although several of the girls hurt themselves during the halftime routine and had to limit themselves and what they could do. Those who had not participated and we who made it through were fine and put on a fantastic show for the fans. We went back to our dressing room near the end of the game, and Carolyn was waiting for us. She called Helen and me to the side and took us to another place before we could change out of our uniforms, indicating we should sit down and rest for a minute. She said she had a favor to ask of us. We both told her we would be glad to help. She motioned for the ladies standing on the sides of the room, and they began to touch up our makeup and hair. Neither of us had any idea what was going on.

"Here's the situation, Helen and Katie. The word is out on you two and your new family. Someone wants to interview you and is waiting for you on the star in the middle of the field. The Cowboy executives approve, and the PR staff is very excited about it. I will be beside you, but off-camera for the whole thing. It could take some time. You will be live on national television. Are you game to give this a try?"

I looked at Helen questioningly, and she nodded. I agreed with her. "Yes, Carolyn. I think we know what to say and what not to say. You guys have taught us well."

"We'll do our best," Helen added.

"Are you ready?"

"Yes, lead on."

She walked with us to the field to mild applause from girls who stayed to see what was going on. A couple of handsome men came over to put mikes on us and gave us the biggest smiles. They were close to our ages and weren't wearing rings. Promising. "My name is Peter, and I am a FOX sound tech."

"I'm Katie."

"Glad to meet you, Katie."

The other one said, "My name is Paul. Is either one of you, Mary?" She and I appreciated the joke. It helped us relax even more.

"No, Paul," Helen liked him, I could tell. He was attracted to her, too, and he touched her breast as he put on her mike, making it look natural. She pushed against him, giving him a thrill. His knees got weak as he left her.

My guy just smiled at me and said, "Break a leg." I kissed him on the cheek as a thank you, and we were ready. Carolyn walked with us to the center of the field.

As Carolyn had said, the temporary stage was set up directly on the star. The lights and camera focused on three chairs with stars on the backrests, one of which held a man who was reading his notes. We walked toward the set with Carolyn at our side and approached the man. As we came nearer, he stood and smiled at us. We both recognized him at once. It was Casey West, a former Cowboy and NFL star, who had called the game from the announcer's booth. Helen and I joined arms and put on our best smiles.

"Hello, girls. Please have a seat." He sat with us flashing his smile as well.

"The cameras are not on yet, and I want to talk with you before we go on the air. Let's see, you are Helen, and he looked at her, so you must be Katie."

"Yes, Mr. West."

"Please, call me Casey."

We looked at each other and held hands.

"Are you nervous?"

"Yes, neither of us has been on live TV without the other girls before."

"I see. You have nothing about which to be nervous. I am going to ask you a few questions, so the audience can get to know you and your amazing story. Is that okay with you?"

"Yes, Casey." Helen nodded in agreement. We looked at the other girls who were watching and saw all of them smiling at us.

"Great. We are about to begin, and this is live TV, so they will cue us when the time comes. Relax and enjoy."

My excitement increased, and I could feel Helen's enthusiasm, as well. A few seconds later, we heard the director counting down, and when he finished, Casey raised his head and looked directly into the camera with the red light on top.

"Welcome back to AT&T stadium, ladies and gentlemen. To begin our post-game show, we have two young ladies here who are sisters and Dallas Cowboys Cheerleaders. Meet Katie Armstrong," a camera moved to get a face shot, "and Helen Armstrong." We could tell they were shooting Helen. She beamed her great smile at the viewers. The camera pulled back to get all three of us in the shot. Casey continued.

"Thanks for joining me on such short notice. It is a delight to have you young ladies and to listen to your story."

"You're welcome," Helen replied.

"It is our pleasure, Casey," I followed. We both assumed the Cheerleader smile just as they had taught us.

Back in Hawaii, Dad told us later. Mom almost fainted when she saw us on TV with Casey. Dad had to hold her up.

"Helen, you are a veteran, right?"

"Yes, Casey."

"And you are new to the squad, Katie?"

"Yes, Casey."

"How do you like being Dallas Cowboys Cheerleaders?"

"It is a dream come true, Casey, a dream of mine since I began dance classes when I was six years old."

"And now that dream has come true, Katie. Congratulations."

I just smiled at him. "Thank you, Casey. Yes, it has."

"I am told that your mother, Jackie, was also a member of the Cheerleaders. Is that right?"

"Yes, Casey. She was a Cheerleader for several years."

Dad said later that Mom got woozy when Casey mentioned her name but came around quickly.

"Your father is also involved? How does he fit into an all-girl group?"

"Just ask any of the girls about our Dad. They are all in love with him. He is like a father to them, and he can dance. They take turns dancing with him."

"Lucky man!" Casey observed.

Mom fainted dead away when she heard that.

"Do you date the players?"

"No. Dating players is prohibited, even though some of them are very hot," the standard answer they had taught us.

"I see. Then are there other men in your lives?"

"Being a Cheerleader takes almost all our time and energy. There are few opportunities to have a steady boyfriend," the standard answer we had also been taught.

"As sisters, are you competitive with each other?"

"No, Casey. We help each other. We live together, eat together, exercise together, and work together on our routines," I told him.

"You might say we are inseparable," Helen added.

"We noticed some new moves in your show today. I don't think I have ever seen such high kicks and straight-leg splits before anywhere."

"We just put those in this past week and call them sky kicks and power splits. We might be the only group who does them."

"I am getting a voice in my ear that our time is almost gone. Is there anything else you want to add?"

We looked at each other. "May we say hello to our Mom and Dad, who are watching from Hawaii?"

"Sure."

"Hello, Mom. Hello Dad. Come home to us soon. We miss you," we said.

Casey turned away from us and back to the cameras. "So, there you have it, folks. Katie and Helen Armstrong, sisters who are both Dallas Cowboys Cheerleaders. Thank you, girls. You are special, indeed."

We just smiled and waved goodbye to the viewers.

"Now, back to the studios in New York."

The cameramen turned off their equipment and began to pack up. Peter and Paul came to take our mikes off. Helen gave Paul his customary thrill, and he swooned. We motioned for the other girls to go over and meet Casey and headed back to the locker room with Carolyn escorting us. She praised our performance all the way. We just smiled. Just as we went under the stands, I looked back and saw Casey surrounded by beautiful girls. He looked like he was in heaven. I motioned for Helen to watch, and she smiled broadly at the scene they were making. Our PR people kept on recording.

Carolyn led us to the little room, and Kelli was already there. "Please have a seat, girls."

We did. Kelli congratulated us on both our performance and our tutoring skills in teaching the other girls. She was beaming at the special kicks and splits and thanked us for our diligence and the resulting show.

Carolyn also expressed her gratitude and gave us each a hug and a kiss on the cheek. Then she told us to dress and go home. She was delighted with the progress the girls were making. "See you tomorrow?"

"You know us, Carolyn. Same time, same routine. We'll be there."

"We need to work off the effects of the performance and get started on next week's activities."

"That's right, Helen. We want to stay loose and limber after our day."

"You might have more company than usual for the day after a game."

"We hope so. Exercising tomorrow will do a lot toward keeping people on track."

"Now, go! Get some sleep and talk with your folks. We have it all on DVD, and you will get yours tomorrow. Sleep well, girls."

"Thanks, Carolyn. I am sure we will," I said as we left the room and walked to our lockers, holding hands and smiling at each other. We dressed and started for the car.

Just outside the locker room, Peter and Paul were waiting for us. "Hi, guys. Thanks for helping us get ready for the interview," I said. Of course, Helen kissed Paul.

"We have a few minutes before we need to go to the airport. Would you like to have a beer with us before you go?"

"Sure. Just one, though." We led them to the bar that everyone walked through to get to the field and took a table. The place was almost empty.

"What will you two have," Peter asked.

"We always drink the sponsor's beer when we are here."

"Four Miller Lite beers, please bartender."

They were cold and tasty.

"You know you two stole the post-game show, don't you?" Peter started the conversation.

"I don't know about that, Peter, but thanks. Our interviewer was one of America's sports heartthrobs, and he was the major personality on the show."

"Not the way I see it," Paul clarified. "Your poise, beauty, and intelligence far overshadowed him."

"Thanks, Paul. We had a blast on-screen with him."

"He liked you, too. You haven't seen the last of him unless I miss my bet."

"He's too old for us. Our father is about his age."

We had an excellent talk, and Peter looked at his watch when we finished our beers and told us they had to go. "We will see you at the next home game, I hope."

"Wouldn't let any other sound man touch me," Helen teased him.

Paul cleared his throat and replied, "Thanks, Helen. It has been a real pleasure working with you. May I call you sometime?"

"I would like that, Paul," and she handed him one of her cards. "Call me here."

"I will, Helen. Until we meet again."

She kissed him goodbye, and they walked back to the field.

"I guess Peter is not interested in calling me," I said.

"You have Brian. I bet he calls after this broadcast."

"Let's go, sister."

We dressed, headed for the car, and soon were on our way, thoroughly satisfied and happy. It had been a unique game.

Chapter Thirteen

Reactions

As soon as we arrived home, Helen and I removed our makeup, showered, and put on some comfortable clothes. No sooner had we finished bathing than the phone rang. "And so, it begins," Helen guessed right. The call was from Honolulu. She answered, "Hello."

"How are our two TV stars?"

"Hi, Dad and Mom. You saw that?"

"Of course. We watched the game in a restaurant, and when Casey came back on and introduced you, your Mom saw you and got the bartender to turn up the volume. Everyone in the restaurant watched after your Mom shouted out that you were our daughters. When you came on, looking fabulous, they applauded."

"We didn't know what was happening until Carolyn stopped us after the game and asked us if we would do it. It seems that the word is out about our family."

"Your Mom almost lost it again when he mentioned her being a former Cheerleader, and when he said what he said about the girls and me, she fainted dead away."

"Mom, are you all right now?" I asked her.

"Yes, girls. I am fine, but it was quite a surprise."

"Did you see how many more of the girls could do the sky kicks and power splits?" Helen asked.

"Yes, Helen. Did you and Katie have anything to do with that?"

"The trainers did it. All the girls are doing our exercise routines now after everyone saw the effects they had on us. They are eating better, too."

"We wish you had been there. When are you coming home?"

"In several days. We should be there later this week," Dad replied.

"We miss you."

"We miss you, too, Helen. Is everything okay there?"

"Yes, Mom. The pool is almost complete, and the horses and Rex are in great shape. I have even started Romeo's training as a show horse. He is such a ham. He loves it."

"I know you must be tired, so we'll let you go. Enjoy yourselves until we get there, and we will be together again."

"Okay, you two. Enjoy the rest of your trip, and we'll see you soon."

"Good night, girls."

"Goodnight," we said in unison. Dad hung up on his end.

"I'm glad they got to see us," I said to Helen.

"Yeah, me too. Want a drink?"

"Yes, it has been quite a day."

"How about Scotch and soda, light, with a lime wedge?"

"Sounds great to me, Helen."

We sat together on the couch, embracing and being close to each other. Having Helen in my arms felt good. "Did you enjoy doing the interview?"

"Yes, how about you?"

"Yes, I did. Most of the time, we were acting, using the script our PR people taught us to answer his questions."

"We did it well, too. I'm glad Carolyn chose us."

"I am too. Maybe we will get to do it again."

"I wouldn't be surprised."

My cell phone rang. "My cell? I wonder who this can be." I answered it.

"May I speak to Katie?" the male voice asked.

"This is Katie."

"Katie, this is Brian."

"Brian? It's good to hear from you."

"Are you busy, or can you talk?"

"I can talk for a while. How are you doing?"

"Just fine, thanks. I saw you and Helen on the game today and was not sure I should call. It was quite a surprise."

"I'm happy you did. Have you been dancing lately?"

"Yes, but it's not the same without you."

"That's sweet, Brian. We do look good together, don't we?"

"Yes, we do. You and Helen look good together, too."

"Thanks. You are nice to say that."

"I saw the part of your interview where you said you didn't have much time for dating and a relationship. Do you have any time for that?"

"Why do you ask, Brian?"

"Because I would like to take you out some time. Would you go out with me, Katie?"

Helen was listening and nodded her head in the affirmative.

"I would like that very much, Brian. What did you have in mind?"

"I know this little dinner club that has a dance floor. We could have dinner and dance. Of course, it is not the kind of dancing we do at DJ's, but it is more intimate and a lot of fun."

"Do you want to slow dance with me, Brian?"

I could see him blushing even though we were talking on the phone.

"Yes, Katie. I want to hold you close and let my romantic side out."

"Wine?"

"Of course."

"Well-dressed waiters?"

"Yes, tuxedos."

"I would love to go out with you, Brian. I have a couple of free nights early next week."

"Would Tuesday night work for you?"

"Yes. Say about six-thirty?"

"That will be fine, Katie. Where do you live?"

I told him and gave him detailed directions.

"Then it's a date?"

"It's a date, Brian. I am looking forward to it."

"So am I, Katie. I'll be there with bells on."

"You can probably leave the bells at home, my dear. Just bring yourself. Good night!"

"Good night, Katie. I'll see you Tuesday night."

"I'll look forward to it." I hung up the phone.

"I have a date, dear sister! My first date in forever, and it's with someone I like."

"Congratulations, Katie." She looked sad.

"Aren't you happy for me?"

"Yes, I am. Brian could be a great guy." She turned away from me with a tear in her eye.

"What's wrong, Helen?"

"I can't help but think it will be our first evening away from each other ever."

I gave her a big hug and tried to comfort her. "Should I see if Brian has a friend who might like to go out with a gorgeous Dallas Cowboys Cheerleader?"

"That would be you, Katie."

"Hang on."

I brought up my call history, found Brian's recent call, and pressed REDIAL. I started ringing. Brian answered.

"Brian, this is Katie. I was talking with Helen, and we realized we hadn't been apart at all for weeks. She doesn't want to be left alone Tuesday night."

"Are you breaking our date?"

"No, no way. Any guy who can dance like you is someone I want to get to know. What I am getting at is if you have a friend who might like to go out with a gorgeous redheaded Cheerleader, we can make it a double date."

"Helen?"

"Yes,"

"I don't think I can find more than five or ten of my friends who would give just about anything they have to go out with Helen. What kind of guy does she like?"

"Here, talk to her. She can tell you much better than I can. Hold on."

"Brian?"

"Hi, Helen."

"Do you know someone who might like to spend an evening with me?"

"Tell me what kind of guy attracts you."

"He should be handsome like you, and a professional. Someone intelligent and can carry on an enjoyable conversation. He must be single, of course, and affectionate. He should have the manners of a gentleman and love to hold hands and touch. Are you available Tuesday night, Brian?"

"I wish I were, but I have a date already, dear Helen."

"Oh, yes. With my sister."

"I have just the guy in mind, Helen. You'll love him."

"A strong case of like will be fine with me, Brian. Does he dance?"

"You might say that."

"Then let's do it."

"You're on. We'll see you Tuesday night."

"Thanks, Brian. You re a dream come true. Good night!"

"Good night, you two. Sleep well."

"We will." Helen ended the call and gave me back the phone.

"I can't believe I am going on a blind date."

"At least we will be together. It should be fun."

"Yes, it should. We both have dates, and they have nothing to do with football."

"Kind of nice, don't you think?"

"Yes, I do."

I moved over close to her and embraced her, kissing her. "Looks like we will share our attachment for life, dear sister."

"Thank you, Katie. You didn't have to include me."

"Yes, I did, Helen. I love you, and if we can be happy together, that's what I want. I think I remember the guy about whom Brian is talking. They were together at DJ's. If it is the same guy, we just might have to swap."

"Or do them together," she said with her devil eyes glowing.

"Now that could be interesting. Are you ready for bed yet?"

"Yes, we have an early morning tomorrow."

"Then let's go. I will undress you and put your nightie on you if you return the favor."

"I can think of nothing I would rather do. Come on."

We undressed and dressed each other and got under the covers in an embrace. My new sister felt so good to me. I was exhausted.

Wouldn't you know it? The home phone rang. I didn't want to answer it but did anyway. It was Carolyn again.

"Katie?"

"Hello, Carolyn. What's up?"

"Is Helen with you?"

"Of course. We just went to bed."

"I'm sorry to call at this hour, but I thought you might want to hear this."

"Go ahead, Carolyn," Helen said sleepily.

"Our servers here have been going on and off since shortly after your interview. The same thing is happening in New York at FOX. They had to go into a 'Denial of Service' mode for quite a while."

"What does that have to do with us," I asked.

"Because emails, tweets, and website hits trying to get in touch with you two are causing the outages. FOX has had over two hundred thousand hits, and we have had almost as many here."

"To us?"

"Yes. Your interview is the talk of the internet."

"What kind of messages are we getting?"

"Everything you can imagine. Marriage proposals, requests for dates, friend requests, and the usual obnoxious comments. The people in New York are ecstatic at the response and are thinking of other ways to get you in front of the public."

"Are you sure it isn't because of Casey?"

"A bare minimum of them. The messages are mostly for you."

We didn't know what to say, so we said nothing.

"FOX wants you in New York to go on FOX and Friends and maybe some other programs. Plus, you are wanted for the late-night talk shows."

"When do they want us?"

"As soon as possible, while you are still on people's minds."

"We have our workouts, practices, and a game this weekend. What do you think we should do?"

"I have reserved one of our aircraft for tomorrow after your workout and lunch. You can fly to New York and do the Tonight Show tomorrow evening. Tuesday morning, you can make an appearance on FOX and Friends and come home immediately after that. We can save the other late-night shows for later dates. The priority is our performance, the PR is important, but we must put first things first."

"We have dates on Tuesday night and don't want to miss them. We haven't been out on a date in a very long time."

"We should have you back in Dallas by lunchtime. If you can postpone your workout and lunch, you can be ready for your dates Tuesday night. Would that work for you?"

"That's why we stay in shape."

"Good girls. I think you will enjoy the experience."

"Who is going with us?"

"I am, and we are taking security as well."

"Company plane, did you say?"

"Yes. Limos when we get there and a gym and spa in the hotel."

I looked at Helen. She nodded her assent.

"We're in, Carolyn. When can we expect the car to pick us up?"

"Come in tomorrow, and we will take you from here after lunch. Bring two uniforms and something to sleep in."

"How about makeup and hair?" Helen wanted to know.

"The pros at FOX will take care of that. Being under the lights on a TV stage is different from being on the field at the stadium. Anything else?"

"Not this moment, but keep us informed about what is going on."

"I will. Now, sleep well and get some rest. We are going to have a busy couple of days, and thanks, girls. I'll make it up to you."

"Goodnight, Carolyn."

"We should tell Brian what's happening.

"Yes, we should, in case of delay on our return," I responded. "I'll let Brian know that we are going out with them at some point."

"We also should tell Mom and Dad so that they can watch."

"Yes. Can we go to sleep now?"

"Yes, dear sister. We are going to need it."

Chapter Fourteen

An Old Friend Leads the Way

We called Mom and Dad and let them know what was going on, and they promised to watch. The Tonight Show was anticlimactic, but the audience appreciated our being there. Carolyn and our security detail took excellent care of us. The makeup artists and hairdressers had done magic, especially with Helen. They brushed and fluffed her red hair, and she looked great. My black hair was a significant feature, and we blew kisses to the audience and smiled our biggest smiles. Jimmy was very kind to us and asked us many of the same questions we had answered during our interview. Even though very little time remained in the show when we went on, we used the chance to promote the Cheerleaders, and he promised to invite us back. Carolyn and security took us to our hotel, and we turned in immediately since we had a very early call in the morning.

We arrived at the FOX studios at five a.m. the next morning, and they directed us straight to hair and makeup for an appearance in the seven o'clock hour. When they finished, we put on our uniforms, and a staff member took us to the green room. We were both very excited. The venue was the outside studio for this broadcast with a substantial audience of fans. The show usually occurred inside with a tiny audience, if any, in the studio. We were glad we had people watching us.

The hour came, and Ainsley announced their next guest. He was none other than Casey. The hosts welcomed him, and he took a seat on the curvy couch with them. "Casey, it is so good to see you again. How have you been?" They came for us at that moment and led us to the hallway down which everyone walked to enter the outside set. We waited as Ainsley continued her conversation with him.

"I am told that you are here with two of your friends from Dallas."

"That's right, Ainsley. I just met them last Sunday, and they are fantastic girls."

"Will you introduce them?"

"Ladies and gentlemen, we are joined on the curvy couch today by the girls I had the privilege of interviewing after the last Cowboy game. May I introduce the Armstrong sisters, both of whom are Dallas Cowboys Cheerleaders? Helen, Katie, come on out."

That was our cue. We linked arms and did the Cheerleader walk onto the set and over to the couch. The director motioned us to sit together beside Casey, but we were having none of that. Helen sat on one side of him, took his arm in hers, and kissed him on the cheek. I sat on the other side and did the same. "Hello again, Casey. We had no idea we would see you again so soon." Both of us moved a little closer to him.

"Hello, Helen. Hello, Katie. When I heard you were coming on FOX and Friends, I immediately volunteered to be your advocate."

"Thanks, Casey. We didn't know you would be here," I said.

"Do I detect something going on here?" Ainsley asked.

"Yes, you do. All the girls, including us, love Casey. He is a Cheerleader ally, and we are delighted to have him as a part of our organization."

"The way you two are holding on to him, it seems that there is more between you."

"There is, Ainsley. Casey gave us our chance on national TV, and our lives have changed dramatically because of him."

"So, which one of you is in love with him?"

"I am," Helen answered.

"That makes two of us," I stated my case.

"I think you are in real trouble, Casey."

"Believe me, Ainsley, he can handle it," Helen said seductively. The audience broke up.

I grinned my most alluring smile at him. The audience applauded again.

"I don't know what to say, girls. All this is such a surprise."

"It's elementary. You are looking at two girls in their early twenties who wish Casey was twenty-five years younger," I tried to clear it up for her. Casey was beaming at all the attention we were giving him.

"What are you going to do about this, Casey?"

"I am going to enjoy it. The sisters cannot go out with me, much to my chagrin. Neither can the other girls. I get to see them at games, but that's all." The audience groaned. "But understand, I care for them, and they care for me. We are great friends, and I hope we will be for a long time to come."

"That's a wonderful story, you three. Will you come back and revisit us?"

We knew that was the end of the interview, and the three of us stood to leave. The last thing we did was kiss Casey real kisses, on the lips, and with more than just a little passion and told him goodbye. The audience roared their approval, and we exited stage left and returned to Carolyn and our security detail.

"Great job, girls. We need to get you back to Dallas, so let's go to our limo and get on our way. You can change here, and she took us to a small dressing room. We were out of our uniforms and into traveling clothes quickly. As we left, the crowd saw us and cheered. We waved to them and boarded the limo, which headed for the feeder airport where the Cowboys plane was waiting.

Carolyn laughed when we began to move.

"What, Carolyn?" She just shook her head.

"Do you two know what you just did?"

"Not really, but it sure was fun," Helen answered.

"You captured Ainsley, Brian, and Steve, the entire audience, everyone who was watching, and especially Mr. Casey West. He is so much in love with you both that he doesn't know how to act around you."

"That was the whole idea, wasn't it?" I asked her.

"Yes. Holding on so tightly had Mr. West soaring above the city, and when it was over, and you kissed him, I thought he was going to swoon and pass out."

"That was our intent, Carolyn. I thought we made a good case for the rest of the girls too."

"You did, but how we are going to keep him away from all of you and out of trouble, I have no idea."

"Let us handle that."

"I am taking you back to Dallas now, and we are going to plot what we are going to do on Sunday to capture the rest of the world."

"That might be ambitious, but count us in," Helen said as she grabbed my hand and squeezed it.

"Can you tell me about the guys you are going out with this evening?"

"Sure, Carolyn. Brian is a corporate auditor and a wonderful dancer," I told her.

"He is bringing one of his friends for me," Helen followed. "They work together. They are young, handsome, and we are so looking forward to having dates again."

"How did you meet them?"

"We met Brian one night when we were out dancing with Mom and Dad. We haven't met his friend yet, but think his name is Doug, according to Brian. He is supposed to be able to dance too. You know us. If a guy can't dance, he has very little chance of getting our attention."

My phone rang. It was from Casey. "Thanks, girls. You made me feel wonderful this morning."

"It was our pleasure, Casey. It seems that every time we meet with you, we get twice as many admirers."

"Are you sure you won't go out with me when I get back to Dallas?"

"We would love to, but you know we can't."

"What is it? My age?"

"That's a part of it, but you should know that we are dating a couple of guys who are very good to us. We are going out with them tonight."

"I see. Then I have no chance with you?"

"You are married, and we don't date married men. Go see your new wife and love on her," I told him. Carolyn nodded her approval.

"Okay, Katie and Helen. I'll see you at the game this weekend. Have a good trip. Goodbye for now." He hung up.

"Did I do all right, Carolyn?"

"Yes, Katie. I think it might be time to run in a gorgeous female announcer for the post-game interview. What do you think about Karen Lotti?"

"It would serve him right. We should nip this in the bud."

"I agree," said Helen. "She would be great."

"I'll see what I can do. In the meantime, try to get some rest. You need it and deserve it. We should be at the airport soon, and we'll be on our way back."

Helen and I moved closer together and embraced. In just a few minutes, we were both asleep with Carolyn looking over us, and a happy feeling in us at what we had done in New York. We had no concerns about what the ramifications might be. We slept on the plane as well. Love field never looked so good to us, and we all got in the limo heading for Frisco.

Just as we left the airport, my phone rang again. This time it was Dad and Mom. "Our TV star daughters strike again."

"Hi, Dad. Did you see us on Fox and Friends?"

"Yes, Katie. You made us proud."

"Thanks, Dad. Where are you two now?"

"Still in Honolulu, but we are coming home tomorrow. We should get there after midnight, but we are coming."

"That's wonderful news, Dad. We have missed you very badly."

"Where are you?"

"We are with Carolyn on our way back to the Star. We are going to have something to eat and do a light workout. Then we might take a nap. We have dates tonight."

"Do we know them?"

"I am going out with Brian, the guy who danced with me at DJ's. He is bringing a friend to Helen. We are going to a dinner place that has dancing too. It should be fun."

"Sounds like it."

"Have fun, Mom and Dad."

"We will and stay away from football players."

Helen and I laughed at that. "Don't worry, Dad. We don't date football players. You know that."

"Those kisses you gave a certain man on TV this morning made us wonder."

"Have no fear. Carolyn takes excellent care of us."

"I thought she might. Okay, we'll see you tomorrow night late. It will be wonderful to be home again and in our bed."

"We are looking forward to your return."

"Goodbye, daughters. Enjoy the evening with your new guys."

"Goodbye, Dad and Mom. We will." They were gone.

We ate first, and our energy came back to us. We did an abbreviated workout, stretched, and did our machines, but didn't push it. Tomorrow we would go back to our regular routines. We felt good as we headed for home. It was still early afternoon, and we had some time before we had to get ready. I noticed the light flashing on the phone, indicating we had a message. I checked it out and saw that it was from Brian.

"Katie, Helen, I am going to have to break our date tonight. My firm had an emergency come up in Chicago, and I must go. Doug is going with me to ensure compliance since it is a Federal issue. The trip could last for several days. I am so sorry, Katie, and I will call you when we get back. Great appearance on FOX and Friends this morning. You made me fall in love with you all over again. Take care."

Helen was listening. "I guess we should tell Carolyn, so she will know our plans fell through. Bummer!"

"Looks like it's just us again."

"Nothing personal, Katie, but I wanted a real man tonight."

"We could go out on our own."

"Call Carolyn and tell her what we are thinking."

"Okay, I will."

"We could go to Al's and eat seafood, then go dancing, or we can just stay here and recuperate from the last two days, after all, it is our last night together."

"I'll call Carolyn," I volunteered.

"Carolyn? It's me, Katie. Our dates stood us up tonight, and we wanted to let you know in case something comes up."

She said, "I am so glad you called. Put this on speaker so Helen can hear too. We have the numbers on your New York appearances. The Tonight Show was so short and late in the program, many people didn't see it, but the FOX and Friends appearance caused quite a stir. You beat every other morning show on TV. Congratulations!"

"That's great, Carolyn. I am glad we could carry the flag for the Cheerleaders."

"There's more. Ainsley is coming to Dallas on Saturday to see how we prepare, and I invited her to the game. She might do the interview we have planned. I think if she could, she would try out for the squad."

"No more ex-players?"

"Nope. Not even one."

"That's music to our ears."

"I thought you liked him."

"Too old, married, self-centered. I don't think so."

"But you made him fall for you today. Are you playing games, too?"

"Aren't we all?"

"I have told you this before, but I'll repeat it. I am so glad you two are on my side."

We both chuckled at that. "Tomorrow, we are going back to our regular routines. We want to focus on getting ready to charm our live audiences and our TV audience. We are not as good as we are going to be, Carolyn, and we hope to take the rest of the squad with us."

"No more TV appearances?"

"Only if they want to come down here."

"You are going to let us handle all the correspondence you two have gotten and are likely to get in the future?"

"Yes. The pros should take that and run with it."

"When are your parents coming home? Do you know?"

"They will be here late tomorrow night."

"No more sleeping together in the big bed?"

We looked at each other. How did Carolyn know about that? "Ours is plenty big enough. How did you know about our sleeping arrangements?"

"I asked Estelle."

"She knows. She even spent some time over here with us in the big bed."

"She misses you two."

"We'll do something about that on Saturday night."

"When your guys get back, let me know. I would like to meet them."

"You mean, check them out?"

"Something like that."

"We will be glad to introduce you. We were thinking about going out for dinner and doing some dancing. Is that all right with you?"

"Where are you thinking about going?"

"Al's for seafood and then DJ's for dancing. Some girls might be there."

"I'll send a car for you and someone to make sure you are okay."

"Thanks, Carolyn. Say around six? We have an active day tomorrow."

"That will be fine. I want you two to have an enjoyable time."

"We have attracted some attention lately, haven't we?"

"Yes, a good thing too, but I am going to make sure my two incredible girls are well-taken care of."

"Tell any of the girls who are still there that we are all descending on DJ's tonight to dance and let our hair down. With security, we should be fine."

"Okay. I might even come myself."

"Would you? That would be great, Carolyn."

"I'll see what I can do. I would love to have a party with my girls as one of them for a change."

"See you there, lady."

"Okay."

"We'll be ready."

"Let's all have a wonderful time."

"We will, especially if you're there."

"Thanks, Katie. I appreciate your saying that."

"We are looking forward to it."

The spa called us, and we fixed a couple of drinks and went out back to take advantage of it. The workers had completed both the pool and the spa, and they worked great now. We relaxed, having no further obligations for the evening. We would have a driver to Al's and DJ's and had no worries. Rex was glad to see us and took up his place on the pool deck. We hoped that someday he would want to join us in the water.

Helen looked so delicious that I couldn't resist taking her in my arms and giving her a big kiss. She kissed me back.

"Let's not get carried away yet, dear sister. We have fun things to do tonight."

"We only have about an hour and a half until our limo gets here. Do you want to start getting ready?"

"Yes. Let's take our time." I kissed her again. "I love you, Helen."

"I love you too, Katie. Let's get ready to have some fun."

"Sounds like a wonderful idea to me."

Chapter Fifteen

A Girl's Night Out

We dressed in our most elegant western outfits complete with boots, jeans, belts with beautiful buckles, and our satin blouses that we had bought together to match each other. We each did each other's hair and makeup and looked fantastic. The limo arrived right on time, and the driver opened the door for us. To our surprise, not only was Carolyn in it but Kelli as well. When we each had a glass of bubbly, the driver drove away and headed for Al's Seafood Restaurant. As usual, the parking lot was full, and he let us off at the door. Our female security guards escorted us into the restaurant while the driver stayed with the limo. Four of our team were already there, sitting around a large table. They were glad to see us, especially Carolyn and Kelli, who didn't go out with the girls very often. We took seats around the table as the waiter came to take our drink orders. Helen and I ordered iced tea.

A few minutes later, several other Cheerleaders came in and walked over to our table. We still had room for a few more. We ended up being twelve. The waiter, whose name was Carlos, returned with our drinks and asked if we had decided. Several of the girls wanted fried shrimp, a couple more wanted peel and eat. Fried oysters were also popular, as was the Mahi dish. I had a thought.

"Carlos, it seems that several of us want to try more than one dish. Why don't you bring three of each of the entrees that people have ordered and put them family-style on the table, so everyone can try what they want?"

"Perfect, Miss Katie. Will there be anything else? Yes. Bring us three dozen oysters on the half shell as an appetizer."

"I'll get those right out."

"Thanks, Carlos."

When he left, Carolyn asked how he knew me. I told her I had been there with my Dad and Mom, and he remembered me from those visits.

Carolyn and Kelli were relaxing with "their girls," and most of them enjoyed socializing with these two leaders of the Cheerleader squad. They fit into the group very well, and before long, we were just one big happy family. Some girls had never eaten raw oysters before, and several were reluctant to try them. I started them off by taking one, putting the horseradish sauce and a little squeeze of lemon on it, and eating it while everyone watched. Several followed my lead to their satisfaction when they realized they were tasty. The three dozen didn't last long. Before I could ask if anyone wanted more, several waiters brought our entrees. They looked good, and their aromas got everyone's attention.

Helen and I stayed with the boiled and grilled dishes accompanied by a small salad with oil and vinegar dressing. Carolyn and Kelli were less selective and enjoyed the fried shrimp and oysters. The Mahi looked terrific, and I decided to have it myself on our next visit. The atmosphere around our table was carefree and enjoyable.

"So, this is what you girls do when you are not at the training table. I should go out with you more often."

"Just wait until we set the dance floor afire at DJ's. The men who go there can dance!"

"Don't share any of our trade secrets," Kelli added.

"I can't promise anything," Helen joked, "if I find a good looking one, I might tell him anything and everything."

"That's my sister. Totally man crazy."

"Yeah, and after all these years."

We finished our meal very satisfied and full of energy for the evening to come. I paid the bill for the entire meal, and we left Al's with our security guards, who motioned for our driver to bring the car around. Helen thanked me for picking up the tab and gave me a kiss right in front of Carolyn and Kelli, who both smiled at us. We reentered the limo and took our places. The drive to DJ's took half an hour, and soon we were walking in the door. The place was busy, but we found a couple of tables and all sat around them. I walked down to the bar and found Jim. He greeted me and asked, "How many bottles tonight?"

"Let's begin with three and go from there," I replied.

"Same as you had the last time?"

"Yes, Jim, that will be fine."

I went back to the table and told the girls the champagne was open and to have a glass. "Whatever you want, after that is on your own."

The DJ put on "The Race Is On," by George Jones, and I dragged Helen to the dance floor and took the lead. The single guys had not shown up yet. I knew that would change. Several other girls wanted to dance, and a group of gorgeous girls was always a magnet. Gradually, everyone found a dance partner and began to enjoy themselves. When the line dances began, we drew a crowd, and the dance floor was full of Cheerleaders and their suitors. A couple of attractive fellows approached Helen and me, and we danced beside them in the line. They tried, but their dancing was not very good.

Nonetheless, we thanked them before we turned and walked back to the table. The champagne bottles were empty, so I decided to get one more. Estelle had joined us, so I thought two more might be even better. I left my seat and walked down to the bar.

"We are going to need two more bottles, please, Jim."

"Okay, coming right up. Jim got them out, and I reached for them, but he didn't give them to me. I'll serve the ladies myself."

I said, "Okay," and turned to go back to my friends, but just then, I bumped into a guy and almost knocked his bottle of beer out of his hands, spilling some, and immediately apologized to him. "I am so sorry. Let me get you another." It was only then that I looked up at his face. He had dark, curly hair, a huge smile, and the bluest eyes I had ever seen on a man. He took my breath away, and I was speechless for a moment. I looked at the table and saw Estelle cracking up and pointing Helen to the guy and me. She whispered something to her, and Helen laughed too.

The guy saved me. "That won't be necessary. Did I get some on you?"

"No, I think I'm all right. So clumsy sometimes."

"My name is Jacob, but everyone calls me Jake."

"Hello, Jake. I'm Katie, short for Katherine. So nice to meet you."

"You guys seem to be having a little party tonight."

I couldn't quit staring at his blue eyes. "Yes, a few of us go out from time to time."

"Well, I don't think I have ever seen that many gorgeous girls together anywhere."

"Thanks, Jake. I'll tell them you said so."

The DJ came on the PA and said, "Now we are going to play a little Willie Nelson. Here's 'Waltz Across Texas.'"

My guy gave me a big smile. "A waltz. Wonderful. Would you like to dance, Katie?"

"I would love to." A waltz? That was unexpected. We went to the dance floor as several couples headed for their seats. I guessed that waltzing was not one of their fortes. He took me in his arms, and we began to dance. The girls were amazed.

Jake was smooth and rhythmic. He knew what he was doing. When people realized we could dance, they stopped whatever they were doing, many of them two-stepping, and watched us. Once our eyes met, we couldn't turn away. He led me around the floor, held me close, and held my hand high so I could twirl as we moved. He had total control of the dance steps, and I wouldn't have had it any other way. "Mamas Don't Let Your Babies Grow Up to Be Cowboys" was the next song, and the waltz set ended with the Woody Guthrie doing the Cowboy Waltz and gave way to "Good Hearted Woman," returning to the two-step numbers. This guy could dance. It was a Willie night. They played "Blue Eyes Crying in the Rain," and slowed things down some. Jacob pulled me close, and I rested my head on his broad chest. That did it for me. I either had to get out of that place or rip off his clothes and rape him right on the dance floor. I chose another option.

"Jacob, you are a wonderful dancer, but I need to go back to my group for a moment. Let me introduce you to my sister, who is an incredible dancer herself and loves to dance with a man who knows what he's doing."

"Okay, but you are coming back to me, Katie, aren't you?"

"Yes, Jake. I don't want to give Helen enough time dancing with you to take you away from me." I motioned for Helen to come over to us, introduced them, and went back to the table, breathless and not knowing what to do with this new man. He took her in his arms, but not as close as he had held me.

Estelle was glowing. "See? What did I tell you? One day you would turn around, and there he would be."

"He can waltz, Estelle."

"I saw that, Katie. He is a wonderful dancer."

"Have you seen his eyes?"

"No, he is too far away, but they look blue to me."

"They are. Intensely blue."

"I think you are gone, Katie. He likes you."

"How can you tell?"

"The way he looks at you and the way he holds, you give him away."

"What should I do?" I said so Carolyn and Kelli would hear and could give me their advice.

"First, catch your breath, settle down. What do you want, Katie?"

"I want to find out if he is as good a lover as he is a dancer."

"Look out," Estelle interrupted. "Helen is bringing him over here." She had his arm crooked in hers as if she didn't want him to get away from her.

"Ladies, give me your attention, please. Let me introduce Jacob Walters, better known as Jake. Jake, meet the girls."

"It is my pleasure to meet you, lovely ladies." They all extended their hands, which he kissed and gave him their names.

"You are Katie," he said, looking at me, "and you are Helen. Would you, by any chance, be the Armstrong sisters?"

"Yes, Jake, we are."

"And the rest of you are Dallas Cowboys Cheerleaders?"

"Yes, we are," Helen answered him.

"Now it all makes sense. How gorgeous you all are, how well you dance, your love for dancing, and your sisterhood in so many ways. I am a lucky guy to have met all of you."

Carolyn broached the inevitable question. "Now that you know about us, tell us about you."

"What would you like to know?"

"Are you married, Jake?"

"No. I am not opposed to marriage. It just has never happened to me."

"What do you do when you aren't dancing?"

"I am in the construction business. Our firm builds many buildings here and in Fort Worth. I am a construction manager and oversee budgets, subcontractors, quality assurance, and the entire construction process."

"Sounds like an enjoyable career. How long have you been doing it?"

"I have spent my entire career in construction and was promoted to the manager about a year ago."

"Where did you learn to dance, Jacob?"

"I was lucky enough to have dated a great teacher, and I took more lessons and love dancing. Besides, I learned very young that women love a man who can dance."

"You are right about that, Jake," I confirmed.

Another waltz came on. Not the usual cowboy song, but excellent anyway. It was "Can I have this dance for the rest of my life?" by Anne Murray. Jacob bowed to Carolyn and asked her if she would like to dance a brilliant move. He knew how to please a woman. She accepted, and he escorted her to the dance floor. A perfect place to enter the waltzing circle came around, and they came together, not too close at first, and began to dance. Jacob fixed his eyes on Carolyn and looked at her as if she were his lover. She moved closer to him, and he held her close with his right hand in the small of her back. Then he bent his left arm so that they could move even closer. When Carolyn realized he was treating her as a lover, being romantic with her, and liked her, she put her head on his shoulder and let him hold her with both arms. She closed her eyes and must have thought of her younger days when she affected all men that way.

As the girls and I watched, Jacob completely captured her affections, and they moved together as one. Carolyn relaxed in the arms of this strong man and gave herself over to him ultimately. They made a lovely couple. Jacob certainly knew how to make a woman feel good. None of us had ever seen her as vulnerable as she was dancing with Jake that night. How did he do it? It didn't matter. I just loved it when he did it for me.

When the song ended, he asked her if she would like to keep dancing. She declined. "I think I should give the other girls a chance."

"Thank you, Carolyn. I enjoyed our dance and look forward to when we can do it again." He walked her over to the table and held her chair for her as she sat down. He had all the right moves down pat. He looked at Kelli, and she wore a big smile. He invited her to dance the next number with him, and she accepted as well. He took her hand as she got up and continued to hold it as they walked to the dance floor. The artist was Billy Ray Cyrus again, and Kelli and Jacob took over the dance floor. She began the Cheerleader routine, and Jacob followed her every move. How the hell did he know how to do it?

"Look at that. Jake is doing the routine with Kelli. He is not following her, either. They are totally in sync." None of us could believe it at first, then Carolyn said, "Don't be surprised by anything this man does. As he said, he loves to dance." Jake had the arm grind into a hip turn, and the quarter-turn move down pat. He looked good. So, did Kelli, of course.

"Come on, girls, they look lonely." I led them into double lines on the dance floor, and we joined in their steps to Achy

Breaky Heart. Everyone else left the dance floor except for two beautiful girls who joined the end of the lines. They were tall, so Kelli moved them into the proper places, and they danced with us as if they had been doing it for years, bringing fond memories to me. Two new prospects? If so, Kelli would take care of getting them together with us for a tryout. We looked so good on the floor that the DJ started the record a second time when the first one ended. Energy flowed through everyone, emanating from us. Smiles of people enjoying themselves were everywhere. After the second playing of the record, we waved at the crowd, and Kelli invited the two dancers to join us at our table. They were out together and unattached. Kelli and Carolyn took them aside and talked with them. The rest of us continued to dance.

The guys seemed to be a little intimidated by our girl group dance. Jacob was the only guy who danced with us. They were standoffish, so we took the initiative and chose our partners. Some of them worked out well, others not so much. However, we all had an enjoyable time. As I hoped he would, Jacob found me again and came my way.

"Katie, would you dance with me again?"

"Yes, Jake. I would love to." We went to the dance floor.

"She is smitten with him," Carolyn observed. She had left Kelli to continue to talk with the two girls.

"That makes two of us," Helen seconded.

"Me too. Jake's amazing," Estelle agreed.

"I wonder if he knows Mike. He works with builders on the large projects."

"Should we ask him?"

"He'll figure it out," Carolyn assured us all. "Look at the two of them. He is as smitten with her as she is with him."

"It's good we will be busy for the next few days. Speaking of which, it is getting late, and we have a big day tomorrow," Kelli observed as she came back to the table after talking with the two new girls.

"I'll go get her," Helen suggested.

"Make sure she tells him how to get in touch with her. If she doesn't, I will," Carolyn volunteered. "I want my girls happy and not mooning over some new lover. They should talk."

Helen walked out to the dance floor, where the two new lovers were still gazing into each other's eyes. "Katie, we have to go. Big day tomorrow."

"Yes, Helen, I know. Here, Jacob, this is my card with all my contact information on it. Mornings are not good because I train then, and tomorrow night we have a big rehearsal. The next two days are good, but Saturday night, we will all be staying together at our hotel, then the game is the next day. Call me when you can, and we'll find some time to get together. We have so much to talk about."

I put my arms around his neck and kissed him lovingly. He didn't expect that but didn't pull away. Instead, he embraced me and returned my kiss. I took one more gaze into his eyes and brightly smiled as I turned and walked to the table where the other girls were already standing. Our escort took us to our cars, and we headed home. I didn't want to leave him, but my euphoria at having met him compensated for my sadness at parting. A smile spread across my face, and I knew he would call me. My unannounced and unexpected encounter with Jacob Walters left me with nothing but good feelings. All my girlfriends could see it. The limo was excellent, and it was terrific of Carolyn to get it for us, but I was floating so high I felt like I could fly home. I was as excited as I had been the night of my first Cheerleader party at the stadium, the night they auditioned me, and I became a member of the team.

When we got to the house, I invited Estelle to stay with us, and she accepted. We would again be three sleeping together. Rex was delighted to see us, and we gave him attention and petted him for a long time. It was not very late, so we talked for a while. Estelle had the grin of a Cheshire cat because it had happened just as she said it would. Helen didn't quite know what to think of the evening. She enjoyed dancing with and meeting Jacob, but she was much less enthusiastic than I was.

"What are you thinking and feeling right now, Sis?"

"I think I should get my mind off Jacob and get back to the role of Cheerleader, but my feelings are much different."

"How so?"

"I'm in love with a man, Helen, for the first time."

"That'll do it," she chuckled.

"What if he doesn't have similar feelings for me?"

"Don't worry, sis. He is crazy about you. All the girls saw it. Carolyn and Kelli saw it, and your team members were snickering when they watched you two dancing. The magic was there." As we prepared for bed, my cell phone rang. It was Jacob.

"I hope it is not too late to call, but I wanted to make sure you got home okay and to tell you what a wonderful evening I had with you and your friends tonight."

"It's not too late, and we all arrived safely. I had a wonderful evening too, Jacob."

"We will have more, Katie."

"I would like that very much. Dancing with you is so much fun. You are outstanding on the dance floor, and you can waltz."

"They say it is the dance of love."

"We must pursue that" I didn't tell him that at one point, I wanted to rip his clothes off and take him right there, in front of God and everyone.

"Next time, we must slow dance with each other longer. That way, I can show you what you do to me."

"I would like that very much. You charmed all the girls tonight. Don't forget them."

"I won't, but Katie, to me, you are the special girl in that group."

"You're sweet, Jacob. Thanks. Now about calling me. I hope you will."

"Somehow, I got the feeling that your schedule would preclude regular calls."

"If I can talk, I will talk to you, Jacob. If I can't answer, call me later or leave a voicemail in my box. Let's get to know each other, dance partner. There are some things you need to know about me."

"I would love that, Katie. Sleep well tonight and have sweet dreams."

"I think I will. I have good memories of dancing this evening."

"Goodnight."

"Goodnight, Jacob."

"I don't believe it," Estelle remarked.

I just sat there, holding my phone close to my breast and gave out a long sigh of satisfaction and delight. "What don't you believe, Estelle?"

"I am seeing up close two people fall in love with each other. Why did you keep him guessing like that?"

"Never reveal your true feelings after meeting someone for the first time. Let Jake keep guessing."

"You know you have a thing for him. Why not let him know?"

"After one evening? I don't think so. Sure, he is a great dancer and very handsome. And he knows how to treat a woman. But I want to know what's underneath his smooth manner and his charm. He hasn't sold me yet, but he is tempting."

"From what we all saw tonight, it looks like I might lose my sister and lover," Helen concluded.

"You are not going to lose either one, dear Helen. I love you, and I love being a Dallas Cowboys Cheerleader and am not going to give either one of those away. Jacob and I just met, and there is a long way to go."

"We'll see."

Chapter Sixteen

A Joyous Reunion

We slept well in the big bed with Estelle and awoke Wednesday morning to an excellent breakfast of our natural foods, changed the bedding for Mom and Dad, and headed for our exercise session mid-morning, a little later than usual. We did a light workout focusing on stretching and flexibility, then had our typical lunch. I wondered all afternoon if Jacob would call, and he didn't disappoint me. His timing was excellent. He knew we had our rehearsal that evening, and we would more than likely be busy. He kept it short, just said hello, and that he wanted to hear my voice. It was good to listen to him, as well. I told him to call back anytime, and that I enjoyed talking with him. He liked that. Still, that nagging feeling that all was not as it appeared to be would not go away. I liked him but needed to know more.

Rehearsal went well, and we headed back home, just Helen and me. Estelle had other plans. We both wanted a soak, so we headed to the spa. It was good for us in that it got our blood flowing and made us even more limber. Our light dinner was gone, so we raided the refrigerator.

Helen and I warmed up some leftovers and sat down to eat. The country dishes were excellent, so we ate heartily and enjoyed reminiscing about the success of last week's happenings. We wondered what Carolyn had in store for us this weekend.

We ate quietly and lost ourselves in our thoughts when we saw headlights coming down the driveway. "They're here." We jumped out of our chairs and rushed downstairs. Mom and Dad exited the limo, and the driver took their bags out of the trunk. We rushed over to them and gave them big hugs and shed a few tears of joy at their return. They both looked fantastic.

"Bring the bags inside, please, driver." He did, and dad tipped him and let him go. Helen and I switched parents, and I hugged my dad, and she hugged mom.

"It's so good to have you home."

"We also are delighted to be here with you two again. It was a fantastic trip, but coming home is always the best part. Let me look at you." He got a surprised look on his face. "You are not the same. You have grown up so much in the last several weeks. Look at them, Jackie."

"My daughters. You are so beautiful. Let me hold you." She embraced us both and cried some herself.

"What smells so good in here?" Dad asked.

"Have you eaten? We were just finishing dinner."

"No, the food at the airport didn't look very good to us. The flight was long coming back from Honolulu, and we had something many hours ago."

"We are eating leftovers, but they are good. Sit down at the table, and we will feed you our version of country cuisine. We must heat it some first. Would you like a drink?" Helen asked.

"Yes, nothing tropical, though."

"How about Scotch, single malt?"

"I would love that," Dad replied.

"Vodka tonic for me with a wedge of lime, please?"

"Coming right up." We made their drinks.

"Dinner will be ready in a few minutes. How was your trip?"

"It was wonderful, girls. We visited some beautiful places, met some interesting people, and ate very well. I got so tired of teriyaki that I had to get your dad to take me to a Wendy's in Honolulu."

"I can understand that," I replied.

"What do you have cooking over there?"

"We have Helen's famous meatloaf, lumpy mashed potatoes and gravy, and green beans, with peach cobbler for dessert."

"That sounds delicious," Mom commented.

I couldn't wait to tell them about Jake. "Mom, Dad, I met a man. He is handsome and is the best dancer I have ever seen. I like him and want to get to know him."

"That's fantastic, Katie. Helen, did you meet someone too?"

"Yes. I met an audio engineer for FOX Sports. His name is Paul, he is very good looking, and he likes me."

"How could he not like you, daughter?"

"Does your guy have a name, Katie?"

"Of course. Sorry not to have mentioned it. Jacob Walters is his name, and he has a way with the ladies. We went to DJ's last night, and all the girls danced with him and fell in love."

"Jacob Walters?" Dad asked. "I know him. Did you tell him who your parents are?"

"No, Dad. it never came up."

"Do you know anything about him, Katie?"

"No, only what I've told you and that he is a construction manager for his company."

"Construction manager? You might say that. Katie, he owns the company."

"He owns it? I had no idea. How much do you know about him?"

"I have worked with him and his company on several projects. Their reputation is excellent in construction circles around here. I'll tell you something few people know. Walters Enterprises was a major player in building AT&T stadium, anonymously, of course. He cut his teeth on that project."

"What a coincidence! It's amazing how things come in circles."

"Yes, it is. When Jacob asks you out, accept his invitation, and go."

"There goes my sister," Helen joked, "I'm losing her to a man."

"You will never lose me, dear Helen. No matter what." I hoped that would be true.

We all chatted a while longer, but Mom and Dad's travels had worn them out, and our busy day and evening caught up with us. We all went to bed, Mom and Dad in their room and us in ours. We didn't wear our nighties. We were together in bed, totally as God created us. We were together again, loving each other, even though our parents were in the next room. We both heard warm sounds coming from them and smiled at each other. They renewed their relationship on their honeymoon trip. We were both thrilled.

We embraced and went to sleep in each other's arms, awaking Thursday morning feeling refreshed, full of energy and enthusiasm for the day ahead. We finished our usual breakfast before Mom and Dad woke up. Now that they had returned, we didn't feel right about using Dad's car. We drove Helen's and arrived just as the early birds started coming in. We scanned our ID's so Carolyn would know we were there and went directly to the exercise room. One of the trainers came in shortly after that.

"Helen, Katie, I would like to watch your workout if I may. We are going to document it and prepare for making a DVD to give to the other girls. It will be our next step in their new workout routines. Okay?"

"Sure, James. You may record it if you wish."

"Today, I just want to take notes. I want the pros to do the video."

"Okay. The first thing we do is progressive stretching together."

We began with our bend over stretches then moved to the wall for back, legs, and shoulders. Next, we got down on the mats and stretched against and with each other. The routine loosened us and relaxed our muscles. Our necks and shoulders needed more work than usual because of the stress of the day and night before. In thirty minutes or so, we were loose and limber and started our exercises. James watched us intently, not saying a word, but examining everything we did.

The elliptical machines came first to get our hearts pumping and the blood flowing. Our stamina also increased in response to the devices. We both got them going very fast, strengthening our legs and hips. The ellipticals toned and shaped our legs as we worked. The way we attacked the machines and the energy we expended surprised James. He still just wrote his notes and remained quiet. It was like he wasn't even there.

Our strength exercises came next. We hit the bench press machines, the leg press, and then the Nautilus. By then, we were feeling the results of our workout and moved our efforts up another notch. Helen and I stayed in rhythm since we always trained together and knew our routine precisely. Over an hour elapsed, and James was still there taking his notes.

Now, we were ready to practice the actual moves we would use on the field. We broke into the Cheerleader walk and stood face-to-face with a gap between us, so we could watch each other and see if either of us had formed any unwanted habits. I sometimes tended to move my hips too much in the walks and marches we did. It was well under control now. We both smiled through our growing fatigue and at how much improvement we had made. The dances to music were next, and Helen started the DVD player. We did our line dances with each other and thoroughly enjoyed dancing together. Helen's long red hair looked great under the lights. We got into the music and the steps until our dance time was over.

Our last exercise was the sky kicks and power splits. Helen started the music again. We stood together with our arms on each other's shoulders as the entire team would do. We picked up the rhythm of the music and got in motion with it doing the Temptation walk. On cue, we began our kicks. Step, step, kick. Then to the other leg, step, step, kick. Because of what we had done previously, we were loose and limber. Our practice involved kicking high enough to raise our legs to a perfectly vertical position that placed our legs right beside our ears. We both nailed it on the first try. After eight kicks, four with each leg, we went down for our power splits, throwing our hair back and turning our heads around, then snapping them back to the front. That was the move the crowd in the stadium loved so much.

After another eight counts, we sprung up into the walk again and tried to look as sexy as possible. We did three more sets of kicks and splits and got to our feet as the music ended. We bowed to the imaginary crowd, then turned and left the room. James applauded us. We returned to do our cool-down sets and gradually returned to normal. The adrenalin and other hormones receded, leaving us with a rush as always. We lived for that natural high.

Our time in the exercise room was approaching three hours. Strangely, none of the other girls had arrived there yet. "Where are the others, James?"

"They are all watching on closed-circuit TV. I didn't tell you because Carolyn didn't want you to have any distractions, so we could see what you were doing exactly. Here they come now."

The doors to the room burst open, and about twenty girls ran through them and over to us. "Here, Katie, let me dry you off," one said. "I'll get you, Helen," another dried my sister. "That was amazing, you two. We had no idea that you were doing all that in your exercise sessions. Where do you get the energy?"

Another asked, "How did you get so limber?"

Another said, "I'll never be able to do all that."

Carolyn came in last. Everyone stopped talking and turned to her. "Katie, Helen, that was a joy to watch, and Cheryl, you *will* be able to do all that. All of you should know that we are changing the training routines for the entire squad. It will not happen immediately, but if you work with us, the entire line will be able to do some incredible things. So, get to work!"

We went to shower, and when we came out, she met us at the training table. "Girls, I want you to meet Greta. She is a dietician and specializes in sports diets. She wants to know what and how you eat. Diet seems to be one of your secrets, and it is a major part of our plan for the girls."

"Hello, Greta, I am Helen, and it is excellent to meet you."

"Yes, it is. I'm Katie."

"Shall we get started?"

"Sure, what do you want to know?"

"Let's begin with your breakfast this morning. It gave you an incredible amount of energy."

Helen told her about the coffee, Greek yogurt, granola, fruit, and juice that were our traditional breakfast foods. She also said we only eat natural foods with no artificial anything in them. She went with us to the food line. We were understandably hungry and got our vegetable protein and our green vegetables along with sides of Extra Virgin Olive Oil with herbs and spices to add flavor. We added whole-grain rolls with pure butter as a carbohydrate, and iced tea, unsweetened. We ate no dairy or intense carbs for lunch. We also avoided any refined sugar or flour. Greta took the same things we did and went back to our table with us.

"Can you explain why you chose as you did?"

Helen began. "Sure, the vegetable protein gives us energy, supplements our muscle mass, and we metabolize it easily. The green vegetables and the EVOO dressing provide us energy and replace much of what we burned off in our workout. The rolls provide us with enough carbs to satisfy us until dinner, and the tea provides easily absorbed caffeine, another source of energy."

I took up the explanation, "Plus, it tastes great, and we can vary our proteins and veggies from day-to-day. We look for foods full of vitamins and trace minerals."

"You eat like this every day?"

"Yes, Greta, we are here for our workout and lunch every day except just before games."

"What do you usually have for dinner?"

"We use dinner to enjoy all sorts of food. Our main course is four ounces of meat or seafood, appropriate carbs, and always our beloved vegetables. Sometimes, on special occasions, we allow ourselves a dessert. Our downfall is Blue Bell ice cream."

"So, you do splurge occasionally?"

"Yes," we both answered with a grin.

"What about alcohol?"

"We prefer champagne, cold and in a flute. When we entertain, we might even have a real drink, but we always have to work off those empty calories the next day."

"I couldn't have designed a better diet for you two myself. I talk and talk, but few of the girls have the discipline to pull it off. Now that we are documenting what leads to your success, I hope it will make a difference. Thank you, girls. You have given me everything I need to start."

"You're welcome, Greta. If there is anything else, you know where to find us."

We continued to eat. It was incredibly nourishing. When we finished, Carolyn came in, walked over to us, and took a seat. We let her begin because she looked as if she had something to say. "You two opened some eyes this morning. James came running into my office as excited as I have ever seen him. He couldn't believe your workout and how easily you did the sky kicks and power splits, which were his designs. Very few have ever been able to do them consistently. You showed him some things he had never even imagined." We just smiled.

"Greta came by just now to show me your diets. She now has the ammunition she needs to convince the other girls how important that is. She went into her office and closed the door so that no one would disturb her. Excellent job, both of you."

We both thanked Carolyn, and Helen told her we did it for the whole team. I nodded in agreement.

"Now, there is something else."

We thought it was about the guys, but we were wrong.

"I want to impose on you both to do another post-game interview."

"With Casey again?" Helen asked. She liked him.

"No, he will be in the booth calling the game, but someone else is going to conduct the interview."

"Not, Joe?" Helen showed her disappointment.

"No. We are taking a different tack this time. Karen will be doing the interview."

"Karen Lotti? What happened to Ainsley?"

"She has another assignment and had to change her plans. Karen will already be here and is looking forward to the interview."

"Yes, not only that, she will be at rehearsal Saturday night and will sequester with you overnight. We are going to give her first-hand access to our pregame routine, something we couldn't do with a male interviewer."

"That's great, Carolyn. We'll show her the ropes ourselves."

"I was hoping you would want to do that. This second interview will catch the eye of every woman in the TV audience, along with the men who want to watch you again."

"The Dallas Cowboys Cheerleaders from a woman's point of view."

"That's the idea."

"When is she getting here?"

"She will get into DFW tomorrow."

"When do we get to meet her?"

"When do you want her to join you?"

"Bring her here, and we will take it from there. We can show her our normal routine and feed her at the training table. That way, she can get the whole picture, something we couldn't do for a guy."

"What about Friday night?"

"Leave that to us. Karen will come away with a great understanding of what we do and how we do it. Mom and Dad will help.

"We will make her feel like she is a part of the organization and could have been a Cheerleader herself if she had chosen to go that way. We are going to do our best to make her an ally of our team."

Chapter Seventeen

A Surprise at Home

When we arrived back home, dad and mom were enjoying the pool and spa, with Rex keeping guard on the pool deck in his usual place. Dad saw us and asked us to join them. We put on our suits and did just that. "This is great! You two did an amazing job."

"All we did was keep track of the crew and let them know we were watching," I said.

"Whatever you did, it worked. The pool and spa are fantastic. We should have built it a long time ago, Jackie."

"We have more incentive now." She smiled at both of us.

They had been out there for a while and were ready to go inside. We went with mom and dad, holding hands and being affectionate. Mom and dad accepted our love for each other graciously. That was good.

We changed into comfortable clothes, and Dad asked us to sit on the sofa so that he could talk to us. His subject surprised us.

"You took excellent care of my car while we were on our trip, but I noticed you took Helen's this morning. I want to do something about that. I think another car is needed, maybe two."

"One will be plenty, Dad. We are always together anyway."

"I think mine is on its last legs," Helen admitted.

"What do you think you need?"

"First, we need something that will get us to and from our exercise sessions, lunch, and other things associated with the Cheerleaders dependably," I explained.

"There is something else. It involves our new friends," Helen added.

She nodded at me to continue. It was so handy to be able to know what the other is thinking.

"You see, when people visit, we will need enough room in the back with one of us driving and the other in the front seat together."

"Do you need an SUV?"

"Yes, mom. When people are here working with us, we will need a larger vehicle. The new one could be smaller, and we could swap with you and use yours if necessary. What do you think, Dad?"

"We could work Jackie's car into the mix."

"We are both going back to work, remember?"

"Oh, yes. There it is, girls. Trade Helen's car on whatever you want. Your mom and I will take care of the cost."

"Thanks, Dad. You are so good to us." We went over to him and gave him a couple of big hugs. We both noticed his scent. The honeymoon had changed him.

"I am happy to have you to do things for daughters. I love you so much."

After a diligent internet search, we found the perfect car for us. It was a white, gently used BMW SUV and had an attractive price. We told Dad what we had chosen, and he called the dealership and made all the arrangements, telling them we, his daughters, would be there soon to pick it up. He told us to take Helen's car with us as trade and sent a funds transfer to the dealership with instructions to put it in his name. He suggested Helen should keep the proceeds from the sale of her car, giving her some money just for her.

We cleaned out Helen's old car and drove it to the dealership, returning to the house in our new ride. It was perfect for us, dependable with plenty of room for passengers. Mom and Dad had left on some errands they needed to take care of, now that they were back with us. We made the BMW ready for tomorrow morning and went inside. It had been a busy day. We had concerns that Carolyn had not called us yet and spent the afternoon relaxing until Mom and Dad came back. We retired earlier than usual because tomorrow was going to be a big day.

Our new BMW took us to the Star Friday morning. Even though the day was young, we began our exercise routines surrounded by ten other girls. Karen had arrived and joined us to see our exercise routines. She had her notebook and took copious notes. "Would you like to join us, Karen?"

"Not this time. I will tomorrow, though."

"Okay, that will be excellent." We began. Our stretches came first.

"Can you show us how you do that?" Cheryl asked.

"Yes, girls. First, we gently do our bend overs to stretch our backs, arms, and necks." If you are doing it right, you can feel your muscles letting go. They formed a line across from us and watched intently, emulating our every move. The stretches went well, and we didn't hurry. The girls limbered up nicely. We did the wall stretches, and then the push/pull exercises together after having the girls pair up. When we finished, everyone felt much better. We went on and took them through all the routines, dance steps, and classic kicks and splits.

"I have not been stretching correctly. My body feels wonderful, and I can do the kicks and splits much easier," Cheryl reported.

"Me, too." Everyone felt much better. We didn't ask them to do the sky kicks or power splits, but we did them, and several tried.

"Don't do too much," Helen warned them, "Carolyn and Kelli wouldn't be happy if half the squad showed up hurt for our rehearsal tomorrow night." They chuckled at her comment. Then she launched into her routine.

Helen took to her workout vigorously, giving it her all. The others tried in vain to keep up. Even I had just to let her go. We watched her and marveled at her stamina and strength. She had a new attitude now that she knew Mom and Dad were back and loved her very much, and our family was together again. She knew the Cheerleaders and directors also took care of her. She smiled as she finished the most fantastic workout I ever saw her do.

We worked them out for two hours more and took them to the cafeteria. "This is how we eat when we are training. We led them through the line showing them the healthiest items and how to flavor them, so they were delicious. Afterward, despite the workout, their energy levels had increased. Helen and I smiled at each other.

It was then that Carolyn came into the room and asked to join us. She wanted to let us know what the plans were. We were eager to learn. She laid it all out for us, and we were excited at what she had planned. Carolyn had explained to Karen that we had offered to take her home with us, so she could get to know our family. She was excited about being with us for the evening instead of all alone in a hotel room. We took her out to the car and took her home to Mom, Dad, and Rex.

Mom and Dad welcomed her gracefully, and Rex was delighted to have another person to give him attention. Karen loved him at once. We found her a swimsuit that fit her well, and all headed for the pool. As she relaxed, she got more comfortable being around us. She asked Mom and Dad about their association with the squad and had a pleasant chat together. Helen and I listened intently. They told her the story of how they met, fell in love, and found Helen and me. It was a fantastic story. Karen took in every word.

Dad grilled tenderloins, and Mom made the sides for dinner. We ate, and they drank, and all had an enjoyable time. Helen and I cleaned up while they talked and returned to the living room and our parents and guest. It got late in the evening, and Mom and Dad decided to turn in, leaving Karen with me with Helen.

"It's getting late, girls. We all have a big day tomorrow."

"That's true, Karen. We should get some rest."

"The only question is what our sleeping arrangements will be."

"We have a bedroom for you, if that is your preference," I informed her.

"That would be fine with me. Is there another option?"

"I don't want to assume anything, Karen, but I thought maybe you might want to sleep with us tonight. You are going to be sequestered with all of us tomorrow night, but tonight, you would make us very happy if you were with us."

"You two sleep together?"

"Yes. We have slept together since before we became a family."

"How did you know about me?"

"We didn't," Helen explained, "but we wanted to take a chance that you might enjoy some female company tonight."

Karen leaned over to her and kissed her lovingly. Helen kissed her back. "Welcome to the family, Karen."

We three went back to the bedroom together and changed into our nightclothes. Helen and I put Karen between us, and I got my kiss too. We snuggled warmly and were soon asleep. She felt very good to us, and we wrapped her in our arms. For that night, we had another sister.

Saturday morning, we saw that during the night, the clouds had gathered, and a light drizzle had set in. We put on our workout clothes, grabbed the things we would need, and headed out. We put Karen through our stretching routine, making sure not to go overboard since she was new to all this. She was in excellent shape, and the stretching felt right to her.

She followed us through the rest of the routine quickly and danced with us enthusiastically as we showed her the steps and moves that were standard for us. She picked up on them soon as her natural sense of rhythm shone through. She was even able to keep up with us through the standard leg lifts and kicks and the traditional splits. When we went into the sky kicks and power splits, she deferred, partly because she needed to take a break and partly because our girl didn't think she could do them. Nonetheless, she watched us very closely.

We took her through our cool-down exercises, and she did them well. "Now, that was a workout!" she exclaimed. "I feel wonderful." She kissed us both sweat and all. We hung around while the others did their routines then went to the training table. The food was excellent as usual, and our appetites had returned. We knew Carolyn had arranged a car for us and headed home to get ready for the practice and party. She was my size, and Helen and I chose her outfit. We did her hair and makeup at the same time we did ours and wore our "sister" outfits, which looked fabulous and were excellent for dancing. No sky kicks or power splits, but we could do everything else. Karen looked fantastic and loved her reflection in the big mirror. I knew she would look even better after our makeup artists and hairstylists finished with her before the game.

Carolyn had arranged for first-class treatment of our new female broadcaster and erstwhile Cheerleader. Security drove us to the practice on Saturday night, went right into the stadium as usual, and let us out at the entrance to the field. A large group arrived before us, and when they saw Karen, and how good she looked, they surrounded us and welcomed her enthusiastically. She beamed in response to all the attention she was getting.

"Are you going to dance with us tonight, Karen?" one asked.

"It would be an honor to have you join us," another added.

"Yes, girls, thanks to Katie and Helen, I learned some moves today. There is no way I can keep up with you, though."

"It'll be fun," Cheryl encouraged her, "and Helen and Katie tell us you can dance. We'll help you if you need it."

"The main thing is to have fun. We will work enough tomorrow." The girls all laughed at that. The back-and-forth banter continued until Carolyn took her place at the microphone.

"Who's ready for a party?" she asked.

Everyone responded enthusiastically in the affirmative.

"Okay. Let's all welcome Karen to our line, and we also have two new prospects with us. Meet Hannah and Cathy." A round of applause ensued. "Positions, everyone. Make sure our guests have their places with us." She cued the DJ, and we took it to the field. Helen and I lead Karen between us, and she assumed the initial position. When the music began, she did the Cheerleader walk with us, and when we all stepped out, she went into the first dance smoothly. As usual, our routines to individual songs came first. She looked great in dancing with us.

When we all joined arms or reached over each other's shoulders, she excelled. The last thing we did was the regular kicks together and in sequence, then to the baby splits. She did the head turns and hair flips very well and bowed along with the rest of us. That night, Kelli added a new twist, which she called the "free dance" in which we could choose our partners and dance together in pairs. Helen immediately grabbed Karen and danced with her before passing her on to me. I did the same thing. One by one, the girls all got their chance to dance with our celebrity sister, and we almost wore her out. She took a short break, and Carolyn brought her a glass of champagne and a bottle of water. She took several sips of the water and went quickly to the champagne. When Karen returned to us, more girls wanted to dance with her, and our new sister obliged them. She became the hit of the party. Everyone liked Karen.

When it ended, our buses took us to the hotel, and we arrived safely in good spirits. Helen and I were inseparable once again, and it felt good to have Karen as our third. We had our dinner together in a dedicated dining room, and afterward, the girls wanted to know more about Karen and her broadcasting activities. She complied, and when the time came to go to our rooms, the girls wanted to continue the discussion. One of the directors came by to check that everyone was there and told us to go to sleep. We had a big day tomorrow. Karen slept with Helen and me for the second night in a row and was becoming dear to us.

When they took us to the stadium, as we were walking in, we saw two familiar faces. It was Peter and Paul waving at us to get our attention. They were waiting for us outside the locker room. We went over to them and gave them huge hugs. Helen kissed Paul again, and I put my arms around Peter's neck and looked up at him longingly. I parted my lips, wet them some, and closed my eyes. Despite his shyness, he got the message and bent his head down to kiss me for the first time. I enjoyed his kiss and kissed him back. Helen and Paul ended their kiss and watched us smiling and holding each other close. Did I see a pair forming? They both had gotten their welcome back kisses, and it felt very good to me. We introduced them to Karen and proceeded to our locker room.

It was good to see Peter and Paul again. The girls knew who they were and weren't surprised that we welcomed them back. Karen gave us a quizzical look, and we could see the questions in her mind. She had not expected our greetings for Peter and Paul.

She was more beautiful in person than she ever was on the TV screen. The whole FOX team welcomed us with smiles and handshakes. We were celebrities to many of them. Karen asked about makeup, so we took her to our locker room. Between Helen and me was a new locker with Karen's name on it. She saw it and hugged both of us with a tear in her eyes. Our next stop was the hairdressers. They began their work with the usual shampoo and blow-dry, styling her hair as they went. Her blond hair gave them a lot with which to work and was gorgeous when they finished. The makeup artists were delighted to have an actual celebrity in their world. She got the full treatment with Nikki's enthusiastic consent. When they finished, all three of us looked fabulous. Karen was amazed at her transformation.

"Stay with us until you have to go to the booth. We'll get someone to take you up the private elevator and introduce you to everyone before you begin. Then come back down the same way, and you can get back to the field easily to start the game."

We took her out with us when we went for our warmups and bonded with her girl to girl. When she left for the booth, we told Nikki we liked her, and she would be an excellent advocate for all of us. She got the message and made sure we met her every need while she was there. The atmosphere was entirely different when Karen was on the job.

We did our usual opening routines, and they went well. The fans were still enthusiastic about us, and we charmed them all through the first half. Both Helen and I were waiting eagerly for our halftime show. Late in the second quarter, we went back to the locker room, took care of the necessities, and rested for a few minutes. Our turn to take the field came again, and we danced and pranced to our positions. The short line was longer this time since more girls could do the advanced routines. The sky kicks went exceptionally well, and when we went into the power splits with all the head turns and hair flips, the crowd went wild. We stayed down for our eight counts, and popped up to our final walk positions, bowed in unison to the applause, and left the field just as the teams were returning. After another brief break, we returned for the second half, very happy with our progress and the performance so far. It showed in our joy until the end of the game. It had been an outstanding performance.

Helen and I made our way back to our lockers. Nikki stopped us again. "Come with me, girls." She took us into the same little room.

"Minor change of plans. Karen wants to interview you as planned, but this time there will be a slight twist. There will be three of you. Interested?"

"Sure, Nikki. No problem." We didn't even ask who the third person would be. We assumed it would be another Cheerleader. She motioned the makeup artists and hairstylists over to us for a touchup and led us back out toward the field. Karen was also having her makeup touched up, and we waited, not seeing the third person. Peter and Paul wired us up for sound, and we went over and sat by Karen. She smiled at us and welcomed us back. We took our seats and relaxed some although maintaining our Cheerleader posture. She started the interview.

"Welcome back to AT&T Stadium for our post-game show, ladies and gentlemen. I am here today with Helen and

Katie Armstrong, whom you met at the last game, but today we have a surprise for you and them. Helen, Katie, how are you today?"

"We are fantastic, Karen, and it is a real treat meeting you," I said as Helen agreed with me.

"Being with you and the other girls these last two days has been a highlight for me, too. I told you I had a surprise for you, so look at your fellow Cheerleaders there on the sidelines and observe."

The group parted, and three Cheerleaders stepped out from the rest together doing the Cheerleader walk. They started into a step-step-knee kick alternating legs as they came closer. I did a double-take. "Helen, that's our mom. Look how good she looks in that uniform with perfect makeup and hair."

"Helen recognized her immediately after I said that and jumped up and ran to her, followed closely by me. We took our positions beside the three and got into the steps they were doing at once. We were dancing with our mom in Cheerleader uniforms, and when into our high kicks, mom was with us all the way. The five of us drew loud applause from the crowd gathered there. It was a highlight of all our lives. Regular splits ended the routine, and mom went down with us perfectly. It was as if she were reliving her glory days as a Cowboys Cheerleader. When we returned to Karen, we kissed her on the cheeks and took our seats a little out of breath. With our mom in the middle, we all held hands. We were so proud of her. Karen took over from us until we could get our breath.

"Now, girls, I said we had two surprises for you, and here is the other one. Look again at the group of Cheerleaders."

We turned back to them, and they parted in the middle again. Two of the girls escorted a tall, handsome man towards us in a Cheerleader trot. We both recognized our dad immediately and got up to run to him. We took him away from the two Cheerleaders who were at his side and grabbed his arms, leading him onto the field. We both kissed him on the cheek and hugged him tightly. I shed a tear. Both of our parents were there with us on national TV. We took him to the last empty chair, which was between mom, who was next to Karen, and us at the end. It was an emotional time for all.

"Ladies and gentlemen in the TV audience, meet the entire Armstrong family." More applause. We even heard the whoops from the bar under the grandstand at field level. Kelli and all the girls were as emotional as we were, smiling through their happy tears.

When things calmed down some, Karen resumed her interview. "Jackie, you certainly don't look old enough to have two grown daughters. Will you tell us how this family came together?"

"Mike is Katie's birth father, although he didn't know until her mother died recently. Katie came down here from Montana to be with her father, and I met her then. Mike and I married, and I adopted Katie, making her officially my daughter. When we met Helen, she was very much alone in life except for the Cheerleaders. Both of us adopted her, and we became a family."

"What an incredible story. Where do you come into the Cheerleader picture, Mike?"

"Ask them," and he pointed to the group of Cheerleaders who had hidden mom and him from us at the beginning of the interview.

"We are going to do exactly that. Who wants to go first?"

Cheryl came forward, and Peter gave her a hand-held microphone. "We all love Mike. He is like a brother to us, and he can dance!"

The next one came forward. "If Mike were closer to our age and single, he would be in real trouble. About twenty of us would go out with him, no questions asked."

"Do all of you feel that way?" Karen asked the group.

A chorus of "yeses" burst from them. Karen couldn't believe her eyes and ears. "I can see that FOX is going to have to get to know all of you better."

"It's a package, Karen. We Cheerleaders are inseparable."

Karen continued the interview, and the TV audience got to know a Cheerleader family. The time allotted for the discussion expired, Karen signed off, and the FOX people again started packing up. Peter and Paul took all our audio devices off and stored them. The girls gathered around Dad. "Thank you, girls. I think you all deserve a kiss."

"I want mine now," Cheryl said as she put her arms around his neck and kissed him lovingly.

Many of the others wanted one too, and Dad obliged until he had taken care of them all. He was beaming brightly. Karen just watched, not believing what was happening right in front of her. She looked over at Mom, not understanding how she could not object to all those beautiful girls making love to her husband. She explained, "It's one of the secrets to our love and now our marriage. Mike is a very desirable man, and I am glad he is attractive to other girls, and these are the best-looking girls in Texas. They love to dance with him. He loves them too." Karen began to understand, although not entirely, but she didn't pursue it further.

We headed for the locker room, inviting her to come with us. She did. When we were out of sight, Helen said, "I want mine too, Karen." She embraced her, and she let Helen kiss her. They were hot together.

"My turn," I said, and she gave me the same with enthusiasm. "Are you going to be able to spend some time in Dallas?"

"I hope so. I like it here."

"We hope so too." She thanked us and went back to the FOX crew.

Mom and Dad came to us next. "How did you get here, Mom and Dad?"

"They brought us in a limo. That's the way we are going home, too."

"Before you leave, we want you to meet someone." Peter and Paul were standing to one side, waiting for us. Helen and I walked over to them and said, "Hi."

"Katie, can I talk with you a minute?" Peter led me away from the others.

"Sure, Peter. What's on your mind?"

"I saw you kiss Karen. Do you like girls?"

"That's a very personal question, Peter. Why do you want to know? If I do, would that affect our friendship?"

"Yes. I can't date a girl who is into other girls."

"I am sorry, Peter. I like you, but that's the way I am."

"I'm sorry, too, Katie. I'm afraid I must call this off. Please forgive me." He turned and walked away.

"What a pisser!"

"Does that matter to you, Paul?" Helen asked him.

"No way. I thought your kissing Karen was beautiful."

"Come with us."

She took him over to Mom and Dad and introduced them. "Paul, this my Mom, Jackie, and my Dad, Mike."

"We're glad to meet you, Paul. Thanks for your excellent work."

"You're welcome. Helen, I will be back soon."

"I'm glad, Paul." She kissed him lightly and let him go.

"Wasn't Peter here, Katie?" Mom asked.

"Yes, but he had a bad reaction to me kissing Karen. He can't date someone who loves other girls, so he left."

"Well, that lets you out, Katie," Dad chuckled.

"Be nice, Mike," Mom admonished him gently.

"Let's all head for the lake, want to?"

"Let us change, and we'll be right behind you."

"Okay. We'll see you later." They headed for their limo, and we went into the locker room. It didn't take us long, and we were on our way too. It had been a good day.

Chapter Eighteen

Romeo Loves His Girls

Helen and I were two again. Peter had exited stage left because he couldn't accept the fact that I am interested in both guys and girls. Paul left Helen because he had to go back to New York, and since we didn't have a home game for two weeks, she would not see him anytime soon. The girls referred to it as the "Cheerleaders Dilemma." Call it what you may, I thought it sucked. We were two girls who turned heads and had great personalities. Besides that, we could dance. And neither of us had a man in our life. How could we change that?

If Estelle were right, the situation would take care of itself as long as we liked ourselves and didn't look desperate to find someone. We both took figurative deep breaths and turned loose of it all. We were looking at two weeks of just being Cheerleaders and being with each other, and both those prospects appealed to us. Mom and Dad were like new people now that they were married and delighted to be together. It made Helen and me believe that if they had finally found their relationship, we would also find ours. Meanwhile, we had the girls and each other. Although not ecstatic, we were content.

A part of that contentment for me was the satisfaction I got from working with Romeo. He was very handsome and took to my training methods quickly and with enthusiasm. I hoped the next two weeks would bring him even further than we had already come. I was training him to be a show horse, and his spirit overflowed. He didn't even wait for me to call him when I went to the corral and barn. I was usually with him in the afternoon, and he began watching for me to come back from exercise and lunch. He regularly beat me to the corral when he saw me coming out to him. He loved for me to ride him bareback, and when we worked together, he accepted the fact that sometimes I was going to put a saddle on him and let him perform.

We worked the barrels, and he was speedy going around them. He knew what to do and loved doing it with me on his back. I also used his natural tendency to show off to teach him moves that a show horse should know. He learned to prance and looked like he wasn't even touching the ground because he was so light on his hooves. I taught him to raise his head, showing his beautiful mane while he raised his tail and arched it in a perfect curve. He learned to move sideways without turning his head and followed my cadence and rhythm. We went from a full gallop to the prance smoothly and without hesitation. He was brilliant and obedient as we worked together. I rewarded him when appropriate and praised him when he did well. We became very close.

It just so happened that I was working with him, with Helen by my side, when Dad came home from work early in the week. He saw what we were doing and stopped the car halfway down the driveway to watch. I had Romeo practicing his cross-legged move to the left, followed by the same step to the right. Dad watched in amazement at what we had taught Romeo to do and how responsive and well-behaved he was under my direction. I saw Dad and decided to let the big horse show off a little. I reined him in and gave him the signal to prance. He threw his head back, raised his tail, and tip-toed across the pasture like he was king of the world. Then I spoke to him and loosened the reins, his cue to leap into his gallop. We circled the pasture, and I stopped him and had him go into his prance again. Dad climbed the fence and came over to us. Romeo wasn't even breathing hard since he had lost a lot of fat as his muscle tone came back. His exercise routine had gotten him in great shape.

"He seems to be in great shape, Katie. How did you do that?"

"It wasn't just me, Dad, Helen has been working with him too. She deserves a lot of the credit."

"You are both working with him now?"

"Yes, and he loves having us take care of him, tell him how handsome he is, and how well he is taking to training.

Come over to the corral, and I'll show you something fantastic." I guided Romeo into the corral and stopped him just short of the barrels. "Time us, please, Helen."

I told Romeo firmly to "Go." He leaped to his racing speed, and we rounded the far barrel and headed back in a figure-eight pattern. He was so smooth going around the barrels and reversing direction. We only had enough space in the corral for a two-barrel course, but I wanted an enclosure that was large enough for the now-standard three-barrel setup, hopefully, soon. In our training, we worked with the two barrels. Romeo was just learning about racing. He loved it! "Wonderful time, Katie. You were two tenths under your previous best. He gets faster every day. My turn now."

I dismounted and handed her the reins. "You both ride Romeo?"

"Yes, Dad. Helen has become quite the equestrian lady."

She mounted him readily and headed for the gate to the pasture. She liked having more room to ride. As soon as she was through it, she turned him to the right and clucked twice to him, his signal for a trot. He was regal and responded to her at once. At the end of the pasture, she turned him around and called for a gallop. She leaned forward on him and let him go. When they got back to us, she stopped him and put him into his prance again, patting his neck and telling him what a good horse he was. The realization hit Dad that his daughters had gained the trust and love of the big horse. She headed him back to the corral and put his reins over the railing. Romeo was panting but still energetic. Dad and I joined them for his bath and brushing. Helen took his saddle off and loved on him. Even after all that, he was not tired.

While Dad watched us, we bathed him head to tail. He loved his baths. We took our time brushing him out, and soon the big palomino was clean again and let us both love on him, becoming affectionate as his girls gave him attention. We put his feedbag full of oats on him, and he ate hungrily. We kept up the praise and petting while he ate. When the oats were gone, he drank from the water trough and washed it all down.

As was his new habit, he stayed there in the corral with us rather than going immediately back to the pasture and the other horses, preferring the attention we were giving him. Dad just shook his head in disbelief. We put Romeo back in the field and started for the house. He whinnied and stomped his right front foot to tell us thanks for loving him and taking care of him. Helen and I both were wearing smiles of pleasure at our outing for the day.

"Now that is a different horse from when we left until now. How did you pull that off?" Dad wanted to know when we were back in the living room.

"Your daughter from Montana knows what she's doing. He fell in love with her first, and he let me into his life gradually. He is astute and loves to show off. All we did was take advantage of his intelligence and taught him steps and poses, just like the directors taught us Cheerleaders."

"Did I miss something?" Jackie had no idea what we were talking about.

"Jackie honey, our daughters have brought that horse to the point that he can race the barrels and do everything to look fabulous in the ring. We might have to start looking for a supplier of show tack and take him in the arena before many people. With either Katie or Helen riding him, he will be fabulous. I can hear the announcer now."

"And now, we present a newcomer to the rodeo, Miss Katie Armstrong, riding Romeo." Or put Helen on him. Either will be fantastic. "In addition to riding their palomino stallion, they are both Dallas Cowboys Cheerleaders."

"Then, whoever is riding him will bring him into the arena and gallop him around once, bringing him to a stop in the middle of the grandstands and put him through his steps and poses. It will be incredible!"

Dad saw the dream we both had.

"First, we should expand the corral for a three-barrel course. Then we can go for fancy, show tack that highlights Romeo's palomino appearance. You two have to get some new outfits, too."

"Isn't this going to be expensive, Dad?" I asked.

"Have no fear. I have wanted to do something like this for a long time. Barrel racing horses can cost over a hundred thousand dollars. We already have one, and ours is show quality too."

"Let's go to a rodeo soon," Helen suggested.

"Look, guys, I still don't have any idea why you three have gone off the deep end about this. Is he that good?" Mom asked.

"He is amazing, Mom. Yes, he is that good," I answered her.

"I must see it before I am getting on board."

"I understand. We still have light in the sky. Why not now?"

"I don't know, girls. You worked him out very well this afternoon. Do you think he is up to it?"

"Trust us, Dad. He is in excellent shape and would love another chance to love on his girls," Helen answered.

"Then, let's go. Come on, Jackie. You are about to be introduced to our show horse."

We went out to the corral, and as soon as Romeo saw us, he ran at a gallop to us. I put a bridle on him and jumped on his back. He shook his head and snorted at us as if to say, "What are we going to do now?" He loved having his girls riding him bareback. I let him prance around the corral for a few minutes looking majestic, and took him out of the corral and around the pasture, allowing him to stretch out and do his stallion thing. At the end of the run, I reined him in and took him through his posing and prancing moves once again. He loved having Jackie there watching him as she never had before.

Next, it was Helen's turn. I dismounted and gave her the reins. "I didn't know you rode, Helen," Mom commented.

"Just watch her, Mom, she is phenomenal."

Helen took him out of the corral at once and let him break across the pasture. She moved forward on his back and picked up his rhythm immediately. Helen was one with Romeo as he trotted with his head held high, and his tail extended. He picked up his feet as we had shown him, and she turned him as he picked up his prance to a canter. With him showing off as he was and Helen's flowing red hair blowing in the breeze, Mom's astonishment showed through. She walked over to the rail and carefully watched as Helen put him through his paces. She then gave him his head and clucked the "Go" signal, and he leaped into his gallop with her riding him like a pro. They made quite a sight. Although her technique and mine were different, Romeo had learned them both and knew who was riding him. Helen yelled out in pure joy as they continued their ride. The horse was in heaven, loving every minute of it.

As dusk settled on us, Helen brought him back into the corral and gave me the reins as she dismounted. She petted Romeo and told him how awesome he was, bringing out a happy whinny from him. He was not even breathing hard. His muscle confirmation showed that he was in great shape. I gave him attention too, and he threw his head, making his mane stand up and look so good. He reminded me of the hair flips we Cheerleaders did in our routine. Helen removed his bit and harness, and we both brushed him. He had just had a bath and didn't need another one. We did feed him, though. I even gave him an apple as a reward for being so obedient to us. He whinnied again and stomped his foot as he left the corral and returned to the pasture. Helen and I walked toward the house with Mom and Dad. We were all quiet. I knew Mom was thinking about what she had just seen.

When we got back inside, Dad made drinks for him and Mom, and we gathered in the living room. Mom spoke first. "Is there anything you two girls can't do?"

"We don't seem to be able to get boyfriends, but aside from that, no. Together, we are unbeatable," I said.

"Now, what about dinner?"

"Let us prepare it for you. You deserve it."

"What would you like to have?" Helen inquired.

"I have a taste for stuffed pork chops, rice and gravy, and baby spinach," Dad responded.

"Sounds great to me, girls."

"Then that is what we will have. Come on, Helen. Let's fix dinner."

We stuffed the pork chops, coated them in flour, and fried them in canola oil. I made the gravy in the same pan with the drippings while the rice cooked. The spinach was very tender, and we cooked it last. The yeast rolls were ready, and we served Mom and Dad their dinner. Helen and I broiled a chop for each of us and added some spinach, and made a couple of salads. It was good and didn't blow our diet. We all four joked, kidded each other, and had an enjoyable time. Shortly after we finished eating and cleaned up, my cell phone rang. I took Helen with me to our room and answered. It was Jacob.

"Hi, Katie. It's a pleasure to hear your voice again."

"Hello, Jacob. You caused a stir among the girls the other night. How did you know our routine for all those songs?"

"I saw you when you were doing them several times, and the steps seemed to go so well with the song, especially Achy Breaky Heart."

"You did well. Carolyn and Kelli enjoyed dancing with someone who knew how, and all the other girls would go out with you."

"There is only one in whom I am interested. Need I say that's you?"

"You did come back to me."

"I had to. There is no way I was going to let you get out of there without talking to me again. What are you guys doing tonight?"

"We rode the horses all afternoon and started thinking about taking Romeo to the rodeo. Dad and Mom are backing us, and we are going to get some new outfits for the horse and us."

"Is your Dad Mike Armstrong?"

"Yes, Jacob. He knows you and your company."

"We have worked together before. Mike knows his business."

"He thinks a lot of you, too."

"Are you and Helen both riding these days?"

"Yes. I told you we were inseparable, I think."

"It's obvious to everyone," he chuckled. "Knowing that, how would the two of you like to go out with me? I know a nice little place with wonderful food and a dance floor, and I could dance with both of you, making me the envy of everyone in the place."

"Oh, Jake. Take us both out together on a date?"

"That's the idea, dear Katie."

"Hold on for a minute. Helen is right here."

"It's Jacob. He wants to ask you something." I gave her the phone.

"Hi, Jacob. What do you want to ask me?"

"Would you join your sister, and both go on a date with me. Dinner and dancing?"

"Yes, Jacob. I would love to go. Do you think you are up to taking care of both of us?"

"It would be a new experience for me, I must admit."

"When do you want to go?"

"How about tomorrow night?"

Helen looked at me and asked, "Tomorrow night, Sis?"

"Sure, why not? Tell him how to get here."

"We live near the lake, Jake. Do you know where the marina is?"

"Yes, I do."

Helen gave him detailed instructions on how to find us, and she gave him her cell number too.

"Six-thirty," he asked.

"We'll be ready. Dressy casual?"

"Yes, that way I won't have to wear a tie."

"Excellent. We are both looking forward to it. You can see where we live and meet the horses."

"Make sure this is okay with your Dad."

"We will make sure both he and Mom are here."

"Then it's a date?"

"Yes, it is a date."

"We'll see you tomorrow evening."

"You bet you will. Have a good night."
"We will, Jake. Goodnight." She ended the call.

Chapter Nineteen

The Girls Have a Date

"Hallelujah, we have a date." Helen and I were ecstatic. "Even if it is with the same guy."

"I don't care," Helen told the truth. "Jacob is great, and I would bet we will have a wonderful time with him."

"I plan to dance very near to him. What kind of music do you think they play at this place?"

"I have no idea where we are going. If there is dancing, maybe it will be a ballroom style."

"It would be nice to take a break from country and western tunes."

"I agree with that. Let's go, tell Mom and Dad."

We found them embracing on the sofa, being affectionate, and enjoying their newfound relationship. Mike and Jackie both looked up when they heard us return.

"You caught us," Dad joked.

"You two are so cute together. Don't worry, we have both been around the block before, but before you take each other to bed, we have something to tell you."

"What's that?"

I took Helen's hand in mine and smiled at her. She took up the narrative. "We have a date tomorrow night." Our smiles showed them we were delighted.

"A date? Both of you?" Mom inquired.

"Yes. Jacob asked both of us to go out with him tomorrow night."

"A double date, but with only one guy. That's a new one on me. Which one of you is the date, and which is the companion?"

"We haven't determined that yet. The last time we saw Jake was the Tuesday before you returned to us. He charmed twenty of us girls, including Carolyn and Kelli. He danced with all of us, especially Helen and me, and is coming here to pick us up and hopes you two will be here."

"He does?"

"Yes, I think he wants our parents to know him better," Helen added.

"I would love to be a fly on the wall, so I could see how you handle this."

"Now, Mom, you know we will tell you everything," I promised.

"We just want to go out dancing with one of our favorite guys, and dinner is a bonus."

"Where is he taking you?"

"We have no idea, but we hope to do some ballroom dancing instead of country/western."

"Waltz, foxtrot, jitterbug, and some slow numbers. I, for one, am going to dance very close to him," I assured them.

"Me too," Helen agreed.

"And when the time comes to take you home, which one of you is going to kiss him goodnight?"

"We both are," we answered in unison.

"And if he has more in mind?"

"We might bring him inside and sit with him on the couch."

"Does he know you are inseparable?"

"Yes. That's why he asked us both out, plus Jake will have one of us on each side of him, and we will show him off."

"I have a feeling he will do the same for you."

"In any event, we will make him feel like a king for the evening."

"We need to go get some rest. It promises to be a big day tomorrow."

"True, Helen. Are you ready?"

"Yes, Katie. Take me to bed now, please."

"Goodnight Mom, Dad. Sleep well, and we'll see you in the morning."

"Goodnight, girls. Yes, tomorrow."

We went to our room and put on our nighties, very happy with our plans and prospects. At last, we had a great guy taking us out. As excited as we were, we went to sleep comfortably in each other's embrace.

"Can you believe the things those girls come up with?" Mom asked Dad.

"They are amazing."

"Do you think this is going to work out?"

"I don't know, but my bet would be on one of them capturing Jake's heart. Katie is the favorite, I think."

"Helen has her charms, Mike. It will be interesting to see what happens."

"Are you ready for bed, Mrs. Armstrong?"

"Yes, Dr. Armstrong. Take me to the big bed."

"With pleasure, dear Jackie. Let's go."

They let Rex in, and he headed directly for his bed in their bedroom and curled up for the night. Soon, after some loving, Mom and Dad also went to sleep in each other's arms. All of us slept until morning.

We awoke to a gorgeous day and elevated expectations. After our usual breakfast, we headed out for our exercise routines and rehearsal of our dance steps. A large group of other girls was there when we entered the gym and were already working. They welcomed us and wanted to show us how well they were doing with their new routines. We could see definite progress. Our mental attitudes must have been apparent because several of them noticed the change in our demeanors, with Estelle being the first.

"Okay, you two. What's going on? You look so happy this morning."

"Believe it or not, we have dates tonight. First ones in a long time," Helen answered her.

"Anyone, I might know?"

"Yes, Jacob asked to take us both out with him together for dinner and dancing."

"That ought to be interesting. How is Jake going to take care of both of you?"

"He did okay the other night with the horde of girls who descended on DJ's. Everyone just loved him."

"So, he narrowed it down to the two of you?"

"That's about the size of it."

"Are you sure he didn't narrow it down to one of you and is taking the other along since you are together all the time?"

"Who knows? He is taking both of us out tonight, and we will just have to see what happens."

"Let's get to work, Helen."

"Okay, sis. Stretches first."

We went through our entire routine. When we got to the dances, all of us there formed our lines and practiced together. It was good to have everyone joining in. It gave a new connotation to our rehearsal time.

Carolyn and Kelli were watching us and came into the room as we finished. "Great work, everyone. You look so good working together."

"Yes," Kelli added. "The exercises and dances bring you all together. Our next rehearsal will be a good one, no doubt."

"Thanks, guys. We enjoy them more when we work together."

"Will you join us for lunch?" Helen asked. We were hungry. Breakfast was gone, and we both needed to eat.

"Yes, we will. After last Tuesday night, we both feel much closer to all of you."

"That's great! We should do that more often. It brings us all together."

"Thanks, Katie. Your contribution to the squad has been invaluable."

"I appreciate that, Carolyn. These women are like family to me."

Lunch was excellent and restored our energy. We all focused on the protein selections to satisfy us and used the salads for the vitamins and minerals in them. After lunch, Helen and I headed home. We had preparations to make before Jacob's arrival for our joint date with him.

"What are you going to wear, Helen?"

"Tonight, I am going to wear a dress with short boots and my gold accessories. Nothing cowboy for this date. Great hair and makeup for a quiet dinner and dancing. Can I dance with him first?"

"Why don't we wait for him to ask one of us to dance. I bet it will be you."

"Do you think so?"

"Yes, sister mine. If our last meeting is any indication, I think he has his eyes on you."

"I don't know, Katie. That is one reason we are going out with him. Should we talk to Mom and Dad about this?"

"What would we say? We don't know much about this, especially how he feels or if he feels anything for us."

I drove through the gate and down to the house, putting the BMW in its covered space. We had no sooner gotten inside that Mom and Dad, who were waiting for us, asked us to come in and have a seat. We looked at each other with knowing expressions on our faces.

"Okay, you two. What are you cooking up now?"

"What do you mean, Dad?"

"He and I both want to know just what you planned for Mr. Jacob Walters," Mom answered.

I reached over and took Helen's hand in mine before we answered.

"Jake knows that the two of us do everything together. We don't know in which one of us he might be interested. Tonight, we hope to find out."

"Yes, Mom. He will have both of us on his arms, and we are going to share him."

"Have you kissed him yet?"

"Yes, both of us. You know that."

"Does he think he is going to get both of you in bed tonight?"

"Mom! How could you think that? Don't you know the two of us well enough to realize that is not even a possibility?"

"Just checking on what you are willing to do to keep him interested. He is quite a catch, you know."

"I hope we have put your concerns to rest. Now, we must take care of the horses before we start getting ready. Rest easy, Mom. We can and will handle what goes on this evening."

We changed into appropriate riding clothes and headed for the barn. Romeo saw us and trotted over to where we were, followed by Blackie and Mandy. All three of them now came to us. We petted them and talked to them, making them very happy that we were back. "Saddles or bareback?" Helen asked.

"No saddles today. Let's just have an enjoyable ride with them. Too bad Estelle isn't here. We could ride all three of them together."

"We can swap mounts and get all three of them some exercise."

"Okay. What did you think about Mom's questions?"

"She is just concerned about us. To her, it is probably like her teenage daughter is going out on her first date."

"Katie, I don't think either of us qualifies for that."

"She will probably stay up until we get back safely, even if Dad goes to bed."

"Probably."

I was riding Blackie, and he was trying his best to emulate Romeo. I patted his neck and praised him. It worked on him too. Then I got up on Mandy and kept Blackie's reins in one hand to lead him around. Helen was glad to be riding Romeo. They liked each other a lot. He anticipated her every movement and looked so proud to have my gorgeous sister riding him. They made quite a pair. I was glad their relationship had developed so well. This evening, I thought to myself, I was going to stand by and watch that happen between her and Jacob. I wanted to know about him.

Our ride ended, and we brushed all three horses out. They got their oats and were very content to return to the pasture. Helen and I were wearing wide grins as we left them. It was time for baths and laying out our outfits for the evening, baths first. As usual, we bathed and dried each other off. We still had plenty of time to get ready and began with doing each other's hair, drying, brushing, and then styling. Helen wanted hers big and fluffy, accenting the red in it. I curled it and made sure it would stay in place. My turn came next, and I went for waviness in mine with full body. She did an excellent job. We were going to look fantastic.

We still had an hour left and started with our makeup. We cleansed just the same as the Cheerleader artists showed us and did our makeup ourselves. They had taught us what worked for us. We were not the same by any means, and both knew what would work for us in a typical restaurant lighting. Helen used a bright red lip color, which she didn't usually do for a performance, but it looked terrific. I went with a darker color than usual but stayed away from the bright red. We checked each other out and gave our mutual approval on the work we had done. Now we were ready to dress. Time was running out for us. Jacob would be here in less than fifteen minutes. No problem, though, Mom and Dad would entertain him until we were ready.

"We need to hurry, Katie."

"No, we don't, Helen. Let him charm Mom and Dad for a while. We will go out to them only when we are ready. Just calm down."

We had not put on our dresses when the doorbell rang. Dad answered it with Mom right behind him. "Jacob, good to see you again. Come on in, boy."

"Thank you, Dr. Armstrong." Dad led him into the living room and gave him a seat.

"Please, Jake. Call me Mike. I think we might get to know each other somewhat better."

"Thank you, sir, Mike, I mean." He turned to Mom.

"Hello, Mrs. Armstrong. It is a pleasure to meet you."

"We are so glad to have you come to visit us, Jake. Helen and Katie will be out in just a few minutes."

"Thank you, Mrs. Armstrong."

"Call me Jackie, Jacob. All my friends do."

"I will, Jackie. Thank you."

"May I ask where you are taking our girls tonight?"

"To a little place not very far from here in North Dallas. The food is excellent, and they play a distinctive style of music for dancing. Its name is Tony's, and it has been around for years."

"I have heard of it. Ballroom dancing is the norm there, I believe."

"Yes, Jackie. That's right. It provides an opportunity to put the country/western music aside for a while in favor of the more traditional dance styles. It should be a lot of fun."

"Then what do you have planned?"

"That all depends on the girls. Would you object, if they agree, to my bringing them back here to end the evening?"

"No, Jacob, that sounds good to us," Dad answered.

"If I know my girls, they might want you to take them to your place instead of coming here."

"We'll see what they say. Ah, here your dates are."

We went out to where they were talking, and Jacob stood up immediately to welcome us.

"My Lord, you two are beautiful tonight." He came to us and gave us each a kiss right in front of Dad and Mom. "How did I get so lucky to go out with you both together?"

"Thanks, Jake. It is our pleasure. May I say how handsome you look?"

"Thanks, Helen. That means a lot to me. Shall we go?"

We took our small purses with us and answered in the affirmative. "See you later, Mom and Dad. Don't wait up for us."

"Okay, Katie. Have a wonderful time."

"We will," and we left on each side of Jake. He opened the door, and the front seat was plenty wide enough to seat all three of us. I slipped into the middle with Helen on my right and Jake on my left, behind the wheel. Before he started up the driveway, I wanted something from him.

"You are not getting away so easily, buster. I want a real kiss, not like the one you gave us in front of Mom and Dad." He complied and gave me a hot kiss with all sorts of romantic implications.

"I want one too," Helen told him. She leaned over me, and he kissed her the same way he had kissed me. "That was a kiss, Jake. Before this evening is over, I want more, please."

"Helen, you and Katie are going to get anything you want tonight. Be careful what you ask for, however. I told your folks I would try to bring you home after dancing and spend some time there with you. I will not be responsible for anything that might happen with us tonight."

"I am not going to ask you yet what you want to happen tonight. Let's see how things go, okay?"

"Okay with me."

Helen and I smiled at each other. He had no idea what was in store for him. My devil came out, and Helen got a lewd smile on her face. Jacob was in big trouble. He kept up the conversation by asking about the Cheerleaders, the horses, and how our appearance on TV had affected us. He got us to talk about ourselves and what we were doing. I tried to turn the tables on him by asking him about his company, his girlfriends, and his life up until then. He didn't hold back from us. Before long, he drove into the parking lot of Tony's and motioned for the valets to take care of the car. They let us out, and we walked arm in arm with him into the restaurant. Escorting us both seemed to please him. The hostess found our reservations and led the way to our booth, which Jake had requested so we could sit on each side of him. We would make sure he was the center of attention.

Chapter Twenty

One Enchanted Evening

"What would you girls like to drink tonight? Champagne as usual?"

"Yes, Jacob, that would be fine. Will you join us?"

"I think I will. Champagne, please waiter."

"Excellent, sir." He gave us menus, but we left them on the table while we talked. When he came back with the wine, we looked at them.

"Does anything look good?"

"Yes. I want to try the scampi with a Caesar salad," Helen told him.

"How about you, Katie?"

"Filet of sole with a chef's salad for me, please."

"Done. I think I will have a small filet. Is the wine all right?"

"Yes, Jake, it is delicious."

"Here's to the two most beautiful and talented girls I have ever known."

"Thanks, Jacob, for taking both of us out tonight," I said.

"I had to. No way I could decide without knowing you both better."

"Decide what?"

"Which one of you I am going to fall in love with."

"Isn't that something that just happens?"

"Yes, and right now, I want you both."

"Tonight, you have us both, so don't blow your chance," Helen kidded him.

The waiter brought our dinners, and we ate with great enjoyment. The food was excellent. As we finished, the music began. The first number was 'In the Mood' by the Glenn Miller orchestra. "Can either of you swing?"

"Let's go," we both said. We hit the dance floor as a threesome. I was on one of Jacob's arms, and Helen was on the other. Yes, we could both dance to this number. So, could

Jake. He twirled us both at the same time, and his rhythm was excellent, as was his footwork. He was as good at this type of dance as he was with the cowboy dances, even better. We danced to all the Miller songs from "Pennsylvania 6-5000" to "Moonlight Serenade" when the music turned to a couple of slow songs such as "Dream Walk" and "To Know, Know, Know You," and Helen and I took turns dancing very close to him. We had his heart beating rapidly, and his sexual desire showed in the bulge we felt in his pants. The music changed back to the Jitterbug with Queen's "A Crazy Little Thing Called Love," followed by more. We needed a break and more of our champagne, so we went back to the table.

A handsome young man came over to us and said, "Hey, Jake. What's shaking?"

"Henry. Good to see you. Out for some fun tonight?"

"Yes, but unaccompanied. You seem to have two of what we all are looking for."

"Really, what would that be?"

"How did you get two gorgeous ladies to go out with you together?"

"Meet my two new lovers. My redhead is Helen, and this is Katie. They are sisters, and they always go together."

"Must be crowded in bed," Henry remarked.

"Excuse us, Jake. I think we will go to the ladies' room to freshen up. It seems that your friend here is already fresh." We got up and left.

"What did I say, Jacob?"

"You have a lot to learn about women with class, Hank. That bed remark offended them. It even offended me. What could you have been thinking?"

"I'm sorry, Jake. I'll just leave you alone with them."

"Apology accepted. Give me a call next week."

"Okay, Jacob. Sorry."

"Forget it."

We returned to Jacob after a brief visit to the facilities, and Henry was not there. "Where did Henry go?" Helen asked.

"His comment about bed embarrassed him, and he left. He is on the other side of the restaurant. Why do you ask?"

"I kind of liked him. He has a sense of humor, that's for sure."

"There he is, right over there. If you want, go to him, and make him dance. He is pretty good."

"Take care of Jake, Katie. I'll be back.

She got up and walked over to where Henry was talking with several other people and tapped him on the shoulder. When he turned around, his eyes lit up, and he stumbled over his words.

"Henry, is that you?"

"Yes, Helen. G-Good to see you again. Would you like to dance?"

"I would like that very much." They hit the floor in rhythm to the music and danced away. Henry could dance, and when they played the first waltz of the evening, he took Helen in his arms and danced romantically with her to "The Blue Danube." He could waltz! Helen was in heaven. She had her guy and didn't have to share him. He had a beautiful smile and held her tight, captivating her at once. They couldn't take their eyes off each other. I wondered what was going on. Helen seemed enraptured by Henry, which suited me fine. She left me with Jacob all to myself. I moved nearer to him and took his hand.

He kissed me, and I put my head under his chin. "Looks as if it is just the two of us now."

"That's the way I wanted it all along," he replied.

"So, it's me, Jacob?"

"Yes, Katie. It has been you ever since our first waltz."

"Why didn't you say something?"

"I needed to see the dynamics among your girlfriends and how you and Helen lived your lives together."

"Tell me about Henry."

"He has his rough edges, but he is a good man, caring, intelligent, and he has an excellent job with many prospects for the future."

"Should I tell Helen anything?"

"No, just let things develop or not. You are both very well taken care of living at home, and with the Cheerleaders, you are safe from anyone. Besides, Helen impresses me as a girl who can take care of herself. Now let's talk about us, you and me."

"What about us? On our first date?"

"I am crazy about you, Katie. I knew it last Tuesday, and I tried my hardest to get to know the other girls. Carolyn and Kelli were wonderful, and I liked them both, but I came back to you. I had to."

"I'm glad you did, but we just met, and I am not sure I am ready for a relationship with all the other things going on in my life. You must be busy, too, owning your own company."

"I guess your dad told you about that. Yes, I own the company, but I can always make time for you. You got to me, Katie. Knowing that, do I interest you at all?"

In answer, I gave him a friendly kiss, because I didn't know what I was thinking and feeling. "Yes, Jake. I am still interested. You seem to be a confident, accomplished man, and you can dance. I want to get to know you and hope things between us will get better from there. I admire what you have done with your life, and you are beginning to get to me."

"I have a chance with you? A beautiful woman who is a Dallas Cowboys Cheerleader and is becoming a star on the TV screen? A woman who kissed Casey West on national TV and has appeared on both the late-night and morning shows? How could you be interested in a construction guy in Dallas?"

"Don't sell yourself short, Jake. You are very handsome, have a fantastic personality, and you know how to dance. Just let me do my thing and be patient, and we have a chance."

"Will you be my steady date? Nights like tonight, parties with my colleagues and clients, and things like that?"

"It's too soon, Jacob. I must do my Cheerleader thing and work with my horses. I want to go slowly, Jacob, but I would be delighted if things developed between us to that extent.

That's the way my Dad won my Mom's heart even when she became a Cheerleader."

"I will talk to them."

"Good, now for the rest of tonight."

"I am going to take you home soon. I promised your Mom that I would."

"My home, or yours?" I kidded him some.

"That question makes a chill run up and down my spine. Would you come to mine?"

"It's too soon, Jake? Even though I love intimacy and I haven't been with a man in some time, I do not know how I feel about you. That type of commitment is not to be entered into lightly."

"There is nothing I would like better, Katie, but there is no way I could let you go back to your home afterward."

"That would be a problem. My parents are very supportive and understanding, but just to not go home would not work. I have more respect for them. I have an idea. Do you ride?"

"Of course. I love to ride."

"Can you get off early some afternoon and come riding with me when Dad and Mom are at work?"

"Hey, I own the company. I can do whatever I want."

"Thursday, then. We'll be back from the Star around noon. Who knows, maybe Helen will want to join us." I chuckled, "riding, of course."

He looked me directly in the eyes and said with all sincerity, "I don't want Helen, although she might do in a pinch." He joked back to me. "I want you, Katie. It is you I am in love with, and I only want to be with you."

"You are in love with me, Jacob? After this brief time we have spent together. How can you be sure?"

"Katie, I am sure. Not only that, but I want to make love to you."

"I am not sure yet, Jacob. As I said, having sex is a big step."

Our conversation ended when Helen and Henry came back to the table. "We need to get home, sister. It's getting late."

"I know. Are you coming with us?"

"Yes. Henry is going to call me soon, and we want to go out together, just the two of us. Is that okay with you?"

"Yes, Helen. Jacob and I have been talking about the same thing. I guess it took a couple of good men to separate us for an evening."

"I guess it did. Are you ready?"

"Let me take care of the tab, and we are off," Jacob agreed.

"Goodnight, Henry. I enjoyed meeting you and dancing the night away. Call me soon."

"Goodnight, Helen. He kissed her and took his leave."

"I like that guy," Helen gushed.

"I am so glad, Helen. We have an early day tomorrow. Let's go."

Jacob took care of the tab, and we left the restaurant. The valet service brought our car, and soon we were on our way. As I predicted, Mom was waiting up for us, and we convinced Jacob to come in for a minute. He didn't stay long. We both kissed him goodnight and accompanied him to the front door. He took off up the driveway and left us with enjoyable memories of the evening. Helen and I smiled at each other and went back inside. Mom wanted to know everything that happened. Our report was straightforward. "We had a wonderful time. The food was excellent, and the dancing was a ballroom theme. Jacob likes me, and Helen met a new guy named Henry. He is handsome and sexy, and he can dance."

"He asked to take me home, but we both left with Jacob. I gave Henry my number and asked that he call me. It was a perfect first date."

"Yes, it was. We both had a wonderful time, but we have an early day tomorrow. We will tell you all about it then if that is okay."

She could see we were tired and sleepy and was okay with us putting her off until tomorrow. At least her girls were home. She could see the smiles we were wearing. I took Helen to bed after we changed into our nighties. We slipped under the covers together. The weather was cooling off, and we wanted to stay warm.

"How did it go with Jacob, sister?"

"He said he was in love with me."

"That was quick," she responded.

"That's not all. Jacob wanted to take me home tonight, to his home, not here. I would have gone if I knew him better, but he said there was no way he could let me go until morning."

"I don't imagine he had cuddling and holding in mind."

"No, he wants me to be his steady girlfriend, and he wants to make love to me."

"What did you tell him?"

"I said I would not stay out all night because my parents expected me home and that I wouldn't do something like that to them."

"Good for you."

"Then I invited him to come here on Thursday after we get back from exercise and lunch to ride the horses, but I had an ulterior motive."

"You want him here without Mom and Dad."

"Yes. I want to be alone with Jake for a while. It has been a long time since I had sex with a man and even longer since I was with one I liked. He may have possibilities."

"You two are way ahead of Henry and me."

"Do you think there might be something there?"

"Honestly, I don't know, Katie."

"I told Jake my sister would be here and to prepare to ride with us both."

"You mean both of us to take him to bed?"

"I am not convinced I want to. A nagging doubt won't go away about Jacob."

"Well, we do everything else together, so why not ride with him and see what develops?"

"We'll wait and see what happens. Is that all right with you?"

"It's the only way to fly. Now kiss me and let's get some rest for tomorrow morning. I need to go to sleep."

She did just that in my embrace, but I wasn't that lucky. The evening with Jake kept going through my mind as did the knowledge of what might happen with him. I was not sure I was ready for that, no matter how long it had been. I felt great conflict. My mind finally shut down, and I drifted off into sleep.

When I awoke, Helen was still asleep, and I tried to get out of bed without disturbing her. I got to the bathroom while she was still sleeping and did my morning routine. I hoped breakfast would wake me up. I went to the kitchen and started the coffee, thinking that would help. As I had my first cup, a sleepy Helen joined me in the kitchen.

"Coffee, sis?"

"Yes, please. You look terrible this morning. Not much sleep?"

"Not enough, that's for sure. We might want to limit our nighttime activities until the season is over."

"I thought we were doing okay last night, but I regret it this morning too."

"Let's have some breakfast and go do our thing. I hope I can take a nap this afternoon."

"We'll take one together."

"Sounds good to me. Let's have some breakfast and go."

We got out to the car and headed for Cowboy Central. On the way, I brought up the conflict that had kept me awake the night before. "Helen, I am not sure I want to get intimate with Jacob when he comes up here."

"Second thoughts?"

"Yes, I couldn't go to sleep last night because I had a conflict about the whole scene. I get the feeling that everything is not as it seems."

"Is it your attraction to me and other girls or something else?"

"I am not in love with him, and I must feel something more than just my desire for sex with a man. What if he is just looking for another conquest? I don't want sex that badly. I want a relationship first, then intimacy. Does that make any sense to you?"

"Yes, sis, it makes a lot of sense to me. What are you going to do?"

"What if I asked Mom to be at home that afternoon? Or, maybe I should just tell him how I am feeling."

"Or both?"

"Would you go to bed with a guy on the second date?"

"No, but I must admit there are exceptions."

"Such as Casey?"

"He might be one of them."

"I understand that. I am just not ready yet."

"Neither am I. Do you realize that since we became sisters, we haven't loved each other as much as we used to? We sleep together, cuddle and hug each other, but something has changed. Can we change it back?"

"I think we need to talk with Mom, lay it out for her, and see what she has to say."

"An all-girl talk like we used to have?"

"Something like that. Mom and Dad think we are invincible, and I doubt if she sees through the facade we put up."

"I think you are right. This evening when mom gets home from work?"

"Yes. If Dad is there, we will just tell him we need to talk alone with Mom. He has always understood that girls need to talk privately at times."

"That'll work. Let's do our exercise thing and have some lunch. We can go take our naps and wait for mom to get home."

"Please forgive me if I seem distracted during our workout. I know things will be running through my mind the whole time."

"Katie, put your mind on your workout and let those other things go. We will take care of them later."

"Okay, Helen. Thanks."

Chapter Twenty-One

A Talk with Mom

"We are so glad you came home early today, Mom. We want to talk to you."

"Make me a rusty nail, and I am yours."

Helen and I pitched in together to make her drink and delivered it to her. "That's good. Thanks. Now, what do you want to talk about?"

"You know that the two of us were lovers before we became sisters. Since then, something, either conscious or subconscious, has held us back from the relationship we once had. Frankly, it is driving both of us wild."

"You sleep together, what's the problem?"

"We had loved on Estelle and Karen when she was here, but not each other." I took Helen's hand in mine, squeezing it. "We want to go back to the way we were before."

Helen resumed the conversation. "What we want to know is whether becoming sisters, legally, although we are not related, is a factor in our love for each other. And, I mean sexual love."

I tried to clarify, "Is it wrong for sisters like us to share our love for each other?"

"The definition of incest is sex with a blood relative or someone with whom you share a common ancestor. Neither of those two conditions applies to you. Legally, it is not an issue. Morally, it might be. Would you have sex with your blood sister?"

"No, of course not, but that is not what we are."

"That's true. What about this is causing you problems?

"We are known widely as sisters. The cheerleaders see us as sisters, and everyone presents us as sisters, even on national TV. What if it got out that we were also lovers?"

"What if it did? What you want to do is not illegal."

"There are moral issues, though, as you pointed out, and we don't want to embarrass the team or you two."

"You are our daughters and will never be an embarrassment to us because we love you both."

"So, what do you advise us to do?"

"Live your lives. Love whom you want to love and, as with any love affair, be discreet. No one else needs to know."

"Are you okay with our being lovers some times?"

"Yes, I back you completely."

"Do you think Dad will feel the same way?"

"Yes, I do. Your dad loves you both very much. Now kiss each other and enjoy being able to be together most, if not all, of the time."

"Thank you, Mom." We both got up and hugged her, then sat back down.

"Now, what is the other question you have?"

Most inopportunely, the phone rang before we could tell her. Helen answered. "Hello, this is Helen."

The person at the other end didn't say anything right away. After a pause, the woman on the other end said, "May I speak with Katie, please?"

"May I tell her who's calling?"

"My name is Melanie, and I know Jacob Walters."

"Just a second, please."

"It's someone named Melanie, and she knows Jacob." Helen gave me the phone, and I turned on the speakerphone, so Helen and Mom could hear the conversation.

"This is Katie."

"Hello, Katie, I'm Melanie. Jacob is my fiancé, and I thought we should talk."

Her statement left me speechless. Jacob's fiancé?

Mom and Helen moved forward to the edge of their seats, not believing what they had just heard.

"Jake hasn't mentioned having a fiancé to me. Is this some sort of joke?"

"I'm afraid it's no joke, Katie."

"I am sorry if I seem to be surprised, but that is just what I am."

"I knew he had a new dancing partner and girlfriend from a mutual friend who was in DJ's when he charmed all the Cheerleaders, and he overheard your name. Then I saw you on Fox and Friends with your sister, and I knew. Talk about being surprised! Jacob was courting a Dallas Cowboys Cheerleader and had impressed several of you with his dancing and personality."

"He *can* dance," I replied. "Melanie, would you like to meet somewhere and talk?"

"Yes, Katie. I would love to meet you and Helen."

"Where are you right now?"

"I'm at work, but I get off in thirty minutes and can meet you. Are you anywhere near North Dallas?"

"I'm on the lake with Helen and my Mom and Dad. Do you know where the marina is?"

"Yes, I do. But before we meet, I need to know something."

"I think I know what it is. Melanie, I have not slept with Jacob and don't plan to do so."

"Thanks for that, Katie. You are not the first girl he has cheated on me with and will not be the last."

"You must care for him very much."

"Not as much as I used to."

"Do you ride, Melanie?"

"Yes, I ride in rodeos regularly."

"We have three horses here. Would you like to come to meet them?"

"That would be fantastic. I had to sell my horse and am always looking for girls like me who love horses and riding."

"Why don't you come here when you get off work? We can visit the horses and would love for you to have dinner with us. How about it?"

"Are you sure I won't be intruding?"

"I think meeting each other would prove to be very interesting. Let me give you to Helen again, and she will tell you how to get here. We'll try to make it a fun evening."

"Okay. Let me talk to your sister."

I gave the phone to Helen, and she gave her directions to our place.

"If it is okay with you, I'll leave now and come see you. Give me half an hour."

"Okay, Melanie. See you in a few minutes." The line went dead on her end.

"Well, Mom, Helen, you must admit that I can pick them. I had a feeling we didn't know the whole story, but can you believe that?"

"That snake. If what Melanie said is true, his life is not going to be very pleasant from here on out. Just leave it to me," Helen promised.

"Mom, what do you think?"

"You knew from the first that something wasn't quite right about this situation, didn't you?"

"I suspected. Something didn't seem quite right to me. I mean, how does a handsome guy who owns his own company, has a great personality, and can dance, not have a girlfriend, right?"

"Wait until the girls find out about this. The word will be out about Mr. Walters," Helen surmised.

"And to think, he almost got us to go to bed with him," I related.

"I can't wait to hear his story," Helen chuckled with delight at the prospect.

"Let's go out to the barn and play with our horses while we wait for Melanie."

"Boots and jeans?"

"Of course. Let's change and get some love from our equine friends. It's the only male attention we can truly trust."

A few minutes later, we walked out to the barn, and Romeo, Blackie, and Mandy galloped over to greet us. We gave them lots of affection and put their bits and harnesses on them. I had been practicing riding Romeo bareback through all his exercises, including the barrels and his show routines. He loved it.

"Do you want to go first, Helen?"

"No, you go ahead. I'll take my turn next."

"Okay." I jumped up on his back and gave him the cue to prance. He looked magnificent. Since the limited space in the corral felt confining, I took him out into the pasture and let him dance. His posing was getting even better. He was a handsome fellow, and he knew it. I talked to him, patted his neck, and let him lead. He had gotten much more muscular now that he was in shape, and I could feel his muscles rippling under me. I lost track of time until a car came down the driveway, and Helen went over to greet Melanie. She got out of the car and leaned on the fence, watching Romeo and me. His spirit and fire caught her eye immediately.

I let him have his head and gave the cue for him to step it up. I turned his head and pointed him out into the pasture. He got the message and, after rearing up on his back legs, leaped into his gallop with one stride. He loved to run. We went around the enclosure twice, and I brought him to a halt, both of us breathing hard, beside Melanie and Helen.

"Let's go run the barrels a couple of times, big boy. Coming girls?"

"Is she going to do the barrels bareback on that horse?" Melanie inquired.

"Yes, it's quite a sight. Park your car over there, and we'll go watch."

"This I have to see."

I reined Romeo in at the start/finish line and nudged him in the sides with my heels. He knew what to do precisely. His first turn was crisp, short, and executed perfectly. He made sure not to unseat me as he did it. The second barrel was as good as the first. I took him around once again and pulled him up.

"Romeo, this is our new friend and horse person, Melanie. Say hello to her."

He whinnied and pawed the ground, moving his head up and down to show his approval of her. Horses know people, and I trusted him to distinguish between the right people and the not so good. He was never wrong. Melanie reached out to pet him, and he loved it.

"May I?" she asked.

"Sure, he is a good ride."

I dismounted and gave the reins to Melanie. She was wearing jeans and boots from work and had no problem getting on him. Romeo knew what she wanted when she gave him his cues. First, she had him prance. Then do his dance with his mane and tail flying as she guided him toward the starting point of the barrel course. Helen moved to caution her, but I held her back with a smile. Melanie showed us there was nothing about which to be concerned.

She took the first circuit of the course at a moderate pace, getting familiar with him. The second circuit, she let him out, and he ran that lap at top speed. Melanie moved with him the whole way. She took him through a third circuit and had had enough. Melanie rode him over to us and dismounted, handing the reins to Helen. She just put the straps over the corral fence and turned loose of him. His training told him to stay there until one of us came for him.

"He's good, Katie. Very good. I loved riding him. How old is he?"

"He is three. We work with him and the others every day to keep them in shape."

"We'll give him his bath, brush them all dry, and feed them. Want to help?"

"Yes, I wouldn't miss it."

I led him and the others over to the fence near the barn, and Helen and I bathed him. We all three brushed them and put on their feed bags. Their water was right beside them too. We removed their halters and got the same "Thank you" from them that we always got and headed for the house. Mom was there, but Dad had not returned yet.

"Mom, this is Melanie. Did you see her ride?"

"Yes, I did. You two might have some competition now."

"I loved Romeo. He is so well-trained and knows just what to do. Riding him was a real pleasure."

"He loves to take care of his girls," Helen offered. And here is another lover. Rex wanted to come in, and we let him. He sniffed Melanie as she showed him her hand and greeted her and the rest of us with a wagging tail and sloppy kisses. He liked her.

The phone rang. It was Dad. He was at one of their favorite restaurants and wanted Mom to join him there. He did not invite us. Imagine that. Mom must have put a bug in his ear.

"That was your Dad. He wants me to join him for dinner and a drink. I'm afraid you three will just have to make do without us."

"No problem, Mom. We will be fine," Helen reassured her.

Shortly, she was gone, not to return anytime soon.

"May I fix you a drink, Melanie?"

"Gin and tonic?"

"Coming up."

I fixed Helen and me a light one of the same, and we sat in the living room. It was only then that I saw the engagement ring on her ring finger. It was awe-inspiring.

"Is that Jacob's ring?"

"Yes. At one point, I thought a matching band might join it. Do you mind me asking about your relationship with Jake?"

"We met him several weeks ago at DJ's. Tuesday night, he took us both to dinner at a place where we could dance."

"He took both of you out?"

"Yes. You might say we are inseparable, and Jake picked up on that."

"He probably thought he could sleep with you both."

"Is he that bad, Melanie?"

"He is a young, wealthy man who usually gets his way."

"How long have you known him?"

"I didn't know him until just recently when he was busy with work he said and couldn't see me. He wasn't working. He was going out with other girls."

"Are you going to break it off with him," Helen wanted to know.

"I want to, but I keep thinking he will come around again."

"We need a plan, girls."

"I am just an administrative assistant in a real estate firm, and I ride horses when I can. I didn't use to be this way. My future was just opening, and then he came along. He had me captured the first night I spent with him."

"Is he a good lover, Melanie?"

"No, but when you consider the whole person, he is quite a catch. And he knows it."

"Those are the worst kind," Helen commented.

"Are you in love with him?"

"Yes, dammit. I wish I weren't."

She began to cry. Helen and I went to her and hugged her. We both knew what she was going through. I know Helen was as glad as I was that we found all this out before it was too late.

"What would you like for dinner, Melanie? We have steak, seafood, Italian, and more in the freezer. Anything you like."

"I would like to have a Waldorf salad. Can you do that?"

"Yes, of course. It is one of our favorites. How's your drink?"

"I would like another if it's not too much trouble."

"There is something you need to know about us, Melanie. We take care of our sisters. It's a Cheerleader thing. We all have each other's back all the time."

"I sense that you two are very close. May I ask how close?"

"We sleep together. Want to see our room?"

"Yes, I would love to."

"Come this way, then." We led her to the back and showed her our room.

"This is so nice. I love the bed. It is so big."

"It sleeps three very comfortably."

"So, Jacob could have slept with both of you?"

"Under no circumstances. The last person to sleep with us was Karen, the Friday night before the last game."

"We have never had a man in bed with us. We like men, but sharing is just not in the cards. We want our own man."

"But you love each other?"

"Yes, we do. Back to the living room?"

"Yes. I would like that."

After we retook our seats, the phone rang. I gave it to Helen. It was Jacob, of all people, and she put it on the speakerphone.

"Hey, Helen. Are you guys ready for tomorrow afternoon?"

"Hi, Jacob. Glad you called. Something has come up."

"Oh, no. And I was looking forward to spending that time with you two."

"We are so sorry, but a Cheerleader's life is full of surprises."

Melanie and I almost cracked up laughing at that.

"Can you find something else to keep your attention?"

"Yes, but I am disappointed. I do have work to do."

"Okay, good. We have company right now, so I have to say goodbye and goodnight."

"Okay, Helen. Can I talk with Katie?"

"Oh, I'm so sorry, but she is outside taking care of the horses. When she comes in, we are going to have something to eat and go to bed. We have a long day tomorrow."

"Is there any way I can see either of you?"

"I'm sorry, Jake. You know we are always together. We are both going to be busy tomorrow."

"How about tonight? I promise to make it interesting."

"You heard me, Jake. We are out of touch for the next several days."

"I am not used to taking 'No' for an answer."

"It's called Cheerleader's curse. Deal with it. When the season is over, we might be able to get our lives back."

"So, you are telling me no for tonight and no for tomorrow?"

"Yes, Jacob. I know it must be frustrating, but that is what it's like dating one of our team."

"But I want to see you."

"Someone here wants to talk to you, Jacob. Hold on." She gave the phone to Melanie.

"Hi, Jacob. Imagine meeting you here."

"Melanie? What are you doing with Katie and Helen?"

"We just ran into each other. We have something in common."

"What would that be?"

"We all love horses. I've been riding with them all afternoon, and your name came up."

"What did they tell you?"

"We all know all about you, Jacob. We shared our experiences where you are concerned."

"Everything?"

"Well, I haven't told them everything about you, but they are learning."

"I can explain, Melanie. Please give me a chance."

"And how are you going to explain me to them, and this ring on my finger?"

"Don't do this, Melanie. You know I love you."

"Do I? You romance every Cheerleader in DJ's, especially them, and we discover what a cad you are, and you want me to believe you love me? I don't think so, Jacob. Do you want your ring back? Do you want to see me again, or have others caught your eye? Do you understand what I am asking you?"

"Don't do something you will regret later, Melanie."

"Right now, all I regret is trusting you and thinking you love me. You know where to find me. Goodnight, Jacob. Have a good life." She hung up on him.

"How did I do?"

"You did great, Melanie. I am proud of you."

"Thanks, guys. You gave me the courage to take care of that situation. Can I come to ride Romeo again?"

"Anytime you want, girl. He needs his exercise as do the others."

"Thanks. I'll call before I come."

"We usually go to exercise and practice in the mornings, but come in the afternoon when you can."

"I will. May I get to know you two better too?"

"Yes, Melanie. We would like that very much."

"I'll call soon, then."

"You do that. We will be glad to hear from you."

We both kissed her, and she went to her car and left us. We both thought it had been an excellent encounter. "Good luck, Melanie," I said as she left. "And thanks."

Chapter Twenty-Two

And Now, What?

We didn't say much for a while, thinking about what had just happened. "Do you believe Melanie?" Helen asked.

"I don't want to, but yes, I think I do. We don't know the whole story, though."

"No, we don't, but I intend to find out."

"How are we going to do that, Helen?"

"We have heard Melanie's side of the story, and at some point, we are going to have to get Jacob's."

"I have an idea. Dad says he knows Jacob, so we should talk to him."

"And Mom said he fell for her when she was a cheerleader. We need to talk with her."

"If Melanie is telling us the truth, we will just have to move on. There is Henry, also Brian, although with Henry being Jacob's friend, I am not sure he is any different."

"Good point, Katie. Sometimes I wonder if there are still any honest men anywhere."

"A true cynic's point of view, sis."

"A realist. Have you ever wondered why I was single when you and I met?"

"It had crossed my mind. I know you like men, so what is it?"

"I was in love with a guy and thought I had found *the one*. It seems that the men I find the most attractive all know it. Lots of girls think they are irresistible and can take away any man from his lady no matter what. The guys never tell us about the 'other woman,' and we find out by accident or someone tells us."

"Then you have been here before?"

"Oh, yes. The Cheerleaders saved me. I was devastated, and it took a long time to get over it."

I embraced her as the memories brought a tear to her eyes. "Naturally, you don't want to go there again."

"No, I don't. I am not going there again. That is why I want to talk to Mom. She found her man and has been able to keep him for many years, the way they talk. I want to know how she does it."

"She told me once that Dad had a 'woman in every port.' And yet, she is still with him. She won out over all of them."

"Call Dad's cell phone. Tell him we need them to come home."

I dialed the number. Mom answered. "Katie, is something wrong?"

"No, Mom. We are okay, but we need you and Dad to come home as soon as you can. We need both of you."

"We'll be there in thirty minutes." She hung up.

"They are coming."

"Good. I'm sure mom and dad can help."

"I think a couple of martinis wouldn't hurt either."

"I don't know any reason why we shouldn't as long as we don't overdo it."

"Come help me make them."

Helen and I both got up and headed for the liquor cabinet. We made them in a shaker with ice cubes to chill them and poured them into chilled martini glasses. After a taste to make sure we had mixed them correctly, we sat back down on the sofa. In a few minutes, we heard dad and mom drive up in front of the house. Mom saw the martinis and knew what was wrong immediately.

"Martinis, is it? Could it be man trouble?"

Dad came in shortly after her. It was a relief to him, seeing we were physically all right. They started to sit in the loveseat, but we would have none of that. We vacated the sofa and told them to sit there. Helen and I put our drinks down and sat in their laps with our arms around their necks, I in Mom's lap and Helen in Dad's. We kissed them on the cheek, and I said, "We need you two to help guide us through a little crisis we are having."

"A little crisis?" Dad picked up on that. "Being out of milk is a little crisis. When you two are both upset, it sounds much more serious than that. Why don't you tell us about it?"

"Yeah, girls. Martinis on the night before you are going to work out? What's wrong?"

"You met Melanie this afternoon. Did you notice the ring she was wearing?"

"No. Your father called, and I left before I got a chance to talk with her."

"She said she was Jacob's fiancé, and he had given her a ring, an engagement ring as she described it."

"Girls, I had no idea," Dad interjected. "Jacob is engaged? I think I might want to check this out further."

"Either that or Melanie is trying to get him back from us two, but she didn't sound that way."

"We don't know whom to believe. Jacob called while she was here, and we know that Jacob gave her a ring which she wore, but we don't know what the state of their relationship is."

"Rex and Romeo both seemed to like and accept her, and they seemed glad to meet her, especially Rex. Romeo is such a ham that he likes anyone who can stay on his back, and you saw her ride, Mom," I explained.

"She is good on a horse," Mom confirmed.

"How far has it gone with him and you two? Dad asked."

"We have not slept with him, thank God."

"So, how can we help?"

Helen explained. "We want to hear your stories. Mom, how you kept Dad interested in you all these years, with all the women who undoubtedly were chasing him."

I said, "And Mom, we need to know what you did to keep Dad interested, despite being a Cheerleader and having your separate interests."

"Yes, maybe your stories will help us. We don't seem to be having much success these days ourselves." That caused smiles all around.

"Why are you in such a big hurry? You are what, Katie, twenty-one, and you, Helen, are twenty-four, approaching twenty-five? When I was your age, your father was married, although it ended badly, except for me. I didn't even know him then. I went through many of the same things you are going through. It seems to run in the Cheerleader family."

"How and when did you realize he was a good man?" Helen asked.

"I knew right from the start. Mike talked to me. He shared his life and bared his soul. It might have been therapy for him, but I knew he was telling me the truth."

"Dad, how did you pry Mom away from the Cheerleaders and all the other things she was doing? What was your secret?"

"Well, Helen, my secret in a word was 'patience.' I loved her, and I knew she loved me. All we had to do was wait until the right time came along. Thanks to you two, that time came."

"Patience?"

"Believe me, girls, *patience is genius*."

"I know you think that's easy for us to say. We found each other amidst all the static and confusion that permeates the relationships between men and women. I saw a lot of others while I waited for your Dad. There are so many attractive people out there, especially in this town. I enjoyed myself and let things take their course and enjoyed every minute of it in the meantime. There are no guarantees in life. You just should live the time you have to the max doing things that make you happy. The right guy might come along, but he might not. Accept that. Be happy with yourself. You must live with you before you are ready to live with someone else."

"Girls, you can have fun with someone and not fall in love with them," Dad observed.

"So, what should we do about Jacob? He attracts us both."

"What do you want to do?"

"We both wanted to take him to bed with us at the same time."

"Helen, that is not going to happen. Remember what I said about emotional involvement? Melanie or no Melanie, I do not love Jacob. He is a great dancer and very accomplished, but the feelings are not there for me."

"No threesome, Katie?"

"No. Do as you wish, but count me out."

"Do you think a threesome is realistic? Could he handle both of you together?"

"According to Melanie, he can't even handle one of us at a time." Helen and I laughed.

"Why do you want to sleep with him?" Mom asked, puzzled.

"He is a great looking man, has a wonderful personality, and is probably the best dancing male we have ever known."

"What does any of that have to do with sleeping with him?"

"OMG! You are right, Mom." Helen and I both saw it at the same time.

"It's his dancing, isn't it?" Dad asked. "Let me tell you a story. When I moved to Dallas, I couldn't dance a lick. I learned everything I know from a great girlfriend whom I never dated but was patient enough with me to help me learn. You have no idea how many hours I spent upstairs by the railing at DJ's practicing the steps by myself. I finally got the rhythm of the two-step, and things just developed from there. Dancing is a matter of learning to move with the rhythm of the music."

"And you both saw him on the dance floor at DJ's. Helen, you, and Estelle danced with him as did several of your girlfriends. Can he dance?"

"He is an excellent dancer," Helen replied. "Any of the girls would love to be his dance partner."

"There you are. A man who can dance has the world in his pocket, and any man can learn to dance if he wants it bad enough."

"What about personality?" I had to ask.

"Does Jacob have a great personality?"

"Yes, he does."

"And what kind of man does he seem to be?"

"I see your point, Mom," I responded.

"And for the other thing, how many attractive guys were at DJ's that night, without considering whether they can dance or have a great personality?"

"Quite a few," Helen admitted.

Mom hugged me tight, and Dad did the same for Helen. "We love you two more than anything, and we want you to be happy, but that comes from within. No guy can make you happy. Your Mom and I can't make you happy. You can be happy together, but you have to get there with each other."

"Thanks, guys. Now for our final question."

"You want to know what role sex plays in all this."

"That's it, Mom. How did you know?"

"I was once your age, and not too many years ago. I remember my hormones raging and how virtually anything made me get wet. I loved riding horses, too."

Both of us blushed at that. Mom knew how stimulating riding could be.

"Having sex with a guy does not make him fall in love with you. It's the other way around. If you love someone and they love you, sex is a normal, natural thing to do. Take you two, for instance. You fell for each other early, and when you knew you shared your love, your affair just happened. You still love each other, and sometimes I think you are in love with each other. Sex between you, even though you are both girls, is perfectly normal and natural for you. You didn't even have to think about it. It just happened. That is the way it should be. Normal and natural. Loving a guy is no different. Ask yourself how the two of you fell in love, and if you are honest with yourselves, you will have your answer."

I kissed my Mom directly on the lips, a loving, lover's kiss.

Helen kissed Dad, although not so affectionately.

"Thanks, you two."

"Yes, thanks," Helen confirmed.

We got out of their laps and went back to our room.

"What do you think we should do?" Helen asked.

"Let's have some fun!"

"I'm all for that," she agreed.

"Give me the phone."

"I looked for recent calls and found the one from Jacob, then hit call back. It rang."

"Katie?"

"Yes, Jacob. Don't say a word. Just tell me, are you engaged to that sweet Melanie?"

"Yes, I am."

"Are you planning to marry her?"

"I don't know."

"What do you mean you don't know?" Helen was listening to the speakerphone.

"I am not sure anymore."

"Don't you think you might want to tell her that?"

"It would break her heart."

"And what do you think you have already done to her?"

"I just danced with you two and had dinner. It didn't go beyond that."

"Not that you didn't try!"

"I am not perfect, Katie. I have my shortcomings, and I know that, but I don't want to hurt anyone."

"Well, you already have, and until you resolve your issues with Melanie, we don't want to see you again. Do I make myself clear?"

"Perfectly. How do I do that?"

"Try thinking about her for a change instead of just yourself. She is a loving, sensitive girl who is madly in love with you. You might want to take another look at your relationship, with her as the most important person instead of you."

"Have you ever seen her ride, Jacob?"

"No. I knew Melanie rode and took part in the rodeos around here, but I have never seen her on a horse."

"Not even when she had her mount?"

"No, never."

"Do you have any idea how big a part of her life that is?"

"How do you know that?"

"We spent all afternoon with her, Jake. Something I understand you haven't done in quite a while.

"I have been so busy with my company that I haven't had the chance."

"You can go out dancing with all of us, but you can't see your fiancé? Sorry, Jacob, that just doesn't fly."

"Okay, let's say that there is no more thrill in our relationship. Melanie seems to be preoccupied these days."

"And here you have two girls who love dancing with you and enjoyed dinner and, under different circumstances, would both go to bed with you, at the same time I might add, but you treat our precious new friend the way you do? That changes everything, Jake. How do we know you wouldn't treat us the same way?"

"I don't know what to say. Both of you, at the same time?"

"Think about it, Jake, we are going to sleep now, and we have an active day tomorrow. If you come up with something, let us know. Otherwise, we have Melanie's back, and we will take care of her if we can. Goodnight, Jacob." I hung up the phone.

"What do you think about all this?"

"Well, Katie, I think we should focus on the things that make us happy and stay out of situations such as Jacob and Melanie are in."

"I agree. We have the Cheerleaders, our three horses, and each other. What more could we want?"

"No more focusing on guys?"

"No. We are two great girls, and somewhere out there are men who appreciate women like us. They will not disappoint us if we just live our lives and do what Dad and Mom told us."

"Always together? Live together, work together, love together, and have fun together?"

"That sums it up."

"What about Jacob?"

"What about Casey?"

"I see what you mean. We can go dancing with Jake, let him take us to dinner, but I have no desire whatever to get intimate with him."

"Neither do I, dear Helen. I don't even want to go dancing with him or go out to dinner. He is off my list as being too risky. We have each other, and if a guy comes along for either of us, we can explore that. But I am not going off the deep end for a guy unless he is honest, straightforward, and unattached. Hell, we are Dallas Cowboys Cheerleaders. We have it made. I am going to enjoy that."

"Where is my phone?"

"Here it is. Who are you going to call at this time of night?"

"Listen, dear sister. I am taking Mom's advice seriously."

Helen searched through her contacts and found a specific number. She dialed it. When I heard the voice on the other end, I knew she was getting herself in over her head.

"Hello."

"Do you have a few minutes?"

"Helen, is that you?"

"Yes, Casey."

"What a surprise! It's good to hear your voice."

"I have been thinking about you ever since Fox and Friends."

"I have had you on my mind since our first interview."

"What are you going to do about that?"

"Is Katie involved in this?"

"No, Casey. It's just you and me."

"Why are you calling me, Helen? I thought there were too many obstacles to our getting to know each other."

"I am not talking about marrying you or even having an affair. I just want to know if you are the man everyone thinks you are. Is that bad?"

"No, Helen. I have hoped you would give me a chance."

"Next time you are here, we just might have to see."

"You mean you would go out with me?"

"Ask me. We will see, but I think I would if it's just the two of us, and we are discreet."

"I would like that very much. May I check my schedule and get back to you?"

"I would like that very much. Sleep well."

"You, too, Helen." She ended the call.

"What do you think, Katie?"

"Truthfully?"

"Yes. Don't hold anything back."

"I think you are out of your mind."

"Could be, but I want to find out about him."

"You have had a crush on him ever since our first interview."

"Was it that obvious?"

"To me, who knows you so well, yes."

"He'll never call."

"Don't be so sure," I told her. Helen just smiled.

"Let's go to sleep, Katie. We need to get up in the morning."

"I'm for that. Let me hold you, and we'll get a good night's rest."

She moved over to me, and we held each other just as we had since the beginning. I might not have had a boyfriend then, but I had my dear Helen. I wondered how long that would last.

Chapter Twenty-Three

Sometimes Things Work Out Anyway

The next day, after our workout and lunch, we came back to the house looking forward to our upcoming Cheerleader activities. Helen wore a smug smile all morning, making several people wondering what her secret was. I hoped she wouldn't be disappointed. We were about to take care of the horses when Melanie called.

"Katie, would you like some help with the horses this afternoon?"

"Certainly, Melanie. We were going out to take care of them when you called. Come on out here."

"I will. I'm fairly close, so I'll see you in about half an hour."

"Okay, girl. We'll be watching for you."

"Melanie is coming to see us again. Let's meet her at the corral."

"Let's go."

When she drove up, we welcomed her and invited her to work with Blackie. He had spirit, and we hoped she would enjoy him. Helen was feeling frisky after her talk of the night before and wanted to take Romeo, leaving Mandy for me. We rode together for a while so that they all got their exercise. As we were giving them their baths, Melanie took the opportunity to tell us something.

"The last time we were together, I didn't get to tell you two the whole story. I apologize for that."

"What do you mean you didn't tell us the whole story?" I asked.

"When Jacob left me and went his separate way, I made a decision. I regained some of my self-respect that I had lost because of him and resolved that I am not going back to Jacob. I realized that a guy I know has possibilities. When I began to get over Jacob, several other guys began to pay attention to me that had stayed away knowing I was involved. They are all rodeo cowboys, and I like being around them. I love to ride with them and watch them do their rodeo things. Jacob never understood about my fondness for horses. They do."

"Why did you keep Jacob's ring?"

"He told me to. He had given it to me and considered it to be mine. It was a parting gift if you know what I mean, a sort of a bribe to let him go."

"Then, you're engagement to him is over?"

"Yes, we are still engaged officially, but my feelings have changed. Jacob wants a second chance for some reason, probably the sex, but I am delighted doing what I am doing and being with an entirely different group of men."

"Did you love him?"

"I thought so, but when I found out who the true Jacob is, I realized I was just after his lifestyle and what he could give me."

"Are you okay, Melanie," Helen asked.

"No, but I will be fine. Clint and the other guys take wonderful care of me. I didn't handle the thing with Jacob very well, but I am sure he will find what he is looking for in a woman, maybe one of you. I am going on the rodeo circuit with the guys, and we will ride at arenas all over the country."

"Your decision is final, then?"

"Yes, Katie. I have made my decision so that I will travel for a while. I hate that because I just met you two and would love to get to know you both better."

"We will miss you, and so will Romeo."

"I'll miss all of you too. Romeo is quite a ride."

"Do you have enough time to help us brush the horses out?"

"Yes, but I have to leave soon. Clint is coming to take me to the horse barn, and we are going to pick one out for me. He says there are some excellent prospects there."

"Do us a favor, Melanie, while you are trying them out, use a saddle."

"I will. Some of the younger horses can be a bit playful with a new rider."

"Yes, we know."

"I still care for Jacob, and I hope you two or someone else will look after him. He needs a woman in his life." She left us with a wave and a smile. I was glad she had decided to take care of herself and be with good people.

"Katie, how about a soak to end the day?"

"That sounds great. Let's go."

Our suits didn't last long after we got in the hot, swirling water. It felt great. I put Helen in my lap and held her tight. When I moved her chin toward me and kissed her, she kissed me back. It was like old times. I caressed her breasts and slid my other hand down to the triangle between her legs.

"Oh, Katie. I have missed this so much."

"No more, Helen. We are back after we chatted with Mom and will love each other for a long time."

It was getting closer to dinnertime, and the sun was going down when the phone rang. Helen got out of the spa and went to answer it. "Hello, this is Helen."

"Hi, Helen. Henry. How are you doing?"

"We are very well, Henry. Just taking a soak in the spa right now. Why don't you come to join us?"

"I would love to. Can I get a raincheck on the spa?"

"Of course. When are you coming to see me?"

"Before they lock you guys up for the game."

"We have a mandatory rehearsal tomorrow night, so that leaves tonight, Thursday, or Friday."

"How about dancing tonight?"

"Short notice, but you might persuade me with the right argument."

"Okay, just me and you, champagne, your choice of ballroom or country/western music. What kind of mood strikes you?"

"I want to be held by a handsome man and just turn loose for a while."

"We can do that. Where do you live?"

She told him. Fortunately, he was familiar with the area.

"Seven o'clock? Yes, Henry. Come take me away."

"I'll see you shortly."

"I'm looking forward to it. Until then." She ended the call with a massive grin on her face.

"He called me, Katie. He finally called me. This evening could be fun."

"Congratulations, sis. Go have fun."

"Will you be all right if I go out without you?"

"Yes, surely. I think a relaxed evening at home with Mom and Dad will be good for me."

"Thanks, Katie. Let's go inside. It is getting chilly out here."

"Okay. I'll get something together for dinner while you start getting ready." She gave a gleeful jump and giggled at her good luck. We went in.

She went to the back while I made turkey burgers for all of us. I expected Mom and Dad to come home soon, and they might be hungry. I made enough for all four of us. Helen came out with her hair fixed and her makeup done wearing her undergarments covered by a robe. I had seasoned the burger patties well, so she just melted some butter over them and ate the whole thing. Henry was right on time. I showed him in and welcomed him while Helen finished creating her most beautiful look. I sat with Henry until she was ready, and when she came out to us, Henry went over to greet her, kissed her, and they were on their way, both smiling broadly. I was alone for the first time in weeks.

The house phone rang again. I didn't recognize the number. "Hello."

"Katie, this is your father. Your Mom is with me."

"Where are you, Dad?"

"We are in New Orleans. This afternoon, I got a call that they needed me on a project here, and I called your Mom and invited her to go with me for some R&R."

"Okay, when are you coming home?"

"The job should take a couple of days, and we are going to partake of the local food and drink. It's a fun place to spend a few days."

"Well, enjoy yourselves, you two."

"We will. Is Helen there with you?"

"No. Helen is out on a date but will be back later."

"I understand. It's good for Helen to go out."

"Yes, it is."

"Tell her we said hello, and you two enjoy yourselves while we are gone. One of us will call you later and let you know when we are coming home."

"Sounds good. Have a Hurricane for me."

"We will, Katie. Goodnight." He hung up the phone.

I let Rex in to keep me company and thought about what I wanted to do. I decided to make myself a drink and relax. I was almost asleep when my cell phone rang. Now, who could that be?

I answered with a yawn, "Hello."

"Melanie said she told you what was happening."

"Jacob, Hi. Yes, she told us this afternoon."

"I couldn't tell you myself because I didn't think you would believe me. It had to come from Melanie."

"Yes, it did. Do you know Clint?"

"No, I have never met him, but she likes him."

"She is very attracted to the rodeo world."

"Yes, she is." He paused. "Katie, does this affect you and me in any way?"

"Yes, Jake. Your holding back from me and what you did to Melanie was a definite factor in what happened to us."

"She is no longer around, Katie, and I appreciate that you would not betray your riding buddy. Do I have any kind of chance with you, Katie?"

"No, Jacob. If there is one thing I cannot stand, it is dishonesty, with a friend or especially with me. I cannot trust you, Jacob, and trust is a major part of a relationship."

"What are you doing tonight, Katie?"

"I have no plans, but you may as well forget it, Jake. I have no intention of seeing you tonight or any night."

"Is Helen there with you?"

"No. Helen has a date with Henry tonight."

"You know he is crazy about her, right?"

"He certainly waited long enough to call her and ask her out."

"He's shy when he feels vulnerable."

"Leave that to Helen. She has a way of instilling confidence in people. My parents aren't here either. They are in New Orleans for a few days."

"You are alone, then?"

"Yes, and I am going to enjoy the evening by myself for a change.

"Will you hear me out, Katie? You have heard Melanie's story, but you haven't heard mine. You seem to have made up your mind about me, but at least let me have a chance to talk to you before you shut me out completely. Will you see me one more time? If, after that, you still want me out of your life, I will kiss you on the cheek, leave, and wish you well."

"Why should I, Jacob? What is it with you. I told you we had no chance, and yet you won't go away. I don't understand."

"Katie, despite the situation with Melanie, and getting so much attention from the other girls. And even though I was able to charm Carolyn and Kelli, none of that means anything. I came back to you that night because I fell in love with you, and I love you now even more than I did then. I loved our date and being with you. You are the woman for whom I have searched all my life, and now that I have found you, I will do anything not to lose you."

I didn't know what to say, so I said nothing.

"Katie, are you still there?"

I make up my mind, and even though I probably would regret it later, I knew I would see him.

"I can offer you a drink and will hear you out. Come now before I change my mind."

"Are you inviting me to come to see you tonight?"

"Yes, Jacob, that is just what I'm doing."

"Are you sure?"

"No, I'm not, but I want us to be friends, at least. I will tell you that I love dancing with you."

"Do you want to go dancing tonight?"

"No. I want to spend the evening with you, talking about things and getting to know each other better. We can go dancing another time."

"Another time?"

"Yes, Jacob. My Dad told me that if you ask me out, I should go, but tonight we have an unusual opportunity just to spend time together, no sister, no parents, and no Cheerleaders. It will be just you and me. I must warn you that this is your last chance, Jacob. Don't blow it."

"I'll be there in just a little while."

"Bring your swim trunks. I like to talk in the spa."

"Okay, Katie, I will. See you in a few minutes."

"Come on, Jake."

"On my way," and he ended the call.

What to wear? He had seen me dressed up and liked that, but tonight, I wanted to be different. I would make no special effort with my hair and no obsession with makeup or my outfit. A DCC jersey and gym shorts would be perfect. I washed my face, put on a little lip gloss, and brushed my hair. I left my feet bare. Did he like me, or was it just the glamorous Cheerleader image that interested him? Tonight, he was getting the everyday, ordinary me. I hoped he would dress comfortably.

I saw his headlights as he drove down the driveway and parked in front of the house. He knocked rather than ringing the doorbell. I opened the door and invited him in, closing and locking it behind him. He took me in his arms and lowered his head to give me a kiss I was reluctant to receive, but I kissed him back, surprised that I enjoyed his affection. It was a platonic, welcoming kiss.

"Have you eaten, Jake?"

"Yes, I grabbed a bite before I left home, but thanks."

"Then, may I fix you something to drink?"

"That I would love. Scotch and soda, please."

I led him by the hand over to the couch and let him sit while I went to make the drinks. I made mine light, but made his full-strength and let Rex in, introducing him to Jacob. The big dog showed his approval with energetic tail wagging and asking for attention. Jacob petted him, and he curled up at Jake's feet. I was amazed that Rex liked him, and his acceptance of Jacob set my mind to thinking.

"Here's to new beginnings," he offered a toast.

"New beginnings," I echoed him.

He was wearing jeans with a nice shirt, and boots He had a thin gold necklace and looked very manly. His outfit matched his personality perfectly.

"You look very good to me tonight, Kate. I like you in comfortable attire. I feel I can be myself and relax with you."

"I am glad, Jake. I spend so much of my time either in uniform or dressed up, both of which I enjoy, but sometimes it is nice to dress down and relax. Would you like to take a dip in the pool or the spa?"

"I would like that very much. Where can I change?"

"Use my room. First on the left."

"Okay. Be right back."

"I'll change too. We'll meet back here in a few minutes."

"First, I want another kiss," he asked politely.

This time, he didn't hold back at all. He opened his soul to me with that kiss, bringing my senses to their height. I was surprised to feel the electricity running through me, and I think he liked it. Thoughts of the soak dissipated as our kiss continued. I was giving in. The more he kissed me, the more excited I got. No man had ever made me feel this way, dammit! I pressed up against his hips and felt the bulge in his pants, and couldn't resist touching him there. He sighed when I did and intensified our kiss. I had to pull back from him, or I would be lost. I was alone with a very sexy man for the first time since I moved to Texas.

Jacob looked deep in my eyes, picked me up in his strong arms, took me back to my bedroom, and put me down on the bed. He had taken total control of the situation, and I was cautiously willing to let him do so. How long had it been? My reservations gave way to repressed passion. He removed my jersey and pulled my shorts off, leaving me completely naked. His jeans fell to the floor as soon as he stood, and I saw a magnificent sight. His penis was erect and looked very good to me. I reached out and took it in my hand, feeling him throbbing and pulsing is his excitement. What was happening to me? I moved over a little, and he got in bed with me, finding the wetness between my legs as he kissed and nibbled my nipples and breasts. I closed my eyes and gave myself to him ultimately. I knew then that I was going to fuck this man.

He moved on top of me and coated his erection with my juices for lube. I spread my legs to ensure he could get a lot on him and then guided him to my vaginal opening. When I gently pulled on him, he got the idea and took me quickly but did not go all the way in. I pushed back on him, and his second thrust buried him deep in my vagina. I saw stars and heard my moans getting louder and louder.

He was gentle at first but became more energetic as we moved together. The feelings he was giving me were familiar, but I had not felt that way in a long time, if ever. This man was a lover, and he was making love to me. I clutched the covers and felt myself responding to him powerfully. He knew how to take me to the top and made it about me and my passion, proving once again that good dancers are usually good lovers. He felt so good deep inside me, and I felt the fires rising in my psyche. He felt it too and redoubled his efforts to bring me to the pinnacle of my passion. It worked. My toes curled, and I wrapped my arms and legs around him, wanting him never to leave that bed. He shifted his hips to get deeper in me, and my orgasm exploded in ecstasy. I gushed around his hardness as I felt him come with me. He buried himself as deep as he could go and filled me with his cum. I came again. He did too. One more load from him and he collapsed on top of me. I kept him inside me as long as possible and then let him roll to my side. I kissed him tenderly and held him tight.

"Jacob, that was wonderful. You are amazing."

"You are special to me, Katie, and I had wanted that ever since our first waltz when we danced so close to each other. Finally, I could do something about it."

"You were loyal to Melanie?"

"Yes."

"You are an amazing man, Jacob. I am so glad things worked out this way. I have had a crush on you since that evening and hoped I could get to know you better, someway, somehow. I was angry with you and what you did to Melanie until I knew the whole story, and I haven't forgotten." I kissed him and asked, "Will you stay with me tonight?"

"Are you sure, Katie?"

"Very sure. I don't want you to leave."

"Isn't there someone special in your life?"

"Just Helen."

"You two seem to have a wonderful relationship."

"We do. We sleep together in this very bed. Does that bother you?"

"No, as long as you don't leave me for her," he joked.

"Some guys are not as accepting as you."

"You also have the other Cheerleaders with whom you spend a lot of time."

"You know they loved dancing with you."

"I just wanted to get back to you as soon as I could."

"And you did. Are you ready for that soak now that we have taken care of our mutual attraction?"

"Sure. Just let me put my trunks on, and we can go."

"No need for that. The pool area is very secluded, and Helen and I don't usually wear anything when we are using either the pool or the spa. I'll get us some beach jackets and towels, and we can just go down there and enjoy another aspect of our being together. You game?"

"Yes. You bet. Let's go."

We did. The spa felt good in the fresh night air. I embraced Jake and held him close to me. He kept me in his arms, too. I loved being naked beside a male body and touching and kissing him. If the water had not already been hot, we would have heated it significantly. I couldn't believe what was happening to us. Would this work out? I hoped so. After a relaxing time, we went back inside. I would have him with me all night long.

Chapter Twenty-Four

Could This Be the Start of Something Big?

We put on robes and slippers to relax again, and I fixed us drinks. Jake would not leave my side and touched me and kissed me repeatedly. I loved his affection and attention. We smiled at each other a lot and couldn't take our eyes off each other. Being with Jacob felt like the most natural thing in the world. I realized that Melanie was wrong about him. He was a fantastic lover and made me feel special.

"Thinking about when Helen comes home, I need to change the sheets on our bed so that she will be comfortable."

"What about us?"

"We will sleep in Mom and Dad's bed in the master bedroom. It is big and can be a lot of fun. Does that sound okay to you?"

"Yes, I like that idea. How long are your mom and dad going to be gone?"

"Dad said a few days, and they will call us when they have decided to return. Would you like to stay here with me until they come back?"

"How could I refuse an offer like that?"

"I love you, Jake, damn me, I do."

"Go make the bed. Want some help?"

"Of course. You need to see what goes on around here."

"I love you too, Katie. Will you introduce me to the horses?"

"Yes, of course. Ours could always use another human to give them attention."

"Maybe before you change the sheets, we should take advantage of them again."

"I'll get a clean towel. Come with me, lover."

"Lead on, my dear. That sounds good."

"I thought you might like it."

"Tell me what you love, Jacob. How can I turn you on totally?"

"I love what we have done already. I have never felt the way you make me feel."

"Get me very wet and gushing. I love it too."

His technique with his fingers was very gentle and stimulating. Much to my surprise, he moved his head between my legs and used his tongue and lips, teasing and gently sucking on my private parts. He was very good at it. Before long, he had me flying on a cloud of desire. This man was a lover, and he loved me. When he entered me, he went all the way this time. I guess I had loosened up some in our previous encounter. I could feel him pressing against the back of my vagina, and the feeling was exquisite. I used my muscles to stimulate him further, and he came violently and dramatically, losing himself in what I was doing to him. I felt myself coming closer and closer until I could hold back no longer. I came immediately after him, and we both tensed and went rigid in our sexual bliss. He took me to orgasm again, and this time, I collapsed under him. He had one more stream to impart to me before his erection receded, and he rolled off me. The towel absorbed much of our fluids.

I moved closer to him, and he took me in his arms and embraced me. He had changed my life in just an evening of dancing, a double date, and an evening together alone at my house. The evening alone was not even over yet. I wanted to wake up with him and make love again. We both drifted off for a while but awoke after recovering from our loving. We even had enough energy to change the sheets on the bed and retreat to the master bedroom and the big bed. It was natural that we went to sleep immediately in each other's embrace. I couldn't remember when I had felt as happy as I did with him holding me in his arms.

The next thing we knew, someone was getting in the big bed with us. Of course, it was Helen. She found room behind Jacob so that he was between us. We both looked sleepily at her, and I said, "welcome home, sis."

"Thanks, Katie. Hi Jacob. Glad to see you again."

"How was the date?"

"It was okay. Henry wanted to take me home with him, but I told him I had an early morning and needed to go home. He understood and brought me back. I like him."

"I am glad," I told her.

"What's going on with you two?"

"We are in love," Jake answered. "I am never letting Katie go."

"How do you feel about that, Katie?"

"I am never letting him go, either. We are together and will remain together."

"Great! I am so happy for both of you. You must tell me what the hell happened to change your mind, Katie. Now, can we get some sleep?"

"Yes, dear sister. You keep him warm from that side, and I will do the same over here, but watch out. He is something else in bed."

"Then Melanie was wrong?"

"Very wrong. This man is a lover."

Jacob kissed me and turned to kiss Helen, and we all three went to sleep. We made quite a threesome and slept very well.

The next morning, we fed Jacob our usual breakfast, and he left for work. He was in Dallas for the week and promised to be home for dinner. We went for our exercise routine and finished with lunch several hours later. I was joyous through it all and felt great despite the drinks we shared and the late night. Fond memories stayed with me all morning, and I knew Jacob would be back with me tonight.

When we returned home, we got a call from Mom and Dad. They had just gotten out of bed after a long night out on the town. They were enjoying New Orleans and all the city had to offer. "How are you guys doing, Katie?" Mom asked.

"We are doing very well. Is Dad there with you?"

"Right here, daughter."

"I have an update on Jacob, Dad."

"Really? What is it?"

"It turns out that he is not engaged after all. Melanie, his erstwhile fiancée, broke it off so she could travel the rodeo circuit with her new boyfriend."

"How did you find that out?"

"She told me and asked for Helen and me to keep an eye on Jake to make sure he was doing okay."

"You are not telling me everything, Katie. What are you holding back?"

"I invited him to visit me last night to talk things out. Helen had a date, and Jake and I spent the evening alone. We used the spa and got to know each other much better."

"Katie, I know I told you if he asks you out, you should go. Is he all right after his breakup?"

"Yes, Dad. It had been coming for a long time."

"How did the evening go?"

"I think I am falling for him, Dad."

"Do you want us to come home?"

"No, not until you are ready. I have Helen with me, and he likes us both. When it comes to dancing, he likes the entire Cheerleader team, but he wants to be with me. Mom, are you hearing this?"

"Yes, Katie. I am happy for you."

"Thanks, Mom. I like him a lot."

"How does he feel about your being a Cheerleader and everything associated with it?"

"He is perfectly all right with it. Besides, he works a lot at his job. He runs that company."

"I know, Katie. It sounds like a situation with which I am very familiar."

"Thanks for blazing the trail for me and advising me on how to handle this affair."

"Did you say affair, Katie?" Dad picked up on what I had said inadvertently.

I paused before answering him. "Yes, I did, Dad. He stayed here last night with me. Helen joined us when she got back from her date. We made quite a threesome."

"I can imagine," Mom commented. "Is she having an affair with him too?"

"No. Jake and I have something special, and Helen has other interests."

"You spent an entire evening apart last night?"

"Yes, until she came home. I think it will be all right if we are not together all the time. We are together quite a lot with all our activities."

"How does Jacob feel about that?"

"He liked sleeping with both of us last night. She kept him warm from the back, and I did the same from the front."

"Is he coming back tonight?"

"Yes. When the workday ends."

"Feed him well, Katie, but not so well that he wants to move in with us," Mom joked.

"We have a long way to go before anything like that might come up."

"Are you happy about all this, Katie?"

"Yes, Dad, very happy."

"I'm glad. We won't worry about you and your sister, at least until we get back."

"Not even then, Dad. Enjoy New Orleans and come home soon."

"We will. You and Helen enjoy yourselves while we are gone."

"We will you two. See you soon."

"Okay. Until later."

"Later."

"I thought they took that rather well," I said to Helen, who had been listening.

"Yes, so did I. Dad and now Mom thinks a lot of him."

"Why didn't you tell them about Henry?"

"There is nothing to tell. I like Henry, but I am not ready for a physical relationship with him."

"Of course, telling them about your other guy would never go over. Mom would tell Carolyn, and that would be the end of that."

"I'm sure they will find out if things begin to happen, but by then, I should know what I want to know."

"Don't let anyone tell you what they think. I listened to Melanie, and she was wrong."

"Let's go feed the horses, and we can come back and take a soak while you tell me all about you and Jacob."

"Okay. Let's change into our riding clothes and go take care of them."

As usual, they all came running to us. Romeo nudged me with his nose and gave me his head. I couldn't resist his request and put his bridle on him before climbing on his back and taking him out of the corral. He was exceptionally playful and started dancing as soon as we cleared the gate. I praised him and patted his neck to encourage him even more. I directed him into a canter, and he was very light on his feet, prancing around, flipping his tail, and letting his mane fly in the wind. He was waiting for my signal to break out into a gallop, so I loosened my hold on the reins and clucked to him. He was ready and did his leap while I held on and moved up farther on his neck. I took him around the pasture several times, and he didn't even get winded. He was in great shape from our working with him.

"Helen, do you want to take a turn on him?"

"Absolutely! He looks full of spirit today."

I dismounted, and he rubbed me with his head again as Helen took the reins. Blackie and Mandy were just hungry, although Blackie snorted a couple of times and stomped his front foot, letting me know that he thought I was taking too long. I put the feedbag on them both. Helen's red hair flowed out behind her as she rode the stallion. They liked each other and made a fantastic picture galloping across the grass. Romeo finally slowed down some, and Helen brought him back to the corral, where we tethered him loosely and got the horse shampoo and water. He loved getting a bath. Then the two of us brushed him dry and made him look incredible. I gave him his apple and put his feedbag on him. Soon he began munching hungrily and finished his oats quickly. I took his bridle off and let him go with a kiss and a few loving pats. He thanked me his usual way and returned to the pasture and the other horses. Helen and I headed for the house.

"It's time for their vet visit and an appointment with the farrier. I'll call and set it up."

"Katie. I want to be here when they come."

"We will both be there."

"Spa now?"

"Yes, I could use a soak."

"Me too, and you can tell me all about Jacob and last night."

"Keep it to yourself?"

"Absolutely. Not even the parents will hear a thing from me."

"Okay. I'll tell you everything."

"That's what I want."

"Bikinis and towels. Let's go."

The bikinis came off as soon as we hit the water. The spa felt so good, and we relaxed in each other's arms. It was different from being with Jake, but I loved Helen, and she loved me. It was still good.

"So, tell me about last night."

"I told him it was over and that he did not have a chance with me. Jacob told me I had not heard the whole story, and he hoped I would listen to him. His argument was compelling. I invited him to come to the house and promised to listen. Against my better judgment, I decided to give him another chance. We shared a platonic kiss, and I sat him down with a drink. One thing led to another, and he kissed me a great kiss, and we embraced. I kissed him back. I invited him to accompany me to the spa, and we went to change, but before we were able to do so, while I was trying to decide what to do, he decided for us both. He picked me up and took me to our bed, where he took off my clothes. I returned the favor, got him hard and wet with my juices, and he took me for the first time. It was splendid. I knew then that Melanie was wrong about him."

"The first time? Tell me more."

"I had almost forgotten what being with a loving man was like, but he showed me plainly. We went to the spa and soaked a while, embracing and touching. We couldn't take our eyes off each other. I wanted him again, so I took him inside, and we made love for the second time in less than an hour. He took me to the heights of my passion and exploded inside me. He showed me his oral skills before the second time, and he knew how to excite a woman, at least this woman."

"Then what happened?"

"We went to sleep together, fully planning another encounter. When you found us, we were glad to have you join us. We kept Jake warm all night. Helen, I have fallen in love with him and he with me. I know it has just been one evening of dancing, with a bunch of our colleagues, a date with the two of us, and last night. He wants us to introduce him to the horses, too. I could spend a lot of time with him."

"Sorry I showed up and ruined your plans."

"Don't be. We had a great evening with incredible sex, and having you join us was like icing on the cake. I am glad you slept with us."

"What time do you think he will come back after work?"

"I don't know, but I think we should feed him well tonight. For enjoyment and to give him energy for us."

"I am not going to join in your romantic activities. You need that man for yourself. It is about time, dear sister."

"We will see what happens, Helen. It's going to take some time to get to know who he is. Besides, how long has it been for you?"

"Are you willing to share your man with me?"

"If I did, would you be interested? He likes you too."

"Is he as good a lover as you say he is?"

"I suspect he is even better, and it will come out as we get to know him."

"Katie, I think you are considering much more than just dating him."

"What do you mean?"

"What are you going to do when he asks you to come to his house and stay there?"

"I like it here."

"Yeah, but Mom and Dad will be back soon, and it won't be our place anymore."

"No more overnight stays?"

"I don't think they would be very enthusiastic about their daughter's lover spending the night with her."

"I see what you mean."

"Do you even know where he lives? A house? An apartment?"

"No, I don't. It hasn't come up."

"Do you know if he has other entanglements in his life?"

"No, I don't."

"But you are enraptured by him."

"Yes. What should I do?"

"You're asking me?"

"Yes, Helen, at least for your opinion."

"I know the throes of passion are potent emotions, and that you have found someone whom you like. Don't let the passion cool down. Use it. Capture Jake and his affections and hold on with all you have and are. If it works out, consider yourself lucky. If not, go on with your life. You are a fantastic woman Katie, and you have everything a man could want. Don't hold back, but be aware that men are just humans too."

"Thanks, sis. I will remember that, but while it lasts, I am going to enjoy it."

"You should. Men like Jake come along only infrequently. He loves you, and he will fall even deeper in love with you. When he asks you to marry him, go with your feelings, and you will know what to do."

We didn't hear him drive up or come in, but suddenly we saw him standing inside the sliding doors. I waved him to come on out, and he joined us.

"Something in a soak, Jacob?"

"With two gorgeous, unclad ladies like you? Where do I sign up?"

"No sign up required, put your clothes on the chaise lounge and come on in."

After a few petties for Rex, in less than a minute, he was in the spa with us. We both hugged and kissed him, although my kiss was much more erotic than Helen's, and he took us both in his arms and embraced us. He wouldn't let go. We hugged him back.

"You are back early, Jake."

"I couldn't stay away, knowing I had you two to come back to."

"Both of us?"

"Yes, how can I choose?"

"You already did, Jacob," Helen answered. "I think I might leave you two alone."

"No, Helen. I don't want you to leave me alone with this guy. Not yet, that is."

"So, while you love each other, what am I supposed to do?"

"Love on us too?"

With that, I embraced her and kissed her erotically and romantically. Then I gave her to Jacob, and he did the same thing. She wouldn't turn loose of either of us and began to cry. "I'm so afraid I am going to lose you, Katie, even to a great guy like Jake. We have become so close to each other with Cheerleaders, becoming sisters, Mom and Dad's marriage and continuing honeymoon, the horses, and all the other things we share."

"Jacob, are you going to propose to me tonight?"

"No, Katie. Not tonight."

"See, Helen, I am not going anywhere."

"And for now, if Jacob agrees, we are going to be three, just as we were when we went out together last time."

"I agree. We are becoming close, and being with both of you is wonderful."

Helen's phone rang. "Hello, this is Helen, what can I do for you?"

"Am I interrupting anything?" the male voice asked tentatively.

"No, we are just sitting here talking about things." She had turned on the speakerphone feature.

Jacob got a surprised look on his face when he recognized the voice and realized who it was calling Helen.

"I know you are not alone."

"Yes, in fact, I am. After the TV show and your goodbye kiss, I haven't been able to get you off my mind."

"So, what are you going to do about it?"

"Take you to dinner?"

"Just me? No, Katie or anyone else?"

"Just you, Helen."

"When are you going to be in Dallas again?"

"Next weekend. I will be in the booth for the game."

"Next weekend? That's over a week away. Who knows what might happen during that time? Besides, I will be with the other girls on Wednesday, and Saturday night, and Sunday after the game, I will need to recover some. When did you want to see me?"

"I'll send a car for you on Friday night to bring you to Dallas. We will have dinner and see where things go from there."

"All right. If we keep a low profile and are unobtrusive, I will come. No press. No cameras."

"Done."

"Okay, Casey. You have a date. Just remember that if anyone in the Cheerleader organization finds out, nothing good can happen."

"Thank you, Helen. I will do as you ask and am looking forward to it."

"Call me when you get to town, so I will know you made it."

"I will. Even before then, if that is all right with you."

"Please do. Have a great evening, Casey. Keep in touch."

"Goodnight, Helen, and thanks again. We will have some fun."

Helen switched her phone off and held it to her breast with a big smile on her face. Jacob was speechless.

"Have you lost your mind completely, sis?"

"Don't worry, Katie? It will never happen. Something will come up."

"And what if it does happen? What if he sends the car just as he said he would, and you meet him for dinner in Dallas?"

"Then I will be able to say that I had a dinner date with him and will go on from there."

"And if he wants to do more than kissing?"

"I'll take care of that when the time comes."

Helen stayed in her mind for the rest of the evening. The dream she had harbored ever since our first interview was all she could think about, at least that is what I thought.

"Are you all right, sis?"

"In my dreams, maybe. In real life, I still don't have a man or a clue."

"Henry liked you. What about him?"

"What did you two do? Fall in love first, then get intimate, or the other way around?"

"We knew we were in love before we ever slept together," Jacob answered.

"Henry wants the sex first, hoping that love will develop. He has a lot to learn about women and relationships, and I don't give lessons."

Chapter Twenty-Five

A Very Confused Redhead

After dinner, we got a phone call.

"Hey, girls!"

"Hello, Dad. How are you and Mom doing?"

"We are fine, and we are coming home."

"That's great. When do you think you will get here?"

"We plan to leave tomorrow morning and should be back sometime in the afternoon. Do we still have a bed we can use?"

"Of course. We'll get it ready for you."

"Is Helen there with you?"

She answered, "Yes, Dad, you know us. We are still inseparable."

"Has Jacob come home after work?"

"Yes, Dad. He just came home."

"Hi, Helen," it was Mom. "Still, inseparable? I'm glad."

"Yes, Mom. Some things have happened since you two left for New Orleans. We will be so glad to have you back. A mom and a dad are essential in a girl's life."

"What are you not telling us, Helen?"

"We have a new addition to our lives. We are now three inseparables."

"Jacob?"

"Yes, Mom, Jacob has joined us."

"I'm so happy for all three of you. You can tell us all about it tomorrow. Do we have a new Son-in-Law, if I may ask?"

"No, nothing like that. We haven't decided what to do with me yet. We could use your input."

"Mom," I said, "he goes to work, and we go do our thing with the Cheerleaders. The rest of the time, we stay together. Jake can ride as well as he dances. We are having a lot of fun together."

"What about Helen?"

"I'm doing great, Mom. Jacob and Katie take excellent care of me. The only thing is we are one guy short."

"That's okay, though. Our bed only holds three."

"So, Jacob has joined you?"

"I told you we were inseparable."

"I can't wait to get back to you. Thanks for telling us about this."

"You know we tell you and dad everything," Helen assured her.

"I get the feeling there is more."

"There is always more, Mom. You two come home, and we'll tell you the rest when we can talk face to face."

"That serious, huh?"

"You will just have to come home, and you can decide whether it is serious or not. We have not decided that yet."

"Does it involve a couple of rings, flowers, and a church?"

"No, Mom. Nobody is getting married. At least not yet."

"How is Melanie?"

"We haven't heard from her since she left with her rodeo cowboy. No doubt, she is fine."

"That's good news. You guys get ready for us. We are coming home tomorrow."

"Will do, Mom. Have a good flight."

"Thanks, Helen, Katie. We'll see you soon. Sleep well tonight."

"We will. Enjoy your last night in the Big Easy. If you can, call us when you get on the ground after your flight."

"We'll try. Until then."

"Until then." The conversation ended.

"I guess we have to come to a couple of decisions, don't we?" she asked.

"Yes, Helen, Jake, we need to be able to tell them what we are doing and what we want."

"Jacob, you start."

"Katie. That is not very difficult for me. I know what I want."

"Okay, go."

"I am doing everything I can do to love you two wonderful ladies, especially you, Katie. You see, I am deeply in love with you, and I love Helen dearly. What I want is to live with the two of you, wherever we can find a place, and stay together. I want to spend all my time with you, although I love my work and riding with you. Three horses, three riders. Whatever your parents say, I am not leaving."

We both kissed him when he said that.

"Helen, the floor is yours now."

"Thanks, Katie. What we are doing is love each other. What I want is what I have, my beloved sister, and our wonderful Jacob. I want to keep on doing our Cheerleader thing and ride the horses with the two of you. What I don't want, but have no doubt created for myself, is a lot of drama in my life. No man is worth that."

"What are you going to tell Mom and Dad about your New York connection?"

"I am going to tell them what is happening and not keep them in the dark about my relationship, if there is one, with a certain football star. What about you, Katie?"

"What I am doing is falling deeper and deeper in love with you, Jacob. What I want is for us to be together until the time comes when Helen finds a man she can love as well. Until then, both of us will love her, and we will sleep together while we find out about ourselves."

"Aside from that, the same as you, Helen. I have just begun my career as a Cheerleader and love it. I want to keep developing Romeo and ride every day. It is also imperative that I don't lose my dear sister."

"Is this the last night we will be able to sleep together now that your parents are coming home tomorrow?"

"No!!" I responded. "Tonight, dear Jacob, would you make love to both of us?"

"Both of you?"

"That's what I said. Both of us."

"You want that to happen before they get back?"

"Yes, Jacob. I want it to happen tonight."

"Don't I have a say in this?" Helen asked.

"Of course, Helen. Is there a problem?"

"Yes. I am not in love with Jacob, and having sex with him is not a priority of mine, nothing against you, Jake."

"I understand, Helen. My being in love with Katie makes me only want her. It may happen for you and me sometime in the future, but for now, my heart is full of love for her."

I loved what I heard from Helen and Jacob. She would sleep with us tonight, and Jacob was going to stay true to me. My tears began to flow. "You two love me very much. Jacob, if you asked me to marry you right now, I would say, 'Yes.' I know now that we three can make it together, no matter what happens."

"Will you marry me, Katherine?"

"Yes, Jacob, I will. There are several married Cheerleaders and see no reason why one should preclude the other."

Helen started to cry, too, as she embraced the two of us. "You guys are going to be fine, but you don't have to do anything quickly. I will be there for both of you."

Jacob took her arms off him and embraced us both. "I love you both more than I have ever loved before. Our lives are going to be great!"

"We will wait until the season is over, and we get a break. Then we will do it. Is that all right with you two?"

"Yes, Katie. My Mr. Right could come along in the meantime, who knows?"

"Yes, who knows? Will you take us to bed now, Jacob?"

"Yes, my dears. The big bed for the last time?"

"Yes, we can change the sheets and things in the morning to get ready for Mom and Dad.

"Sounds good to me."

"If you change your mind about Helen, I will be there to help you out."

"Thanks, Katie, but I have decided."

"Then let's get some sleep."

He escorted us back to the master bedroom, and we changed for the night. As usual, we put him in the middle with each of us on one side of him and holding him tightly. He was still my love, but now he was much more. He was my betrothed, my fiancée. How would Mom and Dad react to that? We would find out tomorrow.

"I must admit that I am perplexed about what is happening to us right now," Helen said when we were all together in the big bed.

"Can we help," Jacob asked her.

"I don't know. Here I am in bed with a gorgeous, sexy man, and for some reason, I am not raping you. What's with that, Jake?"

"You love Katie and me so much that you do not see me as a suitor. You still have your relationship with her, and you are not putting any pressure on either of us. It is an act of love, Helen."

"I don't know, Jake. I think I have my attention on someone else."

"You mean Casey?"

"Yes. I have dreamed of being with that guy ever since our first interview, but no one seems to understand."

"You will find out soon, Helen, and if things don't work out, come back to us. We both love you very much and want you to be happy."

"I will, I promise. Do you think I am foolish?"

"No, Helen, I don't. You need to find out, and you are about to do that."

"Hold me, please, Jake. I need a strong man to wrap himself around me and love me. Tonight, that man is you."

"Katie?"

"Go ahead, Jake. Hold her until she wants you to turn loose. I will be right behind you and will hold you too.

"Thanks, Katie. I am so tired. I may go to sleep quickly."

"I will hold you while you sleep, Helen," Jacob promised.

"That will be nice. Good night you two. I love you both very much."

"We love you, Helen. Sleep well."

We were asleep in each other's arms in just a few minutes, and we slept soundly until morning. We had our usual breakfast and fed Jacob well before he left for work. Both Helen and I hated to see him go, but for very different reasons. I wanted to go back to bed with him, and Helen just wanted to get attention from him. We would have time for both later.

Our workouts were energetic and heated. I was able to keep up with Helen as were several of the other girls. They were coming along very well. The sky kicks and power splits were not as daunting to them as they had been. The trainers had done a fantastic job with all of us. They smiled at our progress all the time, knowing we would have a tremendous performance on Sunday.

"Come guide me through this, Katie, please. See if I am doing it correctly," were common requests from them. We all stayed through lunch. Helen and I were ecstatic about their progress.

When lunch was over, we got in the BMW and headed for home. Much to our surprise, we saw Dad's Lincoln parked in front of the house. "They're home!" exclaimed Helen.

"It looks like it. Let's go greet our folks and welcome them back."

I got out of the car quickly, but Helen was way ahead of me. She rushed into the house, found Mom, embraced her, and wouldn't let her go. She began to cry. "I am so glad you are home. We missed you so much through all that has happened this past week, and now, finally, you are here." Dad went over to them, and Helen embraced him too. He looked at mom over Helen's shoulder with a look of bewilderment, and mom shook her head, letting him know that she didn't have a clue.

"Come over here, Helen, sit between us and tell us all about it."

"The good part is that Romeo loves me, and he responds to me as if we were reading each other's minds. Plus, the girls are getting so good at their routines using our diet and training methods that we are looking fantastic as a group. One mindset governs us all. I'll let Katie tell you the wonderful things that have happened to her before I launch into my problems. Are you sure you don't want a break or something to eat or drink? Maybe we should feed you first."

"We had something when we got home. We took an earlier flight and arrived about an hour ago. Now tell us what's going on." Helen's tears returned.

"I am so happy for Katie, but I don't know what it means for me."

I spoke up. "Mom and Dad, last night, Jacob proposed to me."

"Oh, Honey. I know he must have been devastated when you told him, no, it's too soon, and you don't know each other."

I looked at Helen, needing some support from my dear sister.

She took up the narrative. "She didn't tell Jake no, Mom and Dad. She accepted, and that is the problem. I am going to lose my beloved sister and lover, my soulmate, and I can't face that."

"You told him yes, Katie?"

"Yes, Mom and Dad. I accepted, but on the condition that we wait, and I can stay with Helen whom I love very much, and we can keep doing our Cheerleader things, and keep the horses in our lives."

"A lot of things must have happened while we were away. Are you really in love?"

"Mom, they are crazy about each other. Jake has been our third member since you two left. I have never seen two people who were more in love than they are."

"Are you sure, Katie?"

"Yes, Mom, I am, but I am not going to give up my sister or my life. We must find a way to make it all work out. I cannot give up on Jacob, and I will not give up Helen. And there is the problem."

"You are engaged to Jake, but the three of you are sleeping together?"

"Yes, Mom," answered Helen, "but Jake and I have not engaged in sex and have no plans to do so. Katie loves him, and he loves her. I will not put myself in the middle of their love for each other."

"Mike, we never should have left them. If we can find a way for everyone to get what they want in this situation, it will be magic. What do you think?"

"We need Jacob to be here. What he thinks is crucially important. What time does he usually get home after work?"

"He will be here in time for dinner, which gives us enough time to take care of the horses and give Rex his daily attention. He can come with us out to the corral, and we will see that he also gets his exercise. Let's put on our riding clothes, Helen. Would either or both of you like to join us?"

"I think your Mom and I need a few minutes to talk. Why don't you go on out and we might join you?"

"Okay, Dad. We'll be back shortly." We started for the corral.

"We told them," I said to Helen, "now let's see what they do about it."

"I am not so sure Mom took it very well."

"She did better than I thought she would do. Now we just have to stay occupied until Jake comes home."

Unknown to us, Dad watched us as we went out to the corral. The horses, all three of them, came running to us. "Jackie, would you look at this? Most people must bribe their horses to get them to come to them, but our girls have a horse magnet. All of them are running into the corral, and the girls haven't made a sound. They came when they saw them coming. What else have they done with them?"

Mom and Dad were soon to find out. They all three wanted their bridles and human attention. Romeo was beside himself when I bridled him and hopped up on his back while

Helen took care of Blackie and Mandy. She mounted Blackie with Mandy's reins in her hand so that she would follow along. It was the only way we could exercise all of them when there were just two of us. I gave Romeo his head right out of the corral, and he treated me to an incredibly energetic ride around the pasture and through all his gaits and paces. I praised him the whole way. He was genuinely magnificent that afternoon. We seldom used saddles on them anymore, so we could be touching them and feeling their muscles as we rode. Blackie had picked up on many of Romeo's moves and was handsome as ever going through his paces.

"What have they done, Jackie? Is there any miracle our girls can't perform? They came here to three undisciplined and untrained horses, and now they are magnificent. No wonder Katie doesn't want to give them up."

"I think Helen feels the same way. Mike, they are swapping mounts. Look at Helen and her red hair on Romeo. He works as well for her as he does for Katie. Look at that grin on her face. She loves this!"

"They both do. I see now why Katie put those conditions on her marriage to Jake."

"I hope he gets here soon. They did say he is coming here after work, didn't they?"

"If things are as Katie and Helen describe them, not only will he come here, but I think he will not want to leave. Remember, they are inseparable."

"We will see when he gets here."

"Did you notice they have set the girl's bedroom up with three pillows? And that they have moved a lot of male things in there?"

"Yes, Mike, and it is the most unusual situation I have ever seen. Naturally, it would involve our two indomitable daughters."

"They are creative, for sure. And our girls know how to get what they want."

"Let there be no doubt about that."

"Then what are we going to do?"

"We are going to let them and Jake devise a solution, and we are going to go along with whatever they come up with."

"I do have my limits, Mike."

"I do too, but I know whatever they come up with will be the best thing for them and will be a workable and honorable solution."

"Love does strange things to people."

"Yeah, just look what it did to us."

"You have a point, my dear husband. I just hope they are all as happy as we are."

"I want that for all my girls. That is what makes me happy."

"We'll wait for Jake, and even if we can't solve everything tonight, we will work it out with them. I can't believe how they have grown up so fast."

"Jackie, they are in their twenties. They are still young. It is not their age that impresses me. It's their level of maturity. I love them both so much, and I respect the women they have become."

"I couldn't have said it better."

Chapter Twenty-Six

Solutions

We had given up on Jacob getting there before we let the horses go. We should have had more faith in him. He came driving down the driveway in his pickup this time and stopped when he saw us. He parked by the gate and got out. I was off Blackie in a flash, and Helen came over with Romeo. We just dropped their reins, their signal to stay where they were, and embraced Jacob together, letting him know we were glad to see him back again.

"Shall we show off a little?"

"Definitely. You must have seen Mom and Dad looking out the window at us."

"Yep. I'll ride Romeo, and you can ride Blackie if that is okay with you."

"It's about time they saw what their future Son-in-Law could do. Let's do it."

Jake mounted Romeo, and I did the same to Blackie. We let them out for a short run around the pasture then brought them together on the pasture side of the corral. Jacob stopped Romeo and had him stand while I brought Blackie up beside them. On our signals, they began to dance together. It was like a line dance for people, but it was just the two horses and their riders. We had taught them to dance together, although no one had seen it yet, and they did their routine as if they were Cheerleaders. First was the cross-step into their lateral moves. Then they turned around completely in unison and did their front leg prance. We heaped praise on them, and they responded. Their heads were high, and they both flipped their tails and shook their manes together, the gold and blonde palomino and his black and majestic companion. They did their routines correctly.

"Will you look at that?" Dad said to Mom. "They have taught them to dance together. Look at them. They are doing the same routine as two Cheerleaders. Amazing! And Jacob is riding Romeo, bareback. He is a multi-talented guy, Jackie. I see why the girls love him so much."

"If I hadn't seen that, I would never have believed it."

"I can't help but wonder what else they have in store for us."

"We are about to see. The horses are taken care of, and here they come."

"This should be interesting. Look at the three of them. They look like their hips are joined together."

"Get ready. We are about to hear Jake's side of the story."

We came in the door arm in arm and grinning at each other. That the horses had put on such a good show pleased all three of us. Our efforts had produced incredible results. Jake greeted them, shook Dad's hand, and hugged Mom. "How was New Orleans? Still the same?"

"Yes, Jacob, we had a blast together. We stayed on Bourbon Street in the Royal Sonesta, and everything was right there. Brennan's, Al Hirt's place, and many more. We rode in the horse-drawn carriages and generally behaved like newlyweds, which we were."

"That's great, Jackie. We missed both of you a lot."

"Thanks, Jacob. I am glad you three didn't wait on us. What you have done with the horses is amazing. I've never seen anything like it."

"They are ingenious animals and have come to trust us. Helen and Katie have been working with them for weeks, and I only got to enjoy them the past week or so. I think they like having a male friend and rider."

Dad changed the subject. "The girls tell me that things have happened with you three as well."

Jacob squeezed our hands as we sat with him on the sofa. "Yes, they have captured my body, soul, and heart. I love them both dearly. Katie, no doubt, has told you I asked her to marry me, and she accepted. We all sleep together, and when they are not doing their Cheerleader thing, and I am not working, we are inseparable. I have never been closer to anyone in my life. We have done so much together; it's as if we had known each other for our entire lives."

"Have you thought about what is going to happen to Helen when you and Katie marry?"

"I think about very little else. Whether Katie and I marry or not, we will remain three for as long as we can. Who knows? Helen might find someone who will take her away from us. Until then, we stay together." We both hugged him and kissed him when he said that. "You see, I find myself caught in a quandary, I am in love with them both."

"Then why did you choose Katie instead of Helen?" Mom got to the crux of the matter.

"Helen is not in love with me. Katie is."

The realization soaked into Mom and Dad, and they realized Jacob had chosen wisely. They smiled their understanding with each other.

"What can we do to help make sure you can stay together?" Dad asked.

"Mike! Are you saying you are all right with their living arrangements?"

"For a guy who lived with four girls when he was in college, I can understand from where they are coming. Do you want your place? Where do you live anyway, Jake?"

"I own several properties in North Dallas. Currently, I live in a penthouse townhome that has a wonderful view but is not the place for horses. If we are going to keep working with them, we need to be close by."

"No, you don't need to be close. You need to be here. Jacob, this is Helen and Katie's home as it is ours. We would like it to be yours as well. You don't have to go anywhere. Your home is here with us, and you can continue to live your lives as you wish. When we are on a trip, and we plan to travel a lot, you three can even use our bedroom."

"How much travel do you plan to do," I asked.

"A lot, for as long as we can do it and until we want to be back with our family," Dad explained. "Do you think you can run two related companies at the same time, Jacob?"

"Are you saying you want me to take over Armstrong Consulting while you are gone?"

"No. I am asking if you will take it over permanently."

"May I keep your people?"

"Of course, Jacob. That is one of the requirements. My people must keep their jobs. They will do well for you."

"Yes, Mike. I can consolidate my operations and provide many more resources to our clients. I will be happy to take care of things for you. When are you planning to travel?"

"Immediately. We want to take in South America, especially Brazil, and the Mediterranean countries while the weather is good, then we want to go to Europe. We are continuing our honeymoon for some time to come. I know you three will take care of things around here, and finding someone I can trust to take over my business ventures is the last part of the puzzle."

Mom added, "We are leaving later this week on the first leg of our trip. We must get the proper immunizations, but as soon as we have taken care of that and have done some shopping, we are on our way. We are leaving it all to you while we are gone."

"You are leaving us again so soon?" Helen asked.

"I'm afraid so. Will you all be okay?"

"Yes, Mom, we will be fine. We want you to be safe and have fun enjoying your marriage. Will you be able to see the game this weekend?"

"Probably not. Do you have any surprises for the fans this time?"

"No, since it is the last home game of the season unless the team can get into the playoffs and secure a home game. Otherwise, we begin the offseason and take a break for a while. Of course, Helen and I will continue our workouts and eat lunch at the training table every day. Will you stay in touch?"

"Yes, you know we will, postcards, a call now and then, depending on where we are and what communications capabilities are available."

"Good. Helen and I got up and hugged them both. Is anyone ready for some dinner?"

"I am," Jake replied. "What do we have tonight?"

"Maybe we should all go out one more time before our globe-hopping parents begin their trip."

"I would love to go to Al's again before we leave. I'm sure there will be lots of seafood on our trip, but a little taste of home to see us off will work until we get back," Mom was thinking ahead.

"Sounds good to me. How about you, Jake? Some gulf seafood before we all turn in?"

"I would love it," He answered. "We probably should change out of these horse clothes and clean up some."

"Let's go. I am getting hungry."

"Let's do, Katie." We were ready in just a few minutes. The spa would come later when we returned from dinner.

I ordered the Mahi, and it was delicious. It was large, and Helen and I shared it. We didn't want to overdo it. Our preparations for the upcoming game would begin in earnest tomorrow, and we wanted to be able to lead and support the other girls. We had all come a long way even though I joined the squad in mid-season. Helen and I both had fond memories, especially when Mom and Dad had joined us on national TV. Our bonds were strong, and we looked forward to the appearances we would make, including the calendar. Carolyn had hinted that Helen and I would be on the cover due to our notoriety and would also have pages inside. We had to stay in shape even though the end of the season was in sight.

After an enjoyable time out with our parents, we headed for the spa when we returned home. It was just the three of us since Mom and Dad were tired after their return and wanted to turn in. We said goodnight to them and began to enjoy our evening together. Of course, as soon as we were in the spa, our suits came off, and we enjoyed being naked together. I sat on one of Jake's legs, and Helen took her place on the other one. We both had excellent access to his most essential parts, and he responded quickly to us. I noticed a semi-evil grin on

Helen's face and wondered what was up with her, knowing I would find out later.

"It looks as if we are staying together and will live here with the things we love so much," I observed.

"Yes, our parents are special people. Did dad live with all those girls in college?"

"From what he and Mom have told me, he surely did. All in the same house. Funny thing, though, is that he wasn't dating any of them. He had his other girlfriends."

"Wise man," Jake surmised.

"Another wise man lives here too," Helen kissed Jake. "Do you think you can handle two women, Jake?"

"We are doing all right so far."

She grinned again. What was going on in that lovely head of hers?

"Is anyone ready to go in?" She invited us.

"What? And I sleep with both of you again. I don't think I can do that for more than a couple hundred years more."

"Then follow me." She led him up the steps by his erection, squeezing and caressing him all the way. I followed, amazed at her.

"Towels, everyone," I wanted us to display at least some semblance of discretion with Mom and Dad in the house.

"Do either of you realize how much better I feel knowing that I am not going to lose you or our life together or anything. I will even gain a brother, something else I have never had or dreamed of in my whole life."

"I am relieved too, Helen, that I am not going to lose you or Jake. Mom and Dad understood and agreed with us. Dad gets what he wants, a happy family, and someone capable he trusts to run his company. It is the best of all worlds."

"Yes, and we can keep doing what we love too."

Helen and I put on our nighties, and Jacob slipped on a pair of briefs. We got into the bed in our usual places when Helen asked us, "Would it be all right for me to sleep in the middle tonight? Now that my fear is gone, I want to be held by those who love me."

"Yes, Helen, get in here between Jake and me, and we will keep you warm all night."

"Will you kiss me, Katie?"

"I would love that," and I took her in my arms and kissed her in an embrace. Jake slid closer to her from the other side and cuddled with her making her sigh slowly, knowing we loved her immensely. Jacob turned her head toward him and kissed her too. She reached up, put her arms around his neck, and pulled him down to her. The kiss they shared was anything but friendly. She kissed him a lover's kiss and wouldn't let him go, not that he was trying very hard to get away from her. I finally realized what she had in mind. Jacob and I were going to be three in everything.

I moved my hand down between her legs and touched her there. She was very wet already and moaned at my touch. Jacob figured it out too. He looked at me with a questioning look, and I nodded my assent. I have no idea what he was thinking at that moment.

"Jacob, Katie, this is the night we become three. Make love to me, both of you. I want to give myself to you freely and without fear. I know we will be together now, and I want to feel your touch, Katie, and I want you to make love to me, Jacob."

"Welcome to our love, Helen. I am so glad you made this decision," I replied. Jacob kissed her lips, her breasts, and nipples. I slipped two fingers into her and rubbed her clitoris with my thumb. She began to clutch the covers as we both made love to her and was gushing girl cream from her vagina.

"Now, Jacob, take me now. Let me feel what I have missed for so many years."

He didn't waste any time. When he took his place above Helen, she opened her legs as wide as she could, and he pushed forward. She gasped when she felt him enter and relaxed even more. His second thrust took him farther, even though she was tight, and her vagina was not very deep since it had been so long for her. Jake was very patient and careful. She wrapped her leg around his hips, further spreading her legs to take as much of him as she could. It was clear that my sister was riding the train up the mountain, and Jacob increased his speed and effort to welcome her back to the world of having a man love her. She began to moan with his every push but was less vocal than I had thought she would be. She was with him all the way.

He took her to her climax, and it hit her like an explosion. He came inside her, and they were in sync and completely together. She didn't scream but let the waves of their loving roll over her until she took a break to get her breath and went right back to stimulating Jake with her muscles. He kept doing the same things to her that had been successful, and he was able to hold back when she rose and fell in her lust again. His next orgasm brought her to another climax, and she fell limp under him. Jake reached another and stopped his efforts, lying on her as she panted her satisfaction and let her arms fall to each side. She opened her eyes and kissed him a final kiss. He rolled off her, and I resumed my kisses on her body and her lips. I kissed him, too. They had been wonderful together, and no doubt that she would need time to recover crossed my mind. He kissed her affectionately to let her know how wonderful she had been and how glad he was that we had worked things out for her. I got a couple of towels and began to clean them up. Helen was a mess. Jake was still sensitive to my touch. I did as much as I could without asking them to get out of the bed, and then I took them both in a loving embrace. Our world had changed.

It must have been several hours later that Helen needed to use the bathroom. She woke me getting out of bed, and I accompanied her, embracing her all the way. When we came back to bed, Jacob went too, and when we were together again, Helen was smiling broadly, and she switched places with me, putting me in the middle between them. Jacob smiled at me and kissed me tenderly.

"Katie, you are quite a woman, engaged to me, and you love your sister so much that you let her be with me so that her needs are taken care of as well as your own. What would you like now?"

"This evening has been an emotional drain on me, and all I want is to be held by you two all night and wake up to a new dawn for us."

"I am so full of love and admiration for you right now, Katie, that I will be glad to hold you all night. You and Jacob have changed my life in addition to being here where wonderful things happen to people, and I love you more than anything else."

"When we get our chance again, Katie, Helen and I will do for you what you have done for us. It was a wonderful way to close our triangle."

"I might feel differently in the morning after sleeping with you two all night. I seem to get my horniest early in the morning."

"Do you think your parents will know what we did tonight?"

"Mom will. She reads minds. Whether she tells Dad is a tossup. I want them to enjoy their trip and not worry about us."

"I want that too," Helen supported me.

"I will take care of your Dad's business, and we will do some wonderful things together, our two organizations. Let's go to sleep now, knowing that we are on a new track. It will be a wonderful time for us."

"Yes, it will, Jake, Katie, and thanks to both of you for bringing me back to life. I stayed away far too long."

"Welcome back, Helen," we both kissed her and snuggled together until the morning sun woke us early. I didn't know if Mom and Dad were up yet or not, but it didn't matter. Jake, Helen, and I managed to stay together and even had a beautiful place to live. I kissed Helen awake, and Jacob opened his eyes to our loving.

"Shall we begin our new lives, lovers?"

"Yes, Katie. I am ready."

"So am I, Jacob agreed."

"We must wear clothes this morning, and I think we should dress and go make coffee. If Mom and Dad wake up, great. If not, we will let them sleep. They need to gather their energies for their next destination."

"When do you think they will get underway?"

"My guess would be no later than Thursday or Friday, maybe sooner."

"Let's go get this thing started."

We went to the kitchen clothed and ready for our morning routine. We made a carafe of coffee in the Keurig and set up the cups and amenities. Jacob liked half and half in his. Helen and I went for the jolt of ours being black. I got the yogurt and other items together, and we looked forward to it, even Jacob, who had come to like our diet very much. He could always have a bagel and cream cheese if he wanted when he got to work, but for now, he was satisfied with our energy foods.

We left right behind him with Mom and Dad still asleep. I felt good to get out of there without having to explain anything they might have heard the night before. Jacob was as good as his word. I felt terrific after we made love to each other, and Helen had no inhibitions about taking full part. She did for me what I had done for her before we went to sleep. We were three delighted individuals. Romeo said goodbye to us with a couple of stomps with his front feet and a flip of his tail and mane and went back to grazing with Blackie and Mandy. They knew we would be back.

Helen and I held hands as much as we could on the way to our workout and kept smiling the entire way. We were both sure that Jake would be smiling too. He talked with Dad later in the morning when he asked his okay and help in proceeding to combine the companies. He kept Dad posted as to his progress throughout the day. The merger was seamless. By the end of the day, they completed it. Dad was happy that Jake had taken charge and put things together. He was confident that the venture would be successful and made sure his girls, namely us, had nothing to worry about whatever happened. When we drove up after lunch, he was holding Mom lovingly, and they were both ready for their next adventure. They had their vaccinations done and just needed to pick up some things for their wardrobe before they could get on an airplane and head south on the first leg of their journey.

We went to see Carolyn the next morning and told her they were off again, and that Jake and I were engaged. Helen just grinned when she asked her how she felt about our engagement. My sister said she was delighted and was going to live with us in the interim. We assured Carolyn that nothing was going to happen for quite some time, and she should not worry about losing either of us. When we told her how much the Cheerleaders meant to us, she didn't worry anymore. We also explained it to the girls who were there, and they wished all three of us well. They shed some tears, whether from happiness for me or from sadness, knowing Jake was off the market. We didn't know which. Many of the more astute, especially those who knew us, could see the happiness exuding from me, but no one said anything.

We stayed longer than usual to make sure everyone who needed us could ask us what they needed to know. When we arrived back home, Dad and Mom were out, no doubt, shopping, and the horses greeted us as usual. Helen and I needed to talk first, however, and we went in and put on our suits to take a soak in the spa. When we relaxed in each other's arms again, I asked Helen how she was feeling.

"Katie, I am so happy right now that I feel like I might burst. Aside from a little soreness where our man retook my virginity, I am wonderful. Are you doing all right with what happened last night?" She kissed me lovingly and let me answer.

"Seeing you two together was one of the most beautiful things I have ever witnessed. It was as if I were watching a red-headed version of myself making love to him. I felt his every stroke and thought I was going to come with you when you went over the mountaintop."

"You were right, you know. Melanie was wrong. He is one hell of a lover."

"I hoped you would agree with me. So, now that we have Jacob, what are we going to do with him?"

"We are going to live with him and love him and let him love us as we love each other. It's simple. And I am not going to marry him yet. We are three, and we are inseparable. We will live and love as three. We are all in love with each other, and there is no way for us to go on otherwise. You see, I love Jacob, but I first loved you, and I still do and will for a long time to come. Your special guy might come along tomorrow and capture your heart. If not, you will always have us."

"And we get to continue to live our lives as we have."

"Yes, dear sister. Whatever comes, we three will face it together."

"Are you still curious about our favorite ex-Cowboy?"

"Curious, but not obsessed. I would bet Casey can't even ride a horse, much less dance."

"You might be right, Helen."

"Now that I know we can stay together, my fears are gone. I know you two love me and that I will always have a home. I am so glad I found you, Katie. It was my lucky day. You fit the bill for the squad so well, and we have become so close. Now, Jacob is with us. You are the one who is going to marry him, not me. And our story will go on."

"Yes, Helen. One thing will always be solid. Our love for each other, and we will continue to love our man. We will also take care of our parents and help them enjoy the rest of their lives. They are very proud of us both. We will make them both prouder as we go. Sisters forever?"

"Count me in, Katie. Sisters *and* lovers forever."

Chapter Twenty-Seven

Two Paths Diverged in the Woods

The team made the playoffs as expected, but unexpectedly, they also won home-field advantage throughout. That meant the season could last two more weeks for the Cheerleader squad. Helen and I were ecstatic at the extension and did our best to encourage the other girls to keep up their exercise routines and continue to eat their meals at the training table. Everyone on the squad agreed to keep to their regular performances and looked forward to the playoff crowds at AT&T stadium. Their dance routines remained the same as at the last home game, and they would just practice them to remember them in detail.

Helen's prediction had been right about something coming up with her heartthrob. FOX assigned him to games on the west coast, and he did not revisit Dallas that season. Helen was not surprised and not very disappointed either. She suspected that someone had leaked his plans to visit her, and someone in New York changed them. Karen did come and spent some time with Katie and Helen while their parents toured the Mediterranean. She got to know Jacob too, but no more interviews ensued. The football team lost the first-round game, and the offseason began for the entire organization. Helen and I took a short break. We worked with the horses, soaked in the spa every day, and enjoyed our lives together and with Jacob. Now that his company and Mike's were working under the same roof, business boomed. He learned to delegate so he could spend more time living his life, and I thought our threesome was growing closer together. The home and the big bed were ours, at least while Mike and Jackie were traveling.

After a week or so off, I went back to my usual routine of morning workouts and lunch at the Star, then going home to work with the horses. Helen was tired of the day-to-day routine and wanted to extend her break. She knew her cheerleader career would end someday, and she began to look around Dallas for a paying position that would appeal to her. Jacob helped immensely, even introducing her to some of his colleagues and letting her use one of his vehicles to get around town since I needed the BMW for my workout sessions. For the first time, we spent days away from each other. We all three came back together in the evenings, though, so the inseparable trio was still a threesome. Helen and I were beginning to miss our parents terribly since they were gone so long this time. We just had to be patient and make sure Rex and the horses got their exercise, and the horses kept practicing their routines.

Life was still good for us, although we all felt some restlessness, and our sex lives tapered off some. Helen and Jacob, once they discovered their mutual physical attraction, began to spend more time together even though Jacob was engaged to me. I realized that the situation and our lives were changing.

One evening after my usual routine, Helen and Jacob returned home together. I thought that was unusual, and when they were quiet all through dinner, I suspected something was up. "Okay, you two. What's going on here? Neither of you has said a word since you got home."

Helen answered. "We have spent a lot of time together lately, sis, and I have come to some decisions about my life."

That scared the hell out of me.

"I am going to leave the Cheerleaders and take a job in Dallas. I have had my years with the squad, and, frankly, the routine has gotten to be more than I want to keep doing."

"You can't leave the team, Helen, you are one of the main players. Everyone looks up to you."

"The time has come for me to move into the next phase of my life. The time I have spent in Dallas has shown me that I have skills and talents that I can use to begin a career, and I want to do that."

I couldn't find the words to say, so I looked at Jacob. "Did you have anything to do with this, Jake?"

"Don't blame Jake, Katie, it is my decision, not his."

"You are going to stay here, though, right?"

Jake entered the conversation at that point. "Katie, I am taking Helen to Dallas with me. We are going to live there together. I have to break our engagement."

I was numb. I was losing my fiancé to my sister, and they were moving to Dallas together, leaving me, the horses, and the house? I just sat back in my chair and tried to keep things together. I felt like they had both delivered powerful right-hand blows to my abdomen. Helen began to cry. Much to my surprise and chagrin, Jake embraced her and tried to comfort her. I knew then that I had lost him. I remembered what Melanie had told me about him that he had a habit of cheating on the one who loved him best. I took a deep breath and just sucked it up. I had been down this road before, but never expected it would come from Helen and Jacob.

"What are you going to do, Helen?"

"She is coming to work for me," Jacob answered.

I put a fake smile on my face with a hint of acceptance and resignation. "Now that we are not engaged anymore, Jacob, are you two going to take up together?"

"Yes, Katie. She is moving in with me, and we are going to go on from there."

I stood up and smiled, then gave them my best wishes. Then I said, "After all this, you no doubt understand that I think it is better that you two to leave here now and go about your own lives."

"We understand. Give us a few minutes to get our things together, and we will go."

"I'll leave for a while to give you a chance to pack. It's been great, and I will miss you both. Goodbye, sister, Jake. Have a great life together." I left them there and got in the BMW. I had no idea where to go, so I went to see if I could get in a workout. That always helped me. The girls who exercised in the evening were there, as was Carolyn. She was surprised to see me. Everyone else was too. What had just happened had not sunk in yet, but I knew I was on my own again. It felt lonely at first, but as I did my exercises in total silence, I felt a sense of freedom wash over me. I smiled. Just as I finished the elliptical machine and was about to go to the dance numbers, joining the other girls, Carolyn walked into the room.

"Katie! What are you doing here this time of day?"

"Carolyn, do you work all the time?" I joked with her.

"Sometimes it seems that way," she chuckled and smiled back at me. I didn't say a word about why I was there. "Can I have a few minutes?"

"Sure, Carolyn. I am always available to you."

"Please come to my office."

We left the exercise room, and both took seats in her office. We sat together instead of her behind her desk and me in an opposing chair. I suspected something was up with her too.

"Where is Helen tonight?"

"I have no idea. Somewhere with Jacob in Dallas."

"Is there something you want to tell me, Katie?"

"Helen told me she is not coming back to the Cheerleaders for another season. She is taking a job in Dallas and beginning a career there."

"She is with Jacob?"

"Yes. Jacob broke our engagement, and they left together."

"Are you okay, Katie?"

"No. It hasn't hit me yet. I seem to have lost my fiancé to my sister. How's that for a kick in the teeth?"

"So, you came to workout. That explains it all. Are you going to have dinner with us here?"

"Yes, Carolyn, I don't want to go home alone. At least not yet. I have to sort through this, and here is the place I love most except our pasture with my horses."

"Can you consider a proposition from the Cheerleader Board of Directors?"

"Yes, of course. The cheerleaders are the major part of my life right now."

"May I ask Kerry to join us?"

"She is new here, right?"

"Yes, Katie. She is our new director and is very dedicated."

"By all means. Ask Kerry to join us."

"Before I do, will you answer a question for me?"

"Yes, Carolyn. You know I tell you everything, just as I do my parents."

"Are you planning to audition for next year's squad?"

"Oh, yes, Carolyn. I want to be on the team for as long as possible."

"What if you don't make it?"

"Believe me, Carolyn, I will make it. I know that as surely as I know my name."

"I had hoped you would say that. I'll call Kerry."

She came into the office, hugged me, and sat in the chair beside me. "Helen is not with you this evening?"

"No. Helen left with Jacob, but she will come back. I know it. As soon as she realizes what Jacob is all about, she will be back. And I, we, will be there for her."

"Katie, I must tell you that we were going to make the same offer to her as we are about to make to you. If or when she does come back, we hope we can convince her to accept. She is still a member of this team, and we hope she will audition as a veteran and stay."

I said nothing, but looked down and almost cried, nodding my agreement with Carolyn.

"Katie, some changes took place within the Cowboys organization yesterday and this morning. First, the General Manager stepped down and relinquished his position. He is still the owner but wants to work at the league level and spend less of his time with the team."

I had heard nothing about this and gave her my undivided attention.

"He named one of his children as the new GM, causing a major shakeup at all levels within the organization."

"His son," I postulated.

"No. A person very near and dear to our Cheerleader's hearts, our former President, is the new General Manager."

"Carla?" I guessed.

"Yes, and she has already begun reshaping both the team and the Cheerleaders. For example, your old trainer friend, James, is moving to the other side of the complex and will take the lead with player training. That leaves his position open. We want you to take his place as head trainer for the girls. We hoped that Helen would join you, and we still haven't given up on her. Carla wants the recruits to be the most qualified and best trained Dallas Cowboys Cheerleaders ever. Are you interested?

"Yes. When I pass my audition, I will be both on the field with the girls and working with them here?"

"Yes, that's the idea. A female trainer can do things with the girls that a male trainer could never do. You will be one of them."

"Does this position include compensation?" I had to ask.

"Yes, you will receive a generous salary and all the company benefits just as we do, including health insurance, a pension plan, and an expense account for company expenses. You will spend more time here when the application deadline passes and will help us select the girls we want to bring in and the selection process once they are here. Your activities with them will keep you in shape, and your skills will increase over time."

"I will help select the applicants we want to see, train them, and judge final tryouts. Will I have any authority to make selections, or will my role be advisory?"

"You will have to make decisions all along the way. Give us a great group of girls for next year, Katie. That is what we want you to do."

"Kerry, I will need your expertise and an eye for talent to help me. You must advise me on who, in your opinion, will take direction and work as a team member."

"I had hoped you would say that, Katie. You can count on me."

"I just have one other question. Why me? I haven't been on the team for even a year yet. How did you decide I was the right one for this position?"

"Let me answer that," Carolyn spoke up. "You have attracted a great deal of attention, Katie, with your interviews and as a darling of the camera. Carla picked you and Helen in the hopes that you would join us and help us go to the next level, whatever that may be. Let me add that her choice pleases everyone who has worked with you. You are our girl. What do you say?"

"When do I start?"

"That's our Katie. The applications will start to come in soon, and we will need you then. Now, take some time to enjoy your horses and wait for Mike and Jackie to come home. Of course, continue your workouts and meals as you take on your new responsibilities."

"Can you find Helen, check on her, and try to bring her back to me? To us?"

"We realized she was trying to find a career in Dallas and began looking for her shortly after she didn't show up for her workouts. We have a couple of leads, but Jacob keeps her very close at hand down there. We need to find her more now than ever with all the changes that are occurring."

"I agree. I accept your offer. Now may I return to my routine?"

"Yes, Katie. I hope this has brightened your day."

"It has, but I want Helen back. That will make everything right."

"I understand. We are doing our best."

I didn't hear a word from Helen, which I thought extremely unusual, and tried to focus on other things. A couple of weeks later, as I settled into my new job, loving every minute of it, I was at lunch after a vigorous workout, and still wanted to know about Helen. The film crew was documenting my entire workout routine by routine so that I would be fresh for each segment. I hardly even knew they were there.

Suddenly, Kerry came hurriedly into the dining room and came straight over to me. "We found her. She called Carolyn. Go to her office right now."

I forgot all about my dinnerware and bolted to Carolyn's office. "Good, you are wearing your sweats. Let's go. I'll fill you in on the way."

The security people showed us to the limo, and I recognized Chief Massey, the head of security, immediately in the front passenger seat. With another car trailing us, we hit the toll road and sped toward Dallas.

"Where is she, Carolyn?"

"Do you remember the New Orleans style restaurant your folks took you to?"

"Yes, of course, Guido's. He introduced us to the two bouncers there and made sure they would recognize us when they saw us again."

"That's right. Helen is there, and they are guarding her to keep the pests away. She is safe, Katie. She escaped Jacob and Walters Enterprises and found refuge there. Our security will go in and get her out. We will take her home."

I was so relieved that I started crying uncontrollably. All the fear and tension I had felt for so long emerged through my tears. Carolyn took me in her arms and comforted me. All I could think of was when I would be able to embrace my sister again and for everything to be all right. I knew the limo was going far above the speed limit with lights flashing and the SUV trailing vehicle keeping up as best as they could. I wanted it to go faster. My tears lessened, and I could see that we were entering Turtle Creek. We passed the Mansion, and I saw Guido's just ahead. The driver drove us up to the front door and stopped with very little space between the car and the building. The Chief got out of our car, and security personnel exited the trailing vehicle quickly. I started to get out too, but Carolyn stopped me.

"Let them do their jobs, Katie. She will be here with us in just a few minutes. I'll tell you what is going on. Our guys will introduce themselves to her guards, and they will escort her out to us as soon as they reach the front door."

One of the security personnel exited the building, checked with his associates, and opened the limousine door next to me. The restaurant door opened quickly, and they brought Helen to us. When she saw Carolyn and me as she got in, she grabbed me in a death embrace, her tears flowing down her face. I kissed her passionately and wouldn't let her go.

"We found you, we found you at last. Now we are taking you out of this place and are going home, dear sister."

"Can you ever forgive me?" she asked.

"There is nothing to forgive. I love you, dear Helen, and I thought I was going to die without you." The limo was back on Tollway again, heading north.

"Carolyn, thank you so much. I couldn't find Katie, and you were the only other person I could trust. I knew you would come to get me." She hugged Carolyn with great appreciation and affection. Our family was coming together again.

"After all this, I can promise you something, actually, two things. One, I am never leaving home again, especially with some asshole like Jacob, and two, I am not leaving the Cheerleaders either. I will audition as a veteran just as I have done before, and when the team hits the stadium floor this fall, I am going to be one of the girls." I grinned at Carolyn when Helen said that. She would find out the new plans later, when everyone, including her, knew she was safe again. My sister was back.

The End

Coming Soon

*<u>Finding our Dreams</u>—The Second Book in the Finding
Kathie McDonald Series*

www.ingramcontent.com/pod-product-compliance
Lightning Source LLC
Chambersburg PA
CBHW020905160726
47993CB00005B/1820